Larger
Than
Death

Larger Than Death

A NOVEL BY

Lynne Murray

ORLOFF PRESS

ATHENS, GEORGIA

Orloff Press
P.O. Box 80774
Athens, GA 30608

Orloff Press and colophon are registered trademarks

Printed on acid-free, recycled paper
Manufactured in the United States of America

Publisher's Cataloging-in-Publication Data
Murray, Lynne, 1948–
  Larger Than Death / Lynne Murray
    p. cm.
  ISBN 0-9642949-0-7
  I. Title
PS3515.U585T48 1997
813'.54—dc20   97—67282
                                                    CIP

5 4 3 2 1

Acknowledgments

MANY THANKS—

To the close friends who have sustained me for nearly three decades, Jacqueline Stone, Barbara Landis, Merry von Brauch and the late, great Jean Berk.

To Jaqueline Girdner and Gregory Booi for keeping my dream alive by generously sharing theirs.

To my brother Michael Mitchell Murray, whose sanity and goodness is like a treasure, although for years until we compared notes, he thought he was the black sheep of the family and I thought I was.

To JP for valuable military insights and Naval attitude.

To Jon von Brauch, J.D., Pacific Bell Special Agent, for taking time to provide law enforcement and telephone security reality checks.

To my friends on the Internet alt.support.big-folks, soc.support.fat-acceptance and NAAFA fat-acceptance mailing list who live Eleanor Roosevelt's words, "No one can make you feel inferior without your consent." They never give consent.

And special thanks to John A. Miller and Orloff Press for investing so much energy and good will to bring this book into the light—and for betting on it when others would not.

Chapter One

My name is Josephine Fuller and I've never weighed less than two hundred pounds in my adult life—not counting the chip on my shoulder. Friends sometimes call me Donna Quixote because tilting windmills is what I do for a living. How did I get started? I answered an ad in the *San Francisco Chronicle*.

> *Need person of substance for special assignments: part bloodhound, part bulldog, part lone wolf. Job requires quick study, travel and communication skills. Must genuinely care about the advancement of women.*

As a matter of fact, I was feeling quite concerned about the advancement of women in general and myself in particular at the moment I read the ad. I had just landed in San Francisco for a breather and a much-needed infusion of salaried work after divorcing my husband, a world-class photographer, adventurer, and philanderer.

In other words, I needed a job. Nothing permanent. After all I hadn't stayed in one place for more than a few months for years. My qualifications consisted of a B.A. in psychology (which most employers agreed we could put aside as irrelevant) and six years of marriage. I had done whatever Griffin Fuller needed to keep him going: cook, money manager, photographer's assistant, ghost writer, travel agent, and all the other kinds of helpmeet that a recent ex-wife can't list without bitterness. Griff lived too much on the edge himself to offer alimony, but he was a good job reference.

So at 9:00 A.M. the day after I faxed my letter and résumé I was awakened by a phone call from a brisk tenor voice informing me of the address where I could report that afternoon if I were interested in interviewing. The address proved to be a mansion on a dizzying hill above Union Street. I arrived pink-cheeked after a brisk hike from my hotel on Pine.

"Josephine Fuller, here for a one o'clock appointment," I said to the tall, slender man who answered the door. His hair was bright auburn and his eyes a penetrating blue, which together with a cynical twist to his mouth gave his handsome face a startling intensity. He wore a full-sleeved white shirt and black trousers and looked ready to pick up a fencing foil and resume his role opposite Errol Flynn in a pirate movie. Both ears were pierced. No rings in them. Must be a conservative place, I thought.

"You know you'll be meeting Alicia Madrone?" he asked, cocking his head slightly.

"No."

"You know who she is?"

"More or less." The Madrone name adorned a museum, a hospital, and half a dozen other edifices around the state.

Was he criticizing my gabardine skirt and blazer or counseling prudence in the presence of old wealth?

"You didn't mention who the interview was with when we spoke on the phone," I said evenly. I could almost look him in the eye without hurting my neck. "Is there something else I should know in advance that would be relevant?"

He examined me for signs of sarcasm. "You didn't think to look up the address in a reverse directory or anything like that?"

"No."

He seemed disappointed. Clearly if he'd had the clout to screen candidates he would have installed a revolving door to replace the massive oak one. "By the way, it's Mrs. Madrone, not Ms.," he sniffed. "She prefers it."

"Okay." His boss clearly came from a generation when marrying into the Madrone family was an accomplishment. No doubt it still is.

He turned and languidly gestured for me to follow him up a spectacular staircase. The banister must have been eight inches wide. A series of stained glass windows greeted us at each landing. On the second floor we met a nurse closing a door at the end of the wide hallway. She responded to my guide's interrogatory eyebrow lift with a nod, and I was ushered into an airy, sunlit room carpeted with rugs that looked as if they should be hanging on museum walls. The furniture was sparse but I guessed most of it to be imported and older than the Declaration of Independence. My guide was gone without a word and I stepped toward the woman who sat in a wheelchair next to a heavy mahogany desk that probably had belonged to some Spanish grandee.

Alicia Madrone was in her sixties and narrow as a whippet, with pewter hair pulled into a chignon. Despite the flood of sunshine from the windows that looked out over the Bay, she wore a heavy sweater and wool skirt. The lilac point Siamese on her lap raised his head and stared at me for a moment before settling back down into the blue blanket that matched the color of his eyes.

I reached into my pocket to peel a tissue off the pack I'd brought. I was starting to sweat.

When I stood in front of her, Alicia Madrone motioned me into a straight-backed Mission chair a few feet away. The sharp brown eyes she turned on me seemed to come from a distracted world of pain where the healthy could not and would not want to follow.

"I've met your ex-husband. He took a portrait of me." Her voice was light and very sweet, almost girlish.

Uh oh. "I didn't know Griff did portraits." When I realized my ex-husband's love affairs were a cunningly practiced obsession rather than an occasional temptation, I began to dread meeting women who introduced themselves by announcing they had known him. The next word was like as not to be "biblically." I wondered how soon I could politely terminate the interview.

"You kept your married name. Why?"

"I liked it better than my maiden name, which was O'Toole. I prefer leading a Fuller divorced life. I wouldn't go back to being O'Toole for anyone." A joke was a risk but I would hate to work for someone who didn't know the meaning of the word humor.

Mrs. Madrone blinked, then chuckled, passing my first test. She looked at me a little cautiously, the way people do when they realize you're armed with a sharp instrument. "Ah," she said. "Why did you answer my advertisement?"

"I need work. I would prefer working where there is no temptation to assassinate my boss for criminal stupidity. During my marriage I developed the skills to gloss over an egomaniac's mistakes, but at least Griffin Fuller wasn't an idiot."

"A blunt speaker. Intelligent and arrogant to boot. You've never learned any particular profession. And you like to travel." She shook her head as if wondering what would become of me. Then she shivered. The lemony sunshine

had suddenly stopped warming her. "You must have trav-
elled a great deal with your ex-husband."

"I travel well."

"Can you stay in one place?"

"Yes." I could have said that I wasn't sure where on earth
I belonged. That was the truth, but not her business.

"You seem to be a person of substance," she remarked,
looking me up and down just a shade shy of insolence.

I looked back at her in silence until enough time had
passed for her to take my point.

"Mrs. Madrone, I never let size stop me and I don't allow
anyone to intimidate me. It took awhile, but I learned not
to obsess about being larger than average. In my family it
comes with the genes. Good health, great teeth, and high
IQ. You want any one of the above, you get the whole
package."

For a moment she retreated, then hitched her wheelchair
forward and smiled for the first time since I had met her.
The smile made her seem young again. Clearly she had
once been a dangerous beauty. Those brown eyes remembered pleasure.

For the first time since I'd rung the doorbell and entered
that quiet mansion, I began to feel a glimmer of the spark
her ad had kindled when I read it.

"How did you get such confidence?" she asked.

I told her about Nina.

Chapter Two

People have actually asked if Nina and I were sisters. All fat women look alike, right? The question might have been more amusing if Nina West hadn't been five feet two inches tall, round, blond and curly-haired like one of those naughty cupids the gods send round on errands of love. I, on the other hand, am five foot eight with dark brown hair and eyes, and a body more along the lines of Gauguin's South Sea Island type.

From childhood I was a magnet for the back-handed compliments of those who pretended to be kind by raving about my fine hair and eyes and telling me I was pretty enough for any domestic or commercial use "if only" I lost X-many pounds. Fill in the blank, depending on my weight at the time and the illusions of the person who felt called upon to improve me.

I was fifteen and miserable, walking through Pike's Market in Seattle, when I strayed into Nina's tiny shop. It was a symphony of colors and textures, beautiful clothing that was large enough for me to wear. I could scarcely believe my eyes.

6

Nina was about thirty then. She saw that I was shy and made it a point to say a few kind words that didn't contain any stingers about how wonderful I could be if I weren't what I was. Until that moment, I hadn't realized how desperately starved I was for kindness.

I went to her shop every chance I got, fascinated by her. Despite everything I had heard up to that point about how fat-and-ugly were actually one word, I watched her happily flirt with men and charm women. She let me hang around and made me feel welcome.

Whatever confidence I have in myself with this body began with Nina. Even after I married and went trotting around the globe after Griff, I kept coming back to her the way people gravitate to the ocean, to stand and stare and somehow be soothed by its presence. She always made me feel that anything was possible. She had begun to sell her clothing in boutiques from Seattle to San Francisco and it seemed that every time I visited her she unfolded another layer of creativity: a newsletter, a bellydancing class for large women, even a sculpture project.

"I want to celebrate what real women are like," she once told me with a smile.

Alicia Madrone nodded. "I like your Nina. You and she have to deal with being larger than society prefers. I have to put up with being an old woman, confined to a wheelchair. Even with all my money, can you imagine how easy it is for people to ignore me? Shall I tell you how I cope?"

"Please."

"I say exactly what I think at all times. At my age there's no time to lie or hold back. And I use my considerable financial means to further my own agenda. Do you play chess?"

"No."

"A pity. Too late for you to learn, for my purposes. Most

women of my station pursue bridge, but I find it excessively sociable for my taste. Children?"

"I beg your pardon?"

"Do you have any? It may be illegal to even ask, but I'm hardly worried about being sued."

"No children."

"I neither. No hostages to fortune. When my husband was alive, I believe I regretted that. Now I find that my money is totally available to pursue my own goals." She wheeled her chair a little closer to me so suddenly that the cat on her lap stirred and half opened its eyes. "Many of the candidates for this position had very rigid ideas about what men and women should be or do in this world. They had plans in mind to right those wrongs. Well, I'm not about to hire someone to promote *their* own agenda. If you could work and travel with Griffin Fuller and sleep with him as well for five years, I suspect you must be organized, capable of great self-restraint, and a formidable diplomat. The fact that you had to break away argues that common sense must be working like yeast somewhere in your character. You may have the job—if you think you can do the work."

"You haven't said what the work is yet."

She laughed delightedly. "See?" she said to no one in particular. "A diplomat. She doesn't come close to committing herself."

She jockeyed her chair even closer. She smelled of camphor, perhaps liniment. "I think well of myself and I care about women's suffering. This combination is particularly rare for someone of my age who has money and some portion of her brain still functioning. Where are all the old women who should be grabbing the world by the throat? Society doesn't train us in that direction and it's time someone did. My health does not permit me to get involved directly. Oh, I write checks to the usual organizations," she waved a pale hand dismissively, "but I could give up my fortune entirely and never notice an impact through official channels. I want to see some results for my money, so I'm setting aside an endowment for individuals or small groups of women. I want you to meet them and bring me back reports. Does that sound self-indulgent?"

Before I could answer, she held up her hand.

"Rhetorical question. I don't give a damn what it sounds like. I need someone I can trust to evaluate real life situations before I commit any resources. Afterward I want detailed and accurate reports on the effects of any expenditures. The job demands a certain amount of subterfuge. Will that be a problem for you?"

"I *was* married for six years."

"Yes." She chuckled, "So you were. I believe I've made the right choice." She backed her wheelchair away. "I understand you are living at the Hotel Belvedere?"

"An economy measure." I could tell by the tone of her voice that the once luxurious Belvedere was no longer even close to a nice place by her standards.

"You will report to my assistant frequently by telephone or fax. I'll want a formal report, in person, of your recommendations for each case and the reasons for them. A certain amount of isolation goes with the job. Can you handle that?"

I took a breath to reply, but she held up a hand, "Don't try to answer. If it becomes too much for you, we'll find out. I travel a great deal, you will come to me to report wherever I may be—at the Côte d'Azur or Connecticut or the San Juan Islands. You can have some time off between assignments in lieu of weekends, holidays, that sort of thing. If you wish to establish a permanent residence—I could help you set up somewhere."

Her mention of the San Juan Islands near Vancouver set me to thinking about Nina only a few miles away in Seattle. "Not yet, I guess."

"Very well. If you have any particular requirements, this is the time to say so."

"Just one."

"Yes?"

"If air travel is involved, I need to travel first class or at least business class. Coach seats are not designed for even average size humans."

She smiled politely. I suspected she had never seen the coach section of an airplane. "Very well. Specify your needs to Ambrose Terrell. He's my personal assistant and you'll be reporting directly to him most of the time."

"Ah."

"Struck sparks already, has he? He's very exacting. Perhaps a little too protective of me, but he's eminently capable. Shall we begin?"

*   *   *

Over the next year I spent a few months with a group of ex-nuns running a program for homeless women in Boston. Then I joined a struggling women's book and health food store in Albuquerque. The last six months I worked with volunteers at a carefully concealed shelter for battered women in North Carolina. I had just finished packing to leave North Carolina for the San Juan Islands to deliver my first year's report to Mrs. Madrone when the phone rang.

It was Nina. Her voice was strained.

"Are you okay, Nina?"

"Well—listen, Jo, do you think you could come up here sooner than next week? Now would be good." She laughed, a little, just an echo of her usual rich, sensuous laugh.

"What's wrong?"

"Oh, there's no emergency, it's just something I need to talk to you about face to face."

"Sure, I guess I could." I hesitated and looked at my very rough draft, "It's just that I'm writing this big report that covers over ten months of work and I don't want to screw it up. I really love this job."

There was the briefest of pauses before Nina said, "I understand. It's not something to lose your job over."

"Look if it's urgent, I really will put this report off. Are you sure you're okay?"

Again there was that second of hesitation, but Nina's voice was strong when she said, "It's nothing like that. I'm feeling good. The business is doing fine. I'm happy with my new boyfriend. Maybe because things finally are going so well, I'm thinking of old times and getting sentimental. I miss you, just come when you can."

After we hung up I wanted to call her back and tell her I'd make some excuse and get on a plane to see her the next day. But frankly I didn't know how I could explain it to Mrs. Madrone, and the idea of telling Ambrose I would be late with the report made a chill run down my spine.

Mrs. Madrone's special assistant never warmed to me. I was not about to do less than my best under his critical eye. I knew he was passing along my field updates to his boss because she okayed my suggestions. The day of the actual report came and Mrs. Madrone seemed pleased with it. Then I told Ambrose I was taking the next week off as planned and he took down the information of where to forward my mail.

As I drove the rental car into Seattle I realized that although we spoke by phone every few weeks, I hadn't laid eyes on Nina in the nearly two years since my marriage broke up. I wanted to get an infusion of her splendid vitality.

I never expected to find the police on her doorstep.

Chapter Three

Nina lived in a four-story brick apartment house on the edge of Seattle's Capitol Hill district. The tenants were eccentric by most standards and the cop car might indicate nothing more than a stereo speaker volume dispute. Then again, Maxine, the long-suffering building manager might have accidentally rented to a drug dealer. This had happened once before, but the walls were thin and too many neighbors were born snoops who worked irregular hours to allow crime to root. The dealer didn't last the second month.

Nina's answering machine had taken my first message. I got the machine again on the second call. So I tried Maxine. She told me in her gravelly smoker's voice to go on in. She hadn't seen Nina in a few days. She assumed I had keys. I did.

I said hello to the two policemen coming out of the building. They were both husky men, further burdened by their guns, batons, and two-way radios. The three of us filled the entryway as they watched me ring Nina's bell.

There was no answer. As I started to use the key, the older man stopped me. "You live in that apartment, ma'am?"

"Not exactly," I looked back at my rental car with a couple of suitcases and boxes of paperwork on the back seat. "I'm going to be staying with my friend for a week."

"Would you mind if we came in with you, ma'am? There's been a call about that unit. The manager isn't home and we were just about to go to the realty company to get a key. We just want to make sure everything's all right." They followed me into the hall.

I examined the first one's I.D. carefully. It looked okay. His name was Mills. Oh, the hell with it, he and his partner had a cop car. Those aren't so easily forged.

"You don't mean to search the place, do you? I mean, it's not my place and I couldn't consent on Nina's behalf. I'm just a guest. I haven't even spoken to her since last week when I told her when I'd be coming."

"No, ma'am, we appreciate your position." Mills was the spokesman. The younger guy waited patiently. "Point of fact, we don't have a search warrant, and as you said, you don't actually live there. Unless you think your friend might have something highly illegal sitting on her living room floor—we call that probable cause." The younger man grinned at that. A little police humor. "We just want to make sure your friend hasn't like, had some problems. . . . " Mills concluded, his voice fading out. "Does she live alone?"

"Yes." His tone set off a pang of alarm in my gut. I didn't like the glimmer of concern behind his studied calm face.

As I led the way up the stairs to Nina's apartment, no one said anything. It wasn't obvious from the hall, but when I unlocked the door and opened it, the smell hit us full blast. "Nina?" I called out, choking a little, "are you all right?"

The three of us stood in silence at the threshold.

"No," I said, as if someone had asked me the question.

The policemen exchanged a glance. Mills took out a cigar and calmly lit it. He puffed a time or two. I appreciated cigar smoke for the first time ever. He dragged at the cigar again and walked further into the apartment. I followed him, trying not to breathe too deeply. It was bad. Not garbage. More like a butcher shop on a hot day.

The place was clean. Stacks of the latest issue of the newsletter, boxes labeled "Patterns," and baskets of fabric samples made it clear she did most of her work at home. The blond hardwood floors gleamed under the ornate patterns of rugs in ripe fruit colors. Pictures hung above bookcases on three walls. The wall behind the sofa was covered with a sculpture made from driftwood attached to a fishing net. An old boyfriend of Nina's had created it. She always joked that she kept in touch with that man simply because she was attached to the driftwood. She didn't want him taking it back.

Mills puffed on his cigar, exhaled the smoke and led the way down the central hall from the living room to Nina's bedroom. A tier of shelves in a niche opposite her bedroom door held Nina's small sculptures of robust women. The bedroom door was closed. The smell was worse.

Shattered fragments of white plaster littered the floor. I looked at the shelf for the sculpture Nina loved most. Without thinking I knelt and reached down to pick up the pieces.

"Wait! Don't touch anything."

I looked up. It wasn't until I felt my face start to twitch that I realized I was crying.

"No!" I reached for the door at the same moment Mills caught my arm.

The door swung inward.

The smell of death hit us like a hot, wet curtain. The room was dark. Mills' cigar smoke breath was on my neck.

A sound filled the hallway that welled up from some deep reservoir inside.

"NO!" I yelled in a voice I didn't know I possessed. It made Mills flinch even as he pulled me backward.

The figure on the bed was propped against pillows with her head tilted forward on her chest, arms and legs stiffly extended on the coverlet.

Her bowed head covered the wound, but the blood from her severed throat had poured out over her body and soaked the thin nightgown she wore, so that it clung to her full breasts, belly and rounded thighs like a dress of red-black velvet.

Chapter Four

I saw Nina's pale hair hanging over her face, trailing in that river of red. The whole room went red.

Mills pulled me back. Away. Down the hallway and through the apartment. He handed me off to the other cop. Al. His name was Al. He led me back out the apartment door to the carpeted landing. He guided me to the stairs and sat me on the bottom step. He opened a window onto the stairwell and half leaned out of it breathing deeply. Then suddenly Al turned and raced back into the apartment. I heard him being sick into the kitchen sink. I hoped it was into the sink.

I started to feel a little queasy too. I managed to stand on shaky legs and walked back into the apartment. The bathroom door was half open and I pushed it in with my wrist, trying not to put fingerprints anywhere. I stood in front of the mirror for a few seconds before I realized there was writing on it. Nausea retreated, as a wave of fear prickled the hairs on the back of my neck.

I blundered out of the bathroom and ran straight into Mills.

"There's writing on the mirror. I think it's in blood."

He clenched his cigar between his teeth, took my arm firmly and propelled me out, but I noticed he glanced in the bathroom door as he went past.

KILL THE WHALES! it said on the mirror. For some reason I noticed the shower curtain was missing.

Al came out of the kitchen and joined us on the landing, wiping his mouth on a paper towel.

"Feelin' better, Al?" Mills asked his partner. If I hadn't been there, no doubt he would have said more. Al nodded and looked around for a place to put the towel before sheepishly stuffing it in his pocket.

"That your friend in the bedroom?" Mills asked me curtly, gesturing with the cigar.

I nodded, whispered, "Yes." I started to shiver.

Mills led me to the stairway, motioned me to sit. "Here, put your head between your legs and breathe deeply. Okay?"

I did. "Better, thanks."

"Good. Just rest there a minute." He pulled Al half inside the doorway and he probably thought out of earshot.

"You think it was him? Captain Ahab?" Al asked with an urgency that got my attention. I listened, resting my head on my arms and clasping my knees, sitting on the stair. They cast occasional looks at me as they spoke.

"Well, it sure wasn't a suicide. And whoever did it was either damn lucky or experienced. Most of her blood flowed out over her and into the mattress. Didn't see any on the carpet. The crime lab might find something—"

"That writing on the mirror," Al persisted, "It's the same as the others. And the victim was a fat woman . . . "

Mills glanced over at me and motioned Al down the stairs, "Could be a copy cat, it's not our job. Go down to the car to call Homicide. And bring up some crime scene tape."

I raised my head, suddenly realizing what was missing. "My god, Raoul!"

Both men stopped and examined me with renewed interest, "Who's Raoul?" Mills spoke in a growl around his cigar, "Her boyfriend? He live here too?"

"No. Well, he lives here, but he's her cat."

Mills shook his head in disgust. He was clearly not a cat person. "If there's an animal in there, dead or alive, the lab techs will find it. They'll be going over the place with a fine tooth comb. Meantime let's do everyone a favor and stay out before we destroy any more evidence than we already have."

Al's receding footsteps on the stairs and the bang of the downstairs door were followed by silence.

I sat on the step and thought back to the first time I'd ever seen Nina. How she had welcomed me to that little shop in Pike's Market. My first impression of her was a kind of awe that, although her figure was rounded, she carried her curves with such style and grace that her body seemed to be a force of nature and a perfect expression of her abundant goodness. The sun is round after all. She had hung up tapestries that begged to be touched—I could almost feel the intricate patterns of thread under my fingertips as I remembered them. She also hauled in a couple of benches and topped them with long, green plush cushions she had made. The whirr of the old-fashioned treadle-powered sewing machine underscored our conversations. In those early days she actually sewed while she waited for customers. I remember sitting awkwardly on the bench soaking up her attitude like a cat basking in a patch of sun.

I remembered when I took the job with Mrs. Madrone, I called Nina and offered to move my worldly possessions out of her basement to free up storage space for her. She laughed and asked whether I was going to drag them around the world with me or store them somewhere else.

Then that last conversation. Suddenly it was so clear to

.me that she had been worried, she who never worried. She had asked me to come earlier. I refused. If I had come last week would Nina be alive? Everyone loved Nina. Who could have killed her and written on her mirror in blood?

"Goddamn it, Nina," I muttered under my breath. "I promise you, I'll get whoever did this. I'll make them pay."

Mills squatted down in front of me, "How ya doing?"

I coughed a little on the cigar smoke, "I've been better."

"Excuse me, Miss . . . I didn't get your name."

"Fuller," I said. I noticed he was wearing latex surgical gloves, which somehow looked obscene on him. He held up a piece of Nina's broken statue.

"Miss Fuller, what was this anyway?" He asked. "You seemed to recognize it?"

"I . . . I don't know if I could explain. I could show you a picture of it. In one of her books." I was so shaken that it took a minute to realize he was staring down my neckline.

I got up and went back into the apartment and over to the bookshelf. Mills followed me. When I stretched up to grasp for the book just out of reach, he moved a footstool for me to stand on to reach the book.

It wasn't until I was on the footstool pulling the art book from the top shelf that I realized he could have reached it himself. He obviously preferred studying my ass. Clearly a man who could appreciate the larger figure. That thought cleared my head a little.

I sat on the sofa and put the book on the coffee table. Mills was looking down my neckline again. All right, if he wanted breasts, the statue of the Venus of Willendorf had an abundance.

"There. See?" I tapped the page and Mills reluctantly moved his gaze over to the full page color photo of the small, weathered statue. "Some of them are thirty-five thousand years old. Sort of a Stone Age Venus," I told him. He nodded. He seemed to sense its primitive appeal. "The broken statue from Nina's shelves was a plaster copy she made of the goddess. She said it was a reminder that this body type was once the ideal. These statues were found at sites all over the world. She inspired people with her life-force. Some people still find her compelling."

We both looked at the ancient small figure for a moment. No one would ever mistake that female for a male. Carved in stone she stood straight, blank face under a formal head-dress. Luxuriantly fat, hands folded demurely over gen-erous breasts and belly rounding over plump thighs. Everything to terrify the modern weight watcher.

Al came in with a roll of yellow plastic tape and stood over us. His gaze flickered over the picture on the page and glanced away. He did not find it compelling. I put the book on the end table next to the sofa and the three of us silently left the apartment.

As they unrolled their tape. I sniffled and fumbled in my pockets for a tissue. None was there. I wiped my eyes and nose with the back of my hand and stood up. I took a deep breath.

Then I heard a clumping up the stairs that could only be one person. Mills and Al jumped as an ear-splitting shriek pursued the footsteps up the stairwell. I was glad not to be standing next to the source of the scream.

"What the hell was that?" Al demanded.

"Well, the building manager," I started to say, still a little shaky, but I was cut off by the cigarette-husky voice coming around the stairwell.

"The place is crawling with cops!" Maxine came slowly into view, using her cane for extra dignity. "Oops, sorry, officer." She clapped her hand over her mouth and man-aged to look more like a naughty schoolgirl than a woman of sixty.

Maxine was short and buxom with a jut to her chin that made it clear she was not to be overlooked. Her dark gray hair was salted with white and chopped into a style more commonly seen on teenagers than grandmothers. She wore huge hoop earrings and a plum-colored shirt over crinkled drawstring pants of the same color. She regarded Al and me with impatient bright blue eyes.

"Maxine Gamble," she said holding out a hand first to Mills, then Al, "I'm the building manager down in Apartment One."

When Al let go of her hand, I hugged Maxine, unable to find a word to say.

"The woman who lived in this apartment is dead." Mills told her.

I could feel the news strike Maxine like a blow as I hugged her. Her cane hit the carpet and I kept an arm around her in case her knees buckled as well.

Al retrieved the cane. I could see from the look he and Mills exchanged that they were not thrilled to have two extremely upset women on their hands.

"Watch the door, Al," Mills said. "I'm going to meet the Homicide team, and these ladies can wait in Apartment One—is that acceptable to you, ma'am? We'll need to talk to you but it will be a little while."

"We'll be in Apartment One."

Another shriek bounced off the ceiling from the level below.

"What the hell is that?" Al asked irritably.

"My roommate," Maxine said over her shoulder, "thinks he's an opera star. Come on, Josie, honey, we're in the way here."

We reached Maxine's apartment and Mills went off to talk to the growing crowd of police in the foyer and on the steps. I asked Maxine, "Who is Captain Ahab?"

"Oh my God!" The look in her eyes sent a chill like a glass of ice water down my spine. "Come on," she said. "We'll talk in my apartment."

Chapter Five

Maxine's apartment was opposite the mail boxes and the laundry room on the ground floor of the building. I had been there a few times before with Nina but never alone with Maxine. In contrast to Nina's, Maxine's front room was a jungle of hot-weather plants. A glass-fronted cabinet full of china plates and photos in breakable frames was flanked by two carts of delicate ferns and briskly flowering orchids. A tropical creeper had made its way up one wall and along the ceiling and was determinedly heading toward the front door.

"Sit down, dear," Maxine gestured to a sofa facing a matching armchair and loveseat. "Let me deal with this desperate character."

Another shriek came from a corner of the room where the carpet was protected with a canvas drop cloth and a second layer of white-spattered newspapers. A wrist-thick tree branch hung from the ceiling like a swing. A large green bird swaggered along the branch from foot to foot with a nautical air.

I sat on the sofa to watch from a safe distance. The bird

began a more gentle chuk-chuk-chuk sound as Maxine approached, but he didn't fool me. I had ventured too close in my first encounter and that black beak had nipped a button off my jacket before I realized I was in range.

"I'd forgotten your parrot until I heard the shriek," I said.

"Macaw. He's a Military Macaw," Maxine corrected. "Aren't you, Groucho, you wild thing?"

She picked up a broomstick and held it against his chest, coaxing him to step onto it. He retreated, hanging upside down and squawking in protest, but she stretched up further, revealing one of her few little old lady garments, knee-hi nylons anchored on her lower calf.

"Behave yourself, Groucho!" Maxine said, still holding the broom up. "Don't be a bad bird or night will fall on you very early." Groucho clambered onto the new perch and Maxine's voice grew soft and soothing. She let him climb onto her shoulder and he nibbled her ear. She tickled his long black tongue with one finger as I shuddered, thinking of the damage he could do with that beak. But he seemed in a good humor when she opened the door to his large cage. He sidled in amiably and began climbing down the bars to root around for sunflower seeds among the headlines on the newspapers that lined its floor.

"There! Now, I'd better make enough coffee and tea for everyone. Come on." I followed her into the small kitchen and sat at the table.

I told her what we had found.

"Oh no." Her hands were shaking but she finished filling the kettle and put it on the stove. Then she turned around. I could see the tears streaming down her face and we both hugged each other. She broke away, found a box of tissues on the counter and put it on the table.

"Maxine, who could have done such a thing to Nina, of all people?" I asked after we both used up several tissues.

"I don't know. It makes no sense." She shook her head and turned back to the stove. "I met Nina twenty-three years ago." Maxine said. "My husband had just died. There was no money. Then I found out I was pregnant with my daughter Hope. You've met her?"

"No."

"Anyway, Nina helped me get this job managing the building. She sewed maternity clothes, went with me to the hospital when my daughter was born. She even babysat Hope when I needed a break. Everyone loved Nina."

The tea kettle whistled. Maxine brought a box of green tea from the cupboard and shook it into a dragon-embossed teapot that sat on the counter.

As she poured the water I heard the hall door open and someone came through the front room. An excited female voice called out, "Mama, it's William. He's back!"

"Hope! There's been trouble."

The young woman in black who came through the door stopped speaking immediately.

I glanced at Maxine and saw that she had her hand up in a gesture—was it warning?

Then I looked back at Hope. She had her mother's piercing blue eyes and short, large-chested build, although she had the glow of extreme youth. With such a radical mother she clearly had to rebel further than most. Her hair was cut in calculated geometry and most recently bleached straw blond with dark brown at the roots and a few ghosts of previous colors left here and there for a carnival air. She had the flawless skin and jaded naivete that belongs only to the early 20's. She had matched her mother's hoop earrings with long dangling fish lures and raised the ante with enough skin-piercing steel to set off a metal detector. Her black jacket, turtleneck, and jeans might have looked conservative if it hadn't been for the spiked dog collar that made me uneasy just on general principle.

"Hope, this is Josephine Fuller, Nina's friend—the one who travels all over. Josie, this is my daughter, Hope."

Hope shook hands like a polite school girl. Totally on guard. "Did you see the police car in front?" Maxine asked, putting out cups and pouring tea. Was it my imagination or was there a warning to her daughter in that statement as well?

"I came in the back. No, I don't want anything to drink, I just came to get my stuff and then I've got to go."

"Nina's been killed," I burst out, surprised at myself, but unable to bear another moment of waiting.

Hope gasped and held her throat, staring at me as if I had grabbed her by the dog collar. She looked to her mother, who nodded confirmation. Then she turned back toward the door with a strangled sob and fled. I heard the outside door slam and Groucho's hypershrill screech of surprise.

Chapter Six

Maxine turned back into the room after the door slammed. "They were very close," she said, putting both palms down on the table and standing still for a moment. Then she poured the tea, and handed me a cup. Before she sat down she filled a large coffee pot. Clearly that would be for the police.

The tea had a bitter taste, but it seemed to help. I put sugar in it. Tried again. No. More sugar. Yes. That would do. Milk or cream would have helped, but for the moment I was grateful to be sitting down with a hot distracting liquid to drink.

"Hope came in through the back?" I asked, after a moment of breathing in the hot vapor that rose from the tea. "I didn't know these places had back entrances. Aside from the fire escape." I sipped some more tea.

"When my daughter got a job she moved into one of the two basement units. There's an entrance through the back yard. Used to be all storage down there before it was converted to apartments."

"I've seen the storage space," I said. "Most of my worldly possessions are down there. But we went down the stairs from the front hall. I don't remember a back door."

"It's a couple of steps up to the back yard. It's usually closed, so you might not have noticed it." At last, she sat down at the table across from me.

"So, who is this William?" I put off talking about Nina, the way you turn your eyes away from a raw wound that you know is going to hurt worse once you see it.

Maxine stared at the steam rising out of her cup. "I can hardly keep track of Hope's boyfriends. I think this was the one with the very short hair. I wonder if that's supposed to be wild or mild these days. Knowing Hope, I'd say, very radical. William went away for awhile." She shrugged, "I guess he's back. Now you know as much as I do."

I took a deep breath. I had to ask. "Maxine. One of the policemen mentioned Captain Ahab after I saw this writing on the mirror—"

"You saw writing?" Maxine's shook her head unbelievingly "Oh, dear God, what a nightmare."

"Look, Maxine. I need to know this. Does it have something to do with *Moby Dick*?"

"Huh?" She stared back.

"Oh, come on. Didn't they make you read that book in high school? Okay, if it's not Captain Ahab hunting the great white whale, I haven't a clue what you're talking about."

"Okay." She sighed. "You just got into town. Even the local papers play down the serial killer story. The last thing we need is a copycat killer. Four or five large women in the Seattle area have been killed. Their throats were cut and the killer wrote a message in blood."

"Kill the whales."

"You've heard about it?"

"Only on the mirror at Nina's."

"Well, a local radio talk show host—you know the type who insults everyone to get their attention?"

I shrugged. "There are toadstools like that all over the country these days."

"Well, this radio guy thought it was funny as hell killing large women. He called the killer Captain Ahab and said the guy was on a beautify America kick. He suggested that if the women of Seattle all went on diets to ward off this lunatic, the man should get a public service award. Nina was furious. She helped organize a coalition of size-acceptance and women's groups to picket the station. It was in the local papers, on TV, and on the Internet. There were letters, calls, and boycotts. The radio station got worried and made the talk show guy apologize on the air. Nina was there to accept his apology. She didn't tell you any of this?"

I was embarrassed. "She did say she'd been doing a lot of community work, but I've been working pretty much round the clock the last year. I didn't get all the details."

Maxine nodded. "Unfortunately, the name stuck, even after the radio guy shut up. Some of the newspapers and even the cops call the killer Captain Ahab. I think that makes it worse because there's this implication that a woman is better off dead than fat." Suddenly her face turned ashen. "Wait. Oh, no. It couldn't be!"

"What?"

"Nina's picture was in the local papers. I even clipped it out. I wonder if the killer found her that way."

"If this Captain Ahab guy was the one who killed her. What happened to the radio guy? He might have resented her."

"He moved on to another city, somewhere in Maryland, I think."

"Don't the police always suspect the boyfriend? Nina told me she was seeing someone."

"Mulligan? He wouldn't hurt a fly. Joan from the newsletter group introduced them. You remember Joan. She and Mulligan both work at the phone company. He has the other basement apartment across from Hope's. He's a very gentle man."

The door bell rang. I followed Maxine out to answer it.

"Maxine, we just heard." The couple standing in the hall were holding state-of-the-art bicycles. "The police outside the building told us."

"Jo, these are the Swensons. They live in the top floor unit across from Nina's."

The Swensons wore matching neon biking outfits and helmets dripping from their ride in the rain. The husband held both bikes while the wife hugged Maxine, and after an introduction, greeted me with a double handclasp. Then the wife held the bikes while the husband did likewise.

"Do you need us to feed Nina's cat?" the wife asked. "We can take him for a few nights. Our cats will hate it, but it would be a pity to send that poor thing to the pound."

Maxine and I looked at each other. I hadn't thought of Raoul since Al pulled me out of the apartment.

"We haven't found the cat yet. The police must not have found him either." I said. "If you see him outside, please either bring him here or if you can't get close enough, let me know and I'll try to get him inside. I hope he's okay."

"Poor baby." The wife said.

They turned and headed up the stairs, carrying their bicycles.

"One of these days," Maxine said, "I expect to see those two rappelling up the side of the building with their bikes on their backs, just to get a better workout, you know?" She opened a pack of gum.

"Let me guess, you feel like a cigarette?"

"Seven years since I quit, but those bike people sometimes have that effect on me."

I accepted a stick of gum. "I feel the same way. And I was never even a smoker."

Before I could unwrap the gum, three more tenants came through the front door and hailed Maxine.

Two were men wearing backpacks and carrying camping gear. They were trailed by a lanky red-haired young woman who was all business in a Burberry trench coat, with high-heeled boots to match the briefcase looped by a strap over her shoulder.

"Maxine, the policeman outside told us. What a shock," said the older, dark-haired man, who looked to be in his forties. His beard had an artful strip of silver that made his chin seem to be cleft.

He hugged Maxine. His blond companion, who looked to be in his early twenties, did too, although a little more gingerly. Maxine took the red-haired woman aside. The dark-haired man turned to me. "I'm Val," he said.

I introduced myself.

"This is K. C.," he said, putting an arm around the young man's shoulder. K. C. nodded. He was not merely handsome but painfully beautiful and deeply upset. His jade green eyes swam with tears.

His earrings made me think of Mrs. Madrone's Ambrose, but K. C. seemed to be made of much frailer stock. His lip began to tremble. "We only just got back from our vacation," he said in a teary voice, "And now we'll never see her again." He wiped his face on his sleeve in a suddenly childish gesture.

"Come on, guys," the red-haired woman put an arm around K. C., as she and Val led him upstairs. "We should let Maxine rest." She nodded to me. "I'm in the apartment across the hall, next to the mailboxes, if I can be of any use."

"Now that's an efficient woman," I said to Maxine as she closed the door.

"Yes, that's Beth. She'd better be efficient, she's a company controller. Val's been a tenant here for fifteen years. He's a graphic designer downtown. Now K. C. is . . ."

"Flavor of the month?"

We hadn't even reached the kitchen when the doorbell rang again. Maxine opened it and nearly stepped back onto my feet in surprise at the thin, intense man who was standing so close that he seemed to be trying to look through the apartment's peephole.

The man, just above medium height, wore a grubby raincoat and horn-rimmed glasses fogged with the sudden change from the rain outside. He stared in at us, then seemed to realize he was peering in too closely and backed away.

"Hello, Eric. Jo, this is Eric Shumacher. He lives in the apartment below Nina's."

"Just got in from Florida," he said. "This is one totally jet-lagged guy. Eric's big business trip." Neither of us said anything. This made him twitch a little faster. "Saw the police in front. They said what happened. What a shock. Eric had to come by on the way in. See? Luggage."

"Stop by tomorrow afternoon, dear." Maxine told him. "I'm going to fall on my face when the police get done here and I'll bet Jo is even more tired."

"Eric understands. Tomorrow then." He made a gesture that might have been very close to touching Maxine's arm though it fell short by about three feet.

"'Eric' understands?" I raised an eyebrow after Maxine had closed the door.

"He just talks like that. He's a computer genius. Beth says he refers to himself in the third person to remind himself he's the carbon-based entity called Eric, and not one of his little silicon buddies. He's a strange one, but very quiet. "

"Oh, yeah. They're all quiet." I muttered.

"Jo," Maxine said, looking at me as if she feared talking to myself was a sign of near mental breakdown. "I know you were going to stay with Nina. You're welcome to stay with me."

I sighed soundlessly, "That's awfully nice of you, Maxine, but I know these apartments are so small . . ." I had seen this before. Hospitality arising from tragedy. People who couldn't put together ten minutes of conversation offering their homes to strangers.

"No, no, I insist. Unless you've got family or somewhere else you'd rather go. My guest room is small but you'll want to be here for the funeral and you're welcome."

The prudent thing would have been to refuse and head for the nearest hotel. But I found myself following Maxine when she offered to show me the room, just behind the kitchen. A narrow space with book shelves on one side and a day bed against the back wall. No windows. Claustrophobic but clean. Griff and I had shared far more cramped and unwholesome places in our travels.

"It probably started as a butler's pantry, but we remodeled it for Hope's room. I'll get you some sheets and blankets."

I knew I'd probably regret it. So, I'd get a hotel room then. I was grimly determined to find out who did this to Nina. The building where it happened was the best place to start. That thought gave me a sudden wave of strength that pressed back the grief. I dug in my pocket and came up miraculously with a clean tissue. "Thank you, I will stay a day or so until I get sorted out," I said, wiping my eyes.

We both ran out of things to say. I went to the window and examined the front yard intently, as if expecting the cat to appear. All I saw was the rain. No sign of Raoul. I hoped he had found a dry place to hole up.

The doorbell rang, followed instantly by a firm pounding, as if simply pressing a button were not enough. Maxine and I looked at each other. No question. This time it was the police.

Chapter Seven

The police didn't leave until well after dark. Like the rain, they came and went in flurries through the afternoon and early evening.

Mills and Al were replaced at Maxine's kitchen table by Homicide Detective Gonick and his partner Detective Lasker. Gonick was tall, stout, and sunburned to the same hue as his red hair. He must have been in his late thirties. I kept wanting to ask where he got that kind of sunshine around here. Lasker was pale and a little taller and younger than his partner, with orange tinted aviator shades and a receding hairline. He listened and wrote while Gonick posed questions.

Toward the end of the interview Gonick suggested that since there were no signs of breaking and entering, Nina probably knew her killer. Or, she had let a stranger into the apartment for some unknown reason. With a delicate, "ahem," he told Maxine, "She was discovered in bed in a thin nightgown. Was she in the habit of letting in strangers?"

Maxine had begun to almost visibly boil with twitches

of anger, "She was a healthy girl," she growled with a snap of her smartly barbered gray locks, "I didn't pry into her sex life and she didn't pry into mine."

When they left, still casting slightly mistrustful looks at Maxine, who no longer seemed like such a sweet old gal, Maxine and I began to laugh in hysterical relief. Then a few tears came. They were short-circuited by the telephone, which began to ring early in the evening as people came home from work and heard of Nina's death. I washed coffee cups while Maxine took calls until she finally recorded a short message for her answering machine explaining the situation and turned off the telephone's bell so we could sleep. I was surprised to find that I did sleep.

The next morning I woke up on the squashy mattress of Maxine's daybed, at first feeling only that there was something terrible waiting for me, like waking from a nightmare. Then I remembered. This nightmare was the walking-around wide-awake kind. I grimly pushed aside the emotions that welled up. The only things I wanted, to hug Nina and talk to her, were the things I could not do. I shuffled into the kitchen with the enthusiasm of a newly roused zombie. Fortunately, even after the policemen had consumed a few quarts of her coffee, Maxine still had a generous supply.

A good thing, too. If she'd been out of coffee, I might have totally broken down. But as I meditated over the caffeine I reconsidered my vow to find out who killed Nina.

Okay, so I wasn't well-equipped for finding out anything about violent death. But it went way beyond unfair that such a luminous person should be slaughtered and ugly words about killing whales scrawled in her blood. A wave of anger swept through me, pushing grief ahead of it. I didn't know what I could do, but now I could function.

I tried to dredge up some kind of rational plan. Someone Nina trusted had killed her, perhaps someone I had spoken to last night or even someone who had slept under the same roof last night. Nina was my best friend, but I had to admit to myself, I didn't know much about her other friends. That would be one place to start.

I brought my coffee from the kitchen back to the room where I had slept. My portable office sat stacked on its two-wheeled airport cart, untouched from when I had brought it in from the car the day before. I unstrapped the laptop computer, hooked it up to the ink jet printer, and plugged them both in. I set the briefcase full of paperwork next to the student desk in Maxine's guestroom.

Now there was barely enough space to turn around. On the other side of the door, Groucho gave a cheerful cackle of greeting as I heard Maxine's footsteps. Then in the kitchen, a few feet away, I heard her open a drawer. I quietly closed the door, glad that I had a cellular phone and didn't have to make toll calls or stand at the wall phone in Maxine's kitchen tying up the line.

It was time to call Mrs. Madrone, or actually to call Ambrose, to arrange a little more time off.

Ambrose sounded shocked and genuinely concerned when he heard a close friend had died, and so violently. He asked if I would be in for the next half hour, and said he would get back to me. But it was Mrs. Madrone herself who called a few minutes later. "Jo! I'm so sorry to hear about your friend Nina! What can I do? What about funeral expenses? Do you need help with arrangements? I can lend you Ambrose if you want to turn it over to someone who is not under the stress of mourning. Really, he can be quite comforting in time of need. He has very strong mother hen instincts."

"No, thanks, Mrs. Madrone. I think everything is covered." I had to smile at the thought of Ambrose closing your pores with his brusque wit. She had a point. Ambrose could probably organize a funeral, a wedding, and the

Normandy invasion in the space of a rainy afternoon, but I wasn't sure I wanted him so close just now.

"Well, let him know where and when services will be held. And of course we'd like to contribute to whatever charity she favored."

"That's so kind, Mrs. Madrone. I appreciate it and I'll tell Ambrose when I find out. It will probably take me another week off before I can get back in gear at work."

"Well, so long as Ambrose knows where to reach you. We'll talk soon."

She hung up and a moment later Ambrose called back. After he took Maxine's address and phone number, there was an unusually long pause. "That's in the Capitol Hill district, right?"

"Yes."

"I think I know someone in the building."

"Val and K. C.?"

Another longish pause, "I know Val. Perhaps I should pay a call."

"Sure, Ambrose, why not? Small world, ain't it?"

"Getting smaller every day."

For the first time I could remember, an encounter with Ambrose left me without a desire to slam the phone down hard. I sat staring without really seeing the bookcase in front of me. The paperwork could wait. I picked up my now-empty cup and went around the corner to the kitchen.

Maxine was sitting at the kitchen table, looking drawn and pale, and older than her years. "I heard you talking to someone," she said raising eyebrows that had been plucked off years earlier and never quite re-grew.

"I used my cell phone." I said a little sheepishly, "I had to check in at work."

"You like your work, don't you?" She fixed me with an open stare of her extraordinary blue eyes.

"Yes. I do." I poured myself another cup of coffee, doctored it to drinkability and sat down opposite her. "There aren't too many jobs where you feel like you're helping make things just a little better."

"Ha! You said a mouthful there." Maxine ran a hand through her iron-gray spikes of hair. "You are one of half a dozen people I've met in six decades who could honestly say that."

There was a pause. "Do you know if Nina had any relatives?"

"No, dear. Her parents were both dead. She's from a small town on the other side of the Cascades. If she has cousins or remote relatives, she's never kept in touch with them so far as I know. She always said we were her family. Her friends—the people in the building, at work, the women in the newsletter group. I've asked them over at noon to help plan a memorial service."

"Okay. I guess we'll be able to look at her papers and make sure once the police let us go in . . . Oh no! What about her cat? I hope he's not crouching under a bush in the rain."

"The police would have told us if they found him."

From what I'd seen of bureaucracies I wasn't so sure of that. "I've got to at least go up there and look for him. I've got my keys."

"The police still have my keys. The place is probably sealed. If there is a seal, don't touch it. Come back and we'll call those homicide cops. Maybe they can come in with us to make it all official."

"Good idea."

"Check the backyard first. Nina sometimes let him out the window to the fire escape. He might be out there now scratching to get in. Or he could be in the backyard trying to get in the door down to the basement."

"And you won't mind my bringing him here, with the bird and all?"

"Oh, the cage will keep the cat out and the bird in. If you find him, bring him in. Take an umbrella, it's raining."

The rhododendron bushes grew wildly and luridly magenta back there. "Raoul, here, kitty, kitty." I stood, dripping water from my umbrella and bent down to look under the branches. Nina had told me Raoul had chosen and could in fact pronounce his own name, but in my experience most cats answer to "kitty, kitty" if to anything at all.

No sign of a cat. I went inside by the back door. Tramped through the spooky basement. No sign of life in either basement apartment. I dripped rainwater up stairs, through the foyer and up the main stairs calling softly, "kitty, kitty" at intervals and feeling foolish.

I got to Nina's apartment. The only sign of an official presence was the jagged edge of the yellow crime scene tape that seemed to have been ripped off the doorway. That seemed odd but there was definitely no official seal on the door or notice not to enter.

I listened. Was that a faint movement inside the apartment? I could imagine the cat, creeping from hiding place to hiding place, eluding the police search. And now trapped in there without food or water, trying to get out. I got a grip on the dread that rose up at the thought of facing the apartment again. I put the key in the lock and went in.

It was quiet. A faint sound seemed to come from the bathroom. As I came closer, I noticed a wadded up roll of the yellow crime scene tape outside the bathroom door. If the police had been that careless, no wonder they missed the cat in their search.

"Kitty, kitty." I stood still and listened, straining to hear the sound again. I didn't want to face the bathroom and that writing on the mirror. A faint squeak seemed to come from the linen closet across the hall. I choked out one last "Raoul" and almost turned and ran from the apartment.

But a faint soprano echo, "raw-woul," from the linen closet froze me in my tracks.

"Raoul, is that you? Kitty, kitty, kitty—" I threw open the closet door and heard another micro-mew from behind a stack of towels on the top shelf. At the same time I could have sworn I heard a faint creak of the bathroom door. I took a deep breath and reached up under the towels, where Raoul's nose sniffed my fingers as if to check my I.D.

The creaking door sent my heart pounding with the conviction that someone else was in the apartment. I grasped Raoul by his smokey-gray ruff and pulled him out, protesting and hanging onto towels with every claw. His eyes shone like orange candles in the dark closet as he exploded into a frenzy of snarling, hissing protest. Towels flew right and left but I kept hold of him and a big towel he had hooked onto. He clawed me across the back of the hand and the neck before I subdued him, clutched against my chest and vibrating with a sustained guttural growl. I had no idea an animal any smaller than a St. Bernard could make such a deep, throaty sound.

As we passed the bathroom door he hissed at it. He sure as hell couldn't read the writing on the mirror, but I didn't much like the idea that he seemed to agree with me that there was someone in there. The cat dug his claws through my coat down to skin.

Chapter Eight

I locked the apartment and leaned against the door holding the cat to my heart, which was pounding as if I'd just run a marathon. The apartment had a presence almost as if it were haunted by the violence that had taken place there.

Raoul brought me back to reality with a sudden wiggle and a jump. I thought I had lost him, but once on his feet in the hallway he looked around forlornly and made no move to streak for freedom. He seemed to sense he was an orphan. He meowed plaintively and allowed me to heft him back up and carry him downstairs.

As we entered Maxine's apartment, Groucho spread his green wings in challenge and lunged at us, crashing into the side of the cage and biting the bars. The cat cowered against me in alarm. He could see this was no overgrown sparrow. That beak demanded respect.

Maxine had gone out, leaving a note, 'Went to get a few things for lunch. I'll be back soon.' That reminded me, if I was going to stay a few days, I needed to contribute some groceries.

I set Raoul down and contemplated going back to Nina's

apartment for the cat's food and water bowls. Forget it. I knew I couldn't face that place again.

I borrowed a couple of chipped bowls from Maxine's cupboard and poured milk into one and water into the other. Raoul followed me into the kitchen. A modern predator, he recognized the refrigerator door noise and began to meow urgently. When I put down the bowls, he vacuumed up the milk first, then lapped at the water bowl for quite awhile.

While he did that I improvised a litter box from a cardboard box, a plastic garbage bag liner, and some potting soil from Maxine's plant work bench in the laundry room. Raoul came in to watch. Soon thereafter he proved beyond all shadow of a doubt that he understood the purpose of my improvised kitty latrine.

"Smart cat." I told him. He responded by scratching up the soil enthusiastically. "I only hope I haven't just taught you to start peeing in Maxine's potted plants."

Raoul leaped out of the box, and a second later let out such a hiss that I thought I must have stepped on his tail without knowing it. But when I looked down, I saw I wasn't near enough to have done that. Raoul was crouched down, ears flattened back, his eyes were focused on the wall, beyond which was the front hall. His hair was puffed up and his tail expanded to face some threat neither of us could see. A surge of terror went through me for no apparent reason. I wondered if that presence I had felt in Nina's apartment could have been an actual intruder. The outside door closed. From Maxine's apartment you could hear everyone who came and went.

I ran round to the window facing the front of the building. Through the screen of rain and the branches of thick-leaved trees I saw a tall, square-shouldered figure in a hooded jacket. Damn that hood. It hid the face and even the back of the head from view, although it must have been a man, or a tall, angular woman. The figure got into a blue pickup truck, started it, and drove away.

When I turned back from the window I practically tripped over the Raoul, who was right behind me. His hair had settled back down so that he no longer looked like a threatened porcupine. He followed me back to the guest room. I lay down for a moment on the day bed. Suddenly a mass of aches and pains surfaced that I hadn't felt until then. The cat put his paws up on the bed and gave a meow of inquiry. "Well, I'll forgive you for scratching me, if you'll forgive me for scaring you," I told him. He regarded me steadily for several seconds and then hopped up beside me. His coat was slightly matted. "I'll get a brush for you," I promised. He purred in answer and I slipped into a dream.

In the dream I was trying to take Elvis Presley to detox. I was helping him down the front steps of a mansion very much like Claude Rains' mansion in Rio from the last scene from Hitchcock's *Notorious*. Like Ingrid Bergman in the film he was too drugged to cooperate or resist. I kept encouraging him, "Come on, Elvis, we're going to the Betty Ford Clinic. You'll meet lots of other famous people and you'll feel much better." But it was hopeless. His handlers spirited him away as a crowd of screaming fans drove up.

I woke up. The shrieking was Groucho demanding attention in the front room. The cat had deserted me. I heard him in the kitchen row-ow-owling at Maxine, probably begging food. Maxine said something. A man's voice replied. I got up and went to investigate.

I ran into Maxine herding a short, slender man with dark, fuzzy hair and a much taller blond woman from the kitchen back into the living room, making fussing noises, about tea being no trouble and just sit down. "I'll hear the whistle when the kettle boils," she insisted, waving a hand at me.

"This is Andrew Stack, an old friend of Nina's."

"My god, Josie, Maxine told me you found her." Stack said in a surprisingly froggy baritone. He came over and captured my hand, looking up into my face with moist brown eyes radiating such sincere concern that I forgot for a moment I'd never met the man before. "Call me Andy, Nina always did." It was clear from the regret in his hoarse voice that he cared about Nina.

"Oh yes, Andy. Nina mentioned you. She leased her store site from you." He looked suitably gratified and I refrained from adding that Nina had always referred to him in pitying tones as a workaholic who didn't have a clue what it was like to have a life.

He let go of my hand and began to pace, sizzling with nervous energy, from time to time throwing out a rapid-fire sentence or two. While I didn't catch every word he muttered, I stood back in awe of the constantly changing expressions that came and went across his face. I could almost see sparks flying out the ends of the untidy frizz of black hair. I wondered if he ever stood still long enough to comb it. My question was immediately answered when he ran his hands through it a few times as if to pull it out by the roots. He wore an expensive brown wool shirt and trousers but somehow made them look as if they had been scavenged from Goodwill.

When he paced back close enough to me again, he stopped to squeeze my shoulder. "I heard you found Nina." he said again. "Are you all right?" I gently twisted free and murmured something about being as well as could be expected.

Andy did another lap of the room, examining the knick-knacks and framed photos in Maxine's glass-fronted cabinets. Then he fell back on the sofa between Maxine and the slender blond woman who sat weeping quietly. Maxine heard the kettle whistling and escaped to the kitchen.

I took a closer look at the woman next to Stack. Although he patted her arm, her tears seemed to annoy him. "This is my fiancée, Susan."

I sat down in the chair opposite the sofa and nodded at Susan. It took a moment to realize that the slender but muscular young woman was very beautiful. She wore an ultrasuede pantsuit in the same shade of teal as her eyes, which were rimmed with red from weeping. Her hair was pinned up in a French twist that had begun to spiral down her neck. From time to time she vaguely pushed at the golden spill of hair.

The three of us sat in awkward silence broken by an occasional sniffle from Susan. Groucho was ominously quiet in his corner cage. He stropped his beak on the bars a few times, and I sensed a shriek building in his throat like a thunderclap.

I murmured that I would see if I could help Maxine. I met her at the kitchen door holding a teapot in one hand and a tray of cups. "Get the cookies from the cupboard," she commanded when she saw me, "Put them on another tray with some fruit. I never know what to feed these people. They're health food freaks, but half the time those people are looking for an excuse to fall off the wagon and grab all the sugar they don't get at home."

"Susan definitely looked like she wasn't getting much sugar at home." I said, smiling to myself at my own double entendre as I opened the cupboard. I was getting to know my way around Maxine's kitchen. She cast me a warning look and walked through the doorway, nearly colliding with Andy Stack.

"I came to help too," he said, looking past me into the cupboard. Maxine shrugged and headed toward the front room where Groucho let loose with a piercing shriek.

"The fruit is fine," Stack said, looking over the tray, "But no refined starches." He closed the cupboard. "I won't allow them in the house, in the office, or anywhere around Susan. You know Susan used to be nearly your size when I met her, but she's come along wonderfully on the Stack Program."

"Hey, your domestic arrangements are your own business," I said with a forced neutral tone.

"Did Nina ever tell you about the Stack Program?"

Okay, that was the second offense. "You mean the one where a grown woman can't be trusted in the same room with a pack of cookies?" I said, reaching past him to jerk the cupboard door open and the package of cookies off the shelf. "Maxine wants to be hospitable, you don't have to touch any of it. If you knew Nina, you'd know she was the last person to put up with your kind of bull."

He seized my wrist as I started to dump the cookies onto a plate. "Maybe you didn't know Nina as well as you think you did."

I tried to move away but he was surprisingly strong for a small man and he didn't let go right away. I froze in his grip and glared at him.

"Take your damn hand off me or I'll scream," I said between my teeth. He let go immediately.

He continued as if I had not spoken, "In the Stack Program we teach that accepting yourself just as you are is the first step to becoming who you really want to be."

"And if I already am who I really want to be?"

"You can't be serious." He gazed at me with fascination, as if examining a puzzle he wanted to assemble—or likely to take apart and reassemble, minus some pieces.

"You could be magnificent," he said.

I rolled my eyes in silence. I was weaned on that kind of remark. He started to say something else but I cut him off. "Your program stands for everything Nina hates." I faltered, "Everything she hated."

There was a long silence and Stack looked at me calmly.

"Feel better now?" He restrained me from moving by blocking the doorway. "You're a lot like Nina. Come to the Center and you'll understand how Nina and I could work together." He peered up into my eyes meaningfully and his breath tickled my collar bone. He smelled of peppermint.

I shoved past him carrying the plate of mainly fractured cookies. I put it on the table next to the tea Maxine had poured into cups. He followed bringing the milk.

Susan looked at him and then at me and then at the floor. Maxine had taken an unshelled peanut from a bowl at the end of the table and was pushing it through the bars at Groucho to buy some silence.

Andy stood over Susan and glanced at his watch. Susan hastily put down the cup she had picked up and didn't even glance at the plates of fruit and cookies. Actually the sugar cookies didn't look very appetizing after our tussle over the bag.

"Maxine, we have to be going." Stack reached into his inner coat pocket and pulled out an envelope, which he handed to her. "This is to help with funeral expenses. When you've finalized something, give us a call, okay? I think I can get hold of Nina's old minister from our home-town. And Josie, do come down to see us, I mean that."

After they left, Maxine and I sat for a moment, staring at the cups and saucers and fractured cookies.

"You didn't take to Andy, did you?"

An understatement. I shook my head.

"The man's a millionaire. He's created a franchise chain of diet centers."

"And Nina worked with someone like that?"

"Nina knew people on both sides of a lot of arguments." Maxine smiled wistfully. "I've heard her in some heated debates with Andy. He's contributed quite a lot to the newsletter. She told him she'd take his money and put his name on the list of contributors, but she intended to warn the readers about the diet part of his program."

"I never noticed any diet ads in the newsletter."

"No, of course not. That's why I, for one, never disapproved. She printed announcements of their fitness classes for large women, but she put a disclaimer next to the notice that the Stack Center had a diet program and the newsletter did not endorse it."

I decided not to mention my odd clash with Andy in the kitchen. It wasn't the first time someone had pushed a diet on me one second and made a pass the next.

"What about the fiancée?" I asked Maxine. "Did you ever meet her before?" Maxine brightened a little at the prospect of gossip. We settled down on the sofa.

"You know, he always came to visit Nina and he never brought what's her name, Susan, along. I wonder why."

Judging by the way he jumped on me in the kitchen I could think of one reason he wouldn't bring Susan along when he visited Nina. "Susan must have met Nina somewhere. She sure seemed broken up by the news."

"Maybe she met Nina at Andy's headquarters. Susan works for him as his secretary, and Nina's store is in the courtyard behind the building." Maxine got up and surveyed the coffee table. "We can leave all this out, but we'll need more cups and spoons. The women from the newsletter will be here any minute to talk about Nina's funeral."

"How are you holding up?" I asked her.

She turned her blue eyes in the wrinkled face back to me and grimaced. "I'll survive." Groucho cackled approvingly in the corner.

The first woman rang Maxine's doorbell a few minutes later. I got ready to sit down and help plan a funeral.

Chapter Nine

The first to arrive was the executive, Beth Kent, the burgundy frames of her glasses clashing cheerfully with her carrot-red hair. I'd last seen her walking K. C. and Val upstairs. She looked leaner than ever and businesslike in a Navy blue turtleneck and leggings with black high top sneakers. She brought an apple pie and apologized at length for having bought it in a store.

I took a dripping pale blue raincoat from the next woman who came in. Maxine introduced her as Cora, which was good because the woman was so soft-spoken I could barely hear what she said. It was clear that Cora's sweatshirt and jeans were draped over a breathtaking hourglass figure. She hugged Maxine a long time. Then she pressed my hand between hers and whispered, "Nina helped me accept myself. She saved my life."

Mine too, I thought. I shook my head at the perversity of how we learn to hate our bodies. Cora had the kind of shape that would drive other women crazy from watching men drool over her. But there was something Cora couldn't accept in herself, and Nina had made it easier for her to live in her skin.

Then Joan Leti arrived. I had met her before at Nina's. It was hard to forget Joan. I'm large myself, but Joan must have been nearly four hundred pounds, which she carried on a six-foot frame. A mass of raven curls circled her round face like a dark halo and added another couple of inches to her height. Nina told me a lot of Joan's serenity came from her Samoan roots, where being large is just fine, thank you.

Joan was a woman of few words. Today she took off an iridescent green cape to reveal one of Nina's swirling float dresses that reflected color into her grave face. She folded me and Maxine together into a warm hug that gave real comfort. At the last newsletter meeting I had attended she had brought a meat and taro casserole with coconut that I still remembered. I was pleased to see that she had brought another one with her tonight. I doubted the dish would last the hour. It smelled great.

Patrice arrived next, a majestic African American woman who was nearly as large as Joan and certainly had as much self-confidence. She hung her dripping red raincoat on Maxine's coat rack. Patrice wore blue jeans and a tank top, with a tight sweater over it, her hair woven in braids that flowed down her massive back like a waterfall.

"Have you considered," Patrice said, settling on the sofa next to Joan, "that if it was Captain Ahab who killed Nina, he might be targeting some of the women in our group?"

"No," Joan said, "but thanks for bringing it up. I really needed that."

There was nervous laughter all around, but there was also fear in the room.

"Maxine told me Nina's picture was in the newspapers when that radio DJ made his apologies," I said. "Were any of the rest of you in the picture?"

None of them was.

"We should just be extra careful and not be intimidated," Cora whispered from where she sat on the loveseat next to Beth.

They all stared at her in surprise, "Well, listen to you," Beth said, patting Cora on the shoulder. "You used to be so shy you'd never say boo. Now you're standing up to mass murderers."

"Well . . ." Cora said.

Maxine asked me to bring a couple of kitchen chairs out in case new arrivals overflowed the living room furniture. But everyone seemed to be here. I sat in one of the kitchen chairs while Maxine settled into her easy chair and they set about putting together a notice for the newspapers. They also divided up the responsibility for notifying Nina's network of friends, and the business associates and customers who had become friends. Again it struck me how deeply rooted Nina was in a strong network of people who cared about one another—particularly these women. I admired how simply and directly they divided the work at hand and how they all seemed to agree what Nina would have wanted, but I felt keenly isolated from them and very alone. I hadn't had this kind of circle of women friends since I was in high school. And I didn't know how to begin to make such connections now. I made notes. It was all I could do.

The doorbell rang and I got up to answer it, waving Maxine back to her easy chair. For a moment I thought it might be Hope, standing in the doorway wearing a black leather jacket and pants. Maxine had an instant of the same illusion because she half rose, and then sank back down in disappointment. This kid was taller and a natural brunette, with an overlay of some black-purplish dye. The first thing she said was, "Where's Hope?"

"I wish I knew," Maxine said, popping half a broken

sugar cookie into her mouth. "If you see her, tell her to call me. She left in kind of a hurry. Jo, I want you to meet Scar."

I extended my hand. Scar's thin pale hand seemed to have been soaking in ice water. "That's an unusual name, Scar."

"Short for Scarlett," she said with a yawn, releasing my hand and stripping off her wet leather jacket to reveal an only slightly drier black t-shirt. She slid down to sit cross-legged on the floor with the speed and grace of an oiled snake. I could only stare in admiration. Almost as soon as the group returned to scheduling the memorial services, Scar began to nod and dozed off sitting up. I wondered what kind of drugs she was on, or if she simply led such an active night life that daytime activities held a limited claim on her attention.

Another knock at the door brought the room to silence so abruptly that even Scar woke up. I hadn't realized until that moment how much on edge we all were. At Maxine's nod, I went to answer it and found myself confronting a rain-drenched man of huge proportions. He had longish, blond hair and the face of a discontented bulldog. The women in the room, with the exception of Joan and Maxine, blinked a little at the fierce expression he presented. Maxine launched herself into his arms with alacrity.

"Come in, come in, Mulligan," she said, pulling him into the apartment and standing on tiptoe to pat his cheek, "You did get the news about Nina, didn't you?"

I was standing close enough to be hit by the drops of rain that flew off his coat and hair when he turned his head. I could see there were tears as well as raindrops on Mulligan's face as he nodded. He fumbled with the buttons on his raincoat as he looked around at the women in the room. He was such a strong, primitive presence that we all were compelled to stare back.

Mulligan seemed even more out of it than we were. He looked like an ox who has been stunned with a mallet.

When he spoke, his voice was a light tenor, unexpected coming from such a large, broad frame. "I saw the newspaper at the airport. Who are these people?"

He addressed himself to Maxine and gestured around vaguely, but he was looking at me. I started to blush without quite knowing why. But when I met his eyes, unexpectedly brown for all his blond hair, a sudden widening of his pupils told me that he also had a vision of the two of us thrashing around on crumpled sheets. He blinked and both of us looked away at once.

"You know most of Nina's friends, Mulligan," Maxine said smoothly, although an extra wrinkle in her forehead told me she hadn't missed the reaction between this total stranger and me. "Oh, and this is Josephine Fuller, Nina's friend from out of town."

Mulligan muttered something about, "She mentioned you," and nodded in my general direction without actually meeting my eyes again. I couldn't tell if he was as embarrassed as I, or if it was simply the crushing grief that caused him to stare at the floor. I felt as if my sudden flush of desire had been broadcast on a wide-screen television for the rest of the room to watch. I sat back down on the kitchen chair. This was bizarre. The man said three words and I was about to faint with lust. It had been a long time since I was with Griff, I told myself. And this man had a strong life force. That was all.

"Mulligan?" Joan spoke up. "Hello."

"Oh, hi, Joan," he ran a hand over his face.

"We're planning the memorial service for Nina. You're welcome to stay." Joan gestured to one of the free chairs.

"No." He turned back to the door and raised a hand to the lot of us in farewell, dismissal, or possibly exorcism, "I'll be downstairs. Does Hope know?" He turned back to look down at Maxine, who now seemed even smaller and more frail.

"Yes, dear," she lowered her voice, but I could tell she was saying Hope hadn't been heard from recently.

He nodded thoughtfully and left without another word, a large wet spot on the rug the only evidence of his having been there.

"Who was that?" I asked. Looking around. With some relief I noticed that I wasn't the only woman in the room made breathless by the man's presence.

"That was Mulligan, the bachelor in the basement," Beth said with a chuckle. "Quite a match for Nina, isn't he? Picture Eric in the apartment below, chewing his knuckles, when Nina and Mulligan hit the sack. It must have been like a Viking orgy upstairs."

Everyone laughed at that, but for some reason I looked at Joan. She hadn't gotten as much of a reaction out of Mulligan as she had wanted. What was all that about?

Partly because I was angry with myself for being pleased that Mulligan had responded to me but not to Joan, I asked recklessly, "He must have the key to Nina's apartment, though, don't you think?"

Chapter Ten

Soon afterward everyone went off to perform their appointed tasks and I realized, looking at my notes, that I had none. After Mulligan came in, my attention must have strayed. Before I could ask a few tactful questions about what I might have missed, the doorbell rang and people from the building began to come in.

What happened the rest of the evening was a kind of informal wake. The only honest-to-goodness, official wake I'd been to several years before had involved lots of Irish relatives and lots of Irish whiskey. The final score was two fistfights and one surreptitious sexual encounter culminating in a screaming match that fractured an engagement, all to the accompaniment of puking, blackouts, and rambling, semi-demented reminiscences about the deceased.

The blood alcohol level was lower among those who gathered to remember Nina. However, I did manage to keep the sex and violence ratio going, at least mentally, by wondering whether Mulligan would show up again and speculating on which of the guests might be a serial killer.

Patrice, Cora, and Scar left soon after the Swensons

showed up with a large vat of salad. Joan and Beth stayed on. What I had seen, or at least thought I'd seen, between Mulligan and Joan disturbed me. First of all, I refuse to compete with other women for a man. If a man isn't smart enough to prefer me, then he wouldn't be able to keep up with me in any event. I wish I could honestly say that's why I divorced Griff. But with Griffin Fuller it was a matter of his preferring me along with every other interesting female that crossed his path.

I don't have much staying power in situations that make me cringe. And instantly desiring my dead friend's lover while seeing Joan seem to feel the same way qualified in that category. My instinct was to cope in my usual splendid manner by leaving town. Dangerous as the topic was, I had to consider the possibility that Joan's feelings for Mulligan might somehow be involved in Nina's death. Women have killed for less.

Eric Shumacher arrived carrying two six-packs of Beck's beer. He wore jeans and a black t-shirt with a message on it in convoluted Gothic script. The letters were intricate enough that I spent several seconds squinting at them before I realized that the text was upside down. Whatever the message was on Eric's t-shirt, it was primarily for Eric's own edification. His face was still taut enough to be just this side of twitching. I led him into the kitchen and opened the refrigerator door so he could put in the beer. As he pulled out a bottle for himself, I snagged a bowl of pretzels from the counter and offered him one. "Did you know Nina well?" I asked.

"Couldn't help it." He took a pretzel, snatching his hand back instantly. It was like feeding a shy woodland creature. "This building is very close." Eric took a sip of beer. "In some buildings you don't even know your neighbors. Here you know too much!"

"What do you mean, 'too much'?" I asked curiously.

He crammed another pretzel in his mouth and examined me mistrustfully. He had the childish face and nearly transparent eyelids of a bright child who spends most of his school time bent over and shielding his paper from other kids who might want to copy off of it. I noticed that his nails were bitten bloody.

"Whatever you wanna know. The walls are like paper," he said with a shrug. I wondered if I was making him uncomfortable.

I couldn't help it. If I was making him uncomfortable I wanted to know why. "Are you okay?" I asked.

He glanced at me warily, pushed his glasses up on his nose, and snagged another pretzel quickly, as if I might slap his hand away from the bowl. "Eric wasn't on the ball," he said around the pretzel. "Should have heard something."

"Because your apartment is below hers?" I asked.

"Yeah," he said without meeting my eyes.

"But you've been out of town. You couldn't very well hear anything from Florida."

"No. But she fought with her boyfriend." He raised his beer, spilled some down his shirt. "Could have been him."

"His name is Mulligan, right?"

"Right."

"First or last name?"

"Dunno. Just Mulligan." Eric dropped his empty beer bottle into a grocery bag that was rapidly filling with them, and turned away. He opened the refrigerator, crammed with casseroles and mysterious-looking brown bags people had brought, and began to inspect its contents. "Eric ran into Mulligan at the airport last week heading out. Said he was on his way to Arizona on business. He might have come back early. He's not here now, though," he said as he pulled out another bottle of Beck's and reluctantly shut the door.

"And you heard them fighting? Did you hear what they said?"

"These apartments. They've got floors like soundboards. People on the top floor, the Swensons," he tilted his head toward the front room where the bicyclists in question sat next to Maxine on the sofa, plying her with salad. He lowered his voice, "And Nina. They don't know because no one is above them. But the noise carries down."

Groucho interrupted him with a shriek. "Except for that bird," he said rubbing his forehead. "That carries everywhere. But even little sounds, when someone walks across the floor above, it sounds like a herd . . . Uh, well, you know, Nina was not a small woman," he glanced at me and then at Joan, coming through the door with the empty casserole.

Neither of us was small. He seemed to feel in imminent danger of being crushed like a bug between the two of us. "It was just that, every step she made . . . And when she had company!" He slugged down another dose of beer at the thought.

"The fighting was bad. Not the words but the voices, and when they weren't fighting, you could hear the bed squeak—sometimes the *sofa*. You could hear them panting, for crissake . . ." He seemed a little short of breath himself. "They were . . . like . . . pounding away, on the *floor* sometimes!"

I mentally congratulated Nina. My eyes met Joan's and neither of us could help smiling at the thought of Nina enjoying herself that loudly. But the image was spoiled by the idea of Eric down below with a glass up to the ceiling listening. He raised the bottle to his mouth and drained the rest. He was sweating.

Joan raised her eyebrows and sailed back out into living room again. Somehow she managed to convey misgivings about Eric's manhood without a word. I was impressed. I usually have to use words myself.

"We're all so incestuous here," a voice came from the kitchen doorway.

Eric started violently. "Beth," he said, between violent coughs.

She came into the kitchen, holding an empty platter, and moved aside to let Eric escape to the front room. "Are you sharing that beer, Eric?" She called to his retreating back. "Or is it all for you?"

"Take one," he replied.

She put her platter in the sink, brought a beer out of the fridge, and offered me one as well.

"Is Eric really a computer genius? He seems so easily flustered, it's hard to imagine him functioning in a business way."

Beth rolled her eyes. "Well, computer people sometimes live in virtual reality. I think he's one of those outlaw hackers they hire to keep the other outlaw hackers out of their systems."

"Did he get along with Nina?"

Beth smiled and her sharp brown eyes blurred with emotion, "Nina made most people feel good. Eric seemed puzzled and excited by her all at once. You can just tell he was down there with his ears quivering when she had male visitors. But he would never ask Nina out."

"You think he's was afraid? It seems he's scared of me and Joan."

"I think he was drawn to her, but who knows? Maybe he thinks she'd be stronger than him physically. Maybe the fellas would make fun of him. Lord knows, they probably do enough of that already." Beth turned to the sink and proceeded to wash the platter and the other dishes stacked there. I took a dish towel and dried them and put them away as she spoke. I still wondered if Eric's obsession with Nina might have turned violent.

After a minute I asked, "How is it out there? Are we missing anything?"

Beth shrugged. "When I left, everyone was trying to figure out who had keys to Nina's apartment. Or else who had keys to someone else's apartment who had keys to Nina's."

"Huh?"

"See what I mean about incestuous?"

"You lost me back at the last key change—but okay, who did have keys to her apartment or a way to get them?"

Beth laughed. "Everybody. Well, except for Eric—I wouldn't ask him to feed my cat or walk my dog would you? Except for him, it turns out every tenant had keys to Nina's or could get them from someone else who did," she said with a shrug.

The dishes were all done and the counters cleaned. Beth and I looked at each other. "Maybe with another beer, the rest of the evening will go quicker," I suggested.

Beth brought out another two beers and we went back into the living room.

"Another really weird thing," I heard Maxine say as I found a chair. "We don't know who called the police. The policeman I talked to said a man called to report that a woman was dead in Nina's apartment. Who would have known that?"

Chapter Eleven

I had been hoping Mulligan would walk back in but he never showed up. From Maxine's nervous glances at the door and pulling Scar into the kitchen to grill her before she left, I suspected she had been expecting Hope back any minute. But the evening ended with no sign of the wayward daughter.

It was raining in earnest the next morning when Gonick and Lasker from Homicide arrived to stand over me and berate me about going into Nina's apartment without authorization. Maxine stood in the doorway, looking embarrassed.

"Who the hell do you think you are, taking down a crime scene tape and breaking a coroner's seal?"

I took another sip of coffee and answered evenly. "I didn't remove or break anything. The tape was ripped off when I went up there. I didn't see any coroner's seal. I did see the crime scene tape wadded up in a corner. I figured someone just didn't pick up after themselves when they took it down."

"That's your story, huh?"

"That's the truth."

"You're sure it wasn't you who ripped it down and threw it in the corner?"

"Believe me, I was looking for the coroner's seal and tape because Maxine mentioned that we might have to call the police to get in. There was no posted warning."

"You see!" Maxine leaned forward into the room, "I told you when you called earlier, she wouldn't have ripped down the tape. Someone else was in there. Maybe it was Captain Ahab returning to the scene of the crime!"

Gonick let me know he wasn't buying my explanation. Lasker seconded his discontent by raising his eyebrows and closing his notebook. But they left soon after.

Half an hour later Nina's lawyer called and asked for me by name. I had been staring glumly at the puddles on the window sill and actually considering visiting my stuffy relatives on Vashon Island, which is as close as I ever get to contemplating suicide. The lawyer had suggested setting up a time to meet within the next week. He seemed startled when I begged to come over immediately, but said he could make time for me around 11:30. I dug out my rain hat and trench coat and escaped into the gray morning. The macaw's screeching would have sent me out in a blizzard.

My car was on the street in front. Nina's building was three stories, with two apartments per floor, and counting Hope and Mulligan's smaller apartments in the basement—eight units total. Most of the block contained old houses, some converted to apartments, some looking like comfortable family dwellings. Nina's was the tallest building on the block. At this midmorning hour the street was quiet.

When I started to unlock the car door, I realized it was already open and papers were strewn all over the front seat. Someone had definitely been in the car. The only small consolation was that at least they hadn't smashed any windows. It was a strange kind of petty criminal to have skillfully unlocked the door, taken nothing, and then left papers as evidence of the intrusion. Unless they were trying to scare me, or more likely, unless I had somehow left one door unlocked and some mildly malicious neighborhood kids had gotten in. I picked up the papers—which consisted mainly of gas receipts and maps, and put them back into the glove compartment. Just as I was about to pull out of the parking place, a blue pickup truck drove past.

Nina's lawyer was in a neighborhood near Chinatown—as we used to call it—now christened the International District with sanitized political correctness. The whole downtown seemed to have been injected with Disneyland steroids. But I couldn't very well complain. While the developers had been reinventing Seattle, I had been tagging around after Griff Fuller, seeing the rest of the world. It wasn't my city any longer, if indeed it ever had been.

A few blocks from the polished-up, expensive part of town, I parked and walked. A couple of men in plaid shirts, slouching in a doorway against the rain muttered something as I passed. They looked strapping and reasonably fit. Homeless lumberjacks on sterno. The town had always had its roughneck side. Maybe it had gotten tougher, or maybe the downtrodden element just had more time on its hands.

To get to the lawyer's office I had to take a few steps down from the street. At the bottom of the steps, I took a sharp left turn and was suddenly in an office waiting room confronting a frozen-faced woman with hair bleached nostalgic platinum blonde. Her eyes lit on me with a doubtful air, but she said nothing. It was up to me to state my business. Behind her, in an office with a frosted glass window, I could see outlines of human beings. I told her I had an appointment and gave her my name.

"You're Sam's eleven thirty." From her voice, she had a cold and didn't want to be there.

"I guess so."

"You'll have to wait." She gestured to a couple of horse-hair chairs—the kind of antiques that have survived intact because they have always been too prickly to touch, let alone sit on.

She picked up a sheaf of papers from the desk and began to shuffle through them listlessly, as if looking for the least awful choice in a bad batch. "Coffee?" she added as an afterthought, gesturing at a hot and cold water fountain arrangement with a jar of instant coffee and some paper cups on a shelf above it.

"No thanks."

She sniffed and shrugged. Here in the espresso and latte capital of the Pacific Northwest, they had stumbled across one way to keep office expenses down. I put my coat on the rack by the door and my umbrella in the bucket next to it and treated myself to a cup of cold water. I stayed away from the prickly chairs and walked over to examine the walls instead. One wall held cheaply framed oil paintings of the Cascades and Puget Sound—perhaps from the same estate sale as the chairs. The other wall held a miniature village of carefully constructed cottages arranged along on a shelf. I moved over to inspect those. But as I bent to look more closely, I was interrupted by the woman behind the desk clearing her throat.

"He'll see you now." And indeed the inner door had opened and an Asian man in a tweed jacket came out stuffing some papers into a briefcase, heading for the coat rack.

The lawyer was on the phone in an inner office. He beckoned me in. I sat in the chair across from him. He hung up the phone and reached across the desk to shake my hand. "Sam Foley," he said. He had a file in front of him with Nina's name typed on its label.

He was olive-skinned, tall and solid, losing his hair on

top. Older than Nina, fifty-something, with dark worry rings around his blue eyes.

"This business with Nina," he said, shaking his head. "Do the police have any leads?"

"I'd be the last person they'd tell. They'd be more likely to contact you, being her lawyer."

"They might call when they want to know what's in the will," he said, as if musing to himself. Then he looked back at me and seemed to speculate again on some private matter. "All I know about the case is what I read in the papers." He shook his head. "It's a tragedy," he said, examining his desk top carefully. "I understand you're staying with Maxine, the manager of the building."

"You understand correctly."

"The real estate company feels that Maxine has done a good job for Nina."

"For *Nina*?" Had I missed something?

"Yes. She keeps the apartments occupied and most of the tenants are no trouble. You're sitting on a nice little property there."

"Beg your pardon? I don't understand."

I could see him deciding to dumb it down.

"The will is pretty simple. Except for a few thousand dollars, a house trailer, and some sentimental bequests of furniture and the like, you inherit everything Nina had. She asked that you let a long list of friends take any clothing or keepsakes they want, but she leaves the decisions up to you. You could say yes or no to any of those. Not much cash, a few thousand in the bank. Aside from the lease and inventory on her store, her estate primarily consists of the building. You'll be sharing equally in the rental proceeds with William Turnbow Crain. Do you know who that is? I've known Nina for twenty-five years and I never heard the name before she wrote the will."

I stared at him dumbfounded. "No. I've never heard of

him either." I shook my head in confusion, still taking it all in. "You're saying Nina owned the building? She never mentioned it."

He looked at me over his glasses. "On today's market it's worth close to eight hundred thousand. But her will stipulates that you won't sell it if it means evicting any of the current tenants. Most of them have lived there for a decade or more. Not long by Seattle standards. Maxine has been there over twenty years." He let me have a moment to absorb that. Maxine had said Nina helped her get the job as manager.

"Does Maxine know that Nina owned the building?" I asked.

"No. She might have had reasons to keep it to herself." He raised his eyebrows. I nodded. He turned a page.

"There's a fairly standard clause that if you should die within forty-five days of Nina, this William Turnbow Crain will inherit the whole thing, with the same restrictions on the rental property tenants."

Foley assessed me with those dark-ringed blue eyes. "Let's see. The only other condition, more of a request really, is that you personally speak to certain friends from her home town. They inherit certain of her possessions to remember her by."

He put on a pair of half glasses and glanced down at the first page of the file folder. "The most important one is this William Crain. But there's an Emily Crain who gets a couple thousand dollars and some pieces of jewelry, probably more sentimental value than dollar value there, I'd think. And she wants Granger Crain to have a house trailer she owned, located in Turnbow next to the Old Town, whatever that is. Good luck finding them. The only address I have is a post office box in Twila. I looked it up before you came in, it's up the road off of Highway 90."

He raised his caterpillar eyebrows. His curiosity seemed

so personal. I suddenly wondered if he and Nina had at one time been lovers. "Do you know any of these people?"

"No."

He tilted back his chair and put his hands behind his head. Oh, yes, he had slept with her. From the slight glaze that came over his eyes, it was a treasured memory.

"I wouldn't betray her confidence, but then she never really confided in me on this subject, then or since. Let me think. It was my old office. Tore it down for Pioneer Square. But I had some good times there." Foley smiled at the thought. "I was offering free first consultations. Still am, if you decide you want me to represent the estate." His grin and the laser-sharp blue eyes flashed at me momentarily, then settled back into reverie.

"She walked into my office like an Amazon—not tall but not timid either. Big, blonde, and sassy. She didn't tell me what she needed. She just asked me about the law on patrimony suits. Somehow the thought that she might be pregnant made her even more interesting. I told her I could look up what she wanted that afternoon and give her the information over dinner. She said sure and I bought her as much of a dinner as I could afford in those days and gave her the information. How a suit was filed. Blood tests and so on. It was way before the days of genetic fingerprinting. She took notes and that was the last I saw of her for over a year."

We both sighed at once. "Well?"

His eyes met mine and he laughed, a little shyly, I was amazed at the change in his demeanor. "What?"

"After dinner, did you two get together?"

"No." He didn't seem surprised by the question. "As a matter of fact I began to worry about her. If she were pregnant, I didn't want to get involved in taking care of her. She wasn't the kind of woman I could easily walk away from. Especially because it looked like somebody else just had."

"You didn't see her for a year."

"Actually it was closer to two years."

"Then what?"

"Then she walked back into the office as if no time at all had passed. She'd put on a little more weight, her hair was shorter, and her clothes seemed nicer. And she had fifty thousand dollars in cash to invest in an apartment building. Well, some of it was tied up in her business, she was doing some sewing at home, dressmaking. And selling women's clothes from a shop at Pike's Market."

"I remember that. That's how we met."

"I asked her if she'd ever filed that patrimony suit. She just smiled and said it wasn't necessary. I assumed somebody paid her off. Even then I knew that some questions you just don't ask. I helped her buy the building and I've helped her with her business affairs. But even if you were God Almighty sitting on that Eternal Bench in the sky, I could honestly swear that nothing she ever did was the least bit shady. All totally above-board. I'm a cynical man but from the first moment I met Nina I wanted her to do well. And she did. Nina was nobody's victim."

"Except at the very end."

"Yes. That was so . . . unlike her."

I was amazed that he would imagine she could have any control over such a thing. "Uh, Mr. Foley . . ."

"Sam."

"Sam, how long ago did Nina make this will?"

"You wonder if she had some premonition. Well, it was six months ago. She was in her forties. Most people who own property would have made a will long before that. She brought in her list of bequests and we hammered it out on the computer. Then she sat right where you're sitting and signed it." Foley shook his head and tilted his chair back down to earth.

I decided I liked him.

"You're staying at Maxine's?" he asked.

"For the moment."

"Lucky you." He shuddered at the thought.

"You've met the bird, I see." We both laughed.

"We'll have to talk again." He pulled out a copy of the will and handed it to me. "I've been trying to reach these people. They don't seem to have telephones. I can send a letter to the one post office box I have in Twila. I could send someone out to notify them in person, but it might take some time. It would cost some, which would come out of the estate . . ."

"I'll go. If these people were important enough to Nina that she wanted me to talk to them, the least I can do is tell them in person in case they want to attend the funeral."

"Are you sure you're up to it? I know you've been through a shock." But he looked a little cheered by the idea. Perhaps he couldn't easily spare the staff, or didn't like paying out money to hire someone. "When is the funeral by the way?"

"Day after tomorrow." I gave him the name of the funeral home and he made a note of it. "Frankly, I'd like to get away for a day or so. Where is this town with the post office boxes?"

"It's a little dot on the map on the edge of the Wenatchee National Forest about a hundred fifty miles east. You could get there and back in a day. Here, I'll get a map." He brightened at the prospect and dug out a AAA brochure. Was there ever a man who didn't love a map? Actually, I take that back, I've known one or two. But only one or two.

We were bending over the desk tracing out where the local road left Highway 90 when someone cleared her throat in the doorway. Sam Foley looked up guiltily. It was the blond woman from the front office.

"Your twelve o'clock is waiting, Sam."

"Thank you, Bonnie, sweetheart." He folded up the map, pressed it into my hand, and told me to call anytime. Bonnie, sweetheart, presumably was Mrs. Foley. She didn't move from the doorway.

Bonnie stepped aside with exaggerated courtesy and watched me out the door. For some reason it was the most amusing thing I had seen in a long time. Every so often I observed a couple that made me glad to be divorced.

Back in my car and on the road, I noticed a blue pickup truck in the lane behind me. It looked a lot like the one that had startled me when I was pulling out from the parking place in front of Maxine's. The hooded figure that caused such a drastic reaction in Raoul had driven away in a blue pickup as well. I told myself I was getting paranoid, but I couldn't help glancing back every so often to see if it was still there.

It was.

Chapter Twelve

As I worried more about the pickup that seemed to be following me than where I was driving, I found myself near the Lake Washington Ship Canal. The Toy Duck Cafe, a favorite hangout of Nina's, was only a few blocks away and I decided to go there.

I made a sudden left turn and sighed in relief when the pickup drove on. I parked up the street from the Toy Duck and got out to walk. The rain had slacked off but it was still chilly. As I walked to the cafe, I realized I'd never gone there without Nina.

She must have wanted to give me comfort, even happiness with this bequest, but at the moment I felt as if it were a heavy burden I could scarcely bear to look at, let alone lift.

The worst part was the thought that I was alive and Nina was dead. Something inside me said, "You survived. She was defeated." I hated that feeling, but it was too real to deny. Some deep, primitive human affirmation of the living over the dead. Nina's broken fertility goddess would have understood it. I squeezed that mental coin as I walked till

the imprint was burned in me. I knew if I turned it over—
the other side of the coin said, "Your turn."

Who could have done this to Nina? Was it some twisted
lunatic just racking up notches on his knife handle the way
the police seemed to think? The crazy writing on the mirror
suggested that.

But would Nina have let a casual acquaintance into her
bedroom without even putting a robe over her nightgown?
She must have known and trusted the person. That pointed
to someone like Mulligan. Although Eric and Andy looked
like suspects, neither one had a key so far as I knew, and I
just couldn't see Nina sitting around in a thin nightgown
talking to them. On the other hand if it had been a woman
she knew, Joan for example, Nina would have let her in
without question.

Then there was Mulligan. Why hadn't Nina told me
about him? If only I had asked more questions. Were they
fighting violently, as Eric had suggested? Mulligan had
seemed deeply moved by her death or was he simply torn
with regret at having killed the woman he loved? It couldn't
be Mulligan who killed her. I just couldn't see him writing
that chilling message on the mirror to draw suspicion away
from himself. Unless he really was this Captain Ahab serial
killer stalking large women as victims. First Nina, then Joan,
then me. Hmmm. I didn't feel Mulligan could be a killer, but
that might be my hormones talking—or shouting.

None of it made any sense—yet.

The Toy Duck Cafe loomed ahead with its silly neon rub-
ber ducky sign and a welcoming pool of yellow light pouring through the window onto the gray street. I had been
there frequently with Nina. The owner, Marilyn Toy, was
an old friend of hers. The cafe featured ice cream, excellent
coffees, teas, pastries, and some truly weird children's toys
and wind-up gizmos for customers young and old, mostly
featuring ducks. Marilyn had a thing about ducks.

The cafe had a refreshingly non-politically correct rule: No children under twelve without parents. When a fifth grade future lawyer argued against it, she said simply, "This is not a day care center, kid. If I let younger ones in alone, it would quickly become one."

Today was too cold for ice cream, too early for school children. Marilyn wasn't there either. They must have been opening late because I saw someone flip the sign from *Closed* to *Open* as I arrived.

The place was deserted except for a clean-cut kid tying on an apron. His hair seemed awfully short for a college student. Oh, wait, maybe the latest thing now was Marine boot camp barbers—I can never keep up. As soon as he put on his apron he picked up a book and lost himself in it so thoroughly that he didn't seem to notice my entrance, although the door quacked its duck call signal as usual. I went up to the counter and asked for a latte.

He looked up at me, unsurprised but not too interested. I re-estimated him to be at least twenty-five, with the deep-weathered skin of one who had spent most of his life out-doors. His tanned face had an open, almost blank innocence.

He smiled. I didn't believe it. He laid the book, spine-up on the counter and turned to measure out coffee and froth up milk. The book he had put down was *Eastern Ways for Western Minds* by Reverend Bliss of the Eastways Spiritual Paths.

I made sure I was picking up napkins, spoon and sugar packets from the self-service counter by the time he turned back with the coffee. I didn't want to discuss Eastern religion. I'd done enough of that during the times when I hung out with Nina at her shop. She had a particular weakness for the Eastways people and they came to see her often. I had to admit that what I heard in those days helped when I trailed around India and Nepal with Griff.

The man brought the coffee, moving slowly, as if entranced by the heat and steam. He set it down in front of me, took my money, gave me back change, flashed his shielded smile, and returned to his book. I took my cup to a table where I could look out the window.

I opened my purse and brought out Nina's will, flattening it on the table. Over at the counter the man turned a page, absorbed once more in his book. I read the will through once, then I examined the section where she talked about delivering bequests to the three people named Crain. Their only address was the post office box in Twila. Seeing the name again after seeing the book the man behind the counter was reading reminded me where I had heard of Twila before. I took out my Washington State map.

Over the years I'd seen several news stories about conflicts between the Eastways group and residents of a small town in the foothills of the Cascades. That town was Twila. I had never had a reason to look it up on a map before. The small circle on the map legend indicated "a population of less than 1,000." Nina's tiny home town.

The door quacked for another customer's entrance. I looked up and saw Maxine's daughter, Hope, come in. Hope greeted the man behind the counter with a kiss. Could this be the wandering William? I watched to see if Hope would recognize me, and sure enough when she glanced around and saw me, she froze in shock.

I waved and started to stand up but she put up her hand as if to ward me off. "No, I don't want to talk to you!" With a wild look at the man behind the counter, she turned and rushed out the cafe door.

I turned to the man. "Your name wouldn't happen to be William would it?" I asked.

He allowed himself only a slight smile, "As a matter of fact it is."

"William T. Crain?" I asked, glancing at the paper, to make sure I got it right.

"Nope." He smiled grimly. "It's William Smith."

I shrugged. Maybe he was lying, or maybe it was just too easy for the first William I ran into to be the one I was looking for. After all, why should Nina give half of her money to Hope's boyfriend?

William was still staring at me with a disturbing intensity. "You sure scared Hope. Who are you?"

I introduced myself and explained how I knew Maxine and Hope. "I only met her once before. But every time I see her, she runs away."

He shook his head. "No idea." Now that the questions didn't concern him, he didn't seem interested. "Hope is just flighty. I usually let her babble on until her tape runs out. I can't tell whether she finds my presence soothing or boring." He looked at me patiently but his eyes kept flickering down to his book.

"Is she staying with you?"

"Sometimes."

"Could you ask her to check in with her mom to let her know she's okay? She just vanished without a word."

"I'll give her the message. She is over twenty-one, you know."

"Yes. Did you know that a woman who lived in her mother's building was murdered?"

"Nina West. I heard about that." His hand ran over the book as if he could read it in Braille while talking.

"Are you an ESP member?"

He flashed me that awful shallow smile. "I guess you could call me a renegade Eastways member. I was born into it. And I keep coming back to it. But I have to ask questions and that makes some people nervous."

"Do most of the members live communally? I don't know

a lot about it except that there are those spiritual dorm things, ashrams—what is it they call them?"

"They're called retreats or farms if they're in the countryside. Missions if they're downtown trying to haul in converts. Brown rice is cheap." He pushed his book aside and leaned back against the wall next to a display of wind-up duck toys, as if deciding to give me his attention for the moment. "There are several degrees of commitment. My parents were totally gung ho. Lived on a retreat in the countryside with a large group during most of my childhood. They raised organic everything including kids, and meditated hours and hours every day." He curled his lip back from beautiful teeth. "If they could see me here serving caffeine to flesh-eaters . . . Well, my parents hoped I'd turn into a fanatic like they were. But," he shrugged. "I didn't."

"You say your parents are deeply involved with Eastways? Did they know Nina West? If they were friends, they might want to come for Nina's funeral day after tomorrow."

He looked at the floor. "Money is really tight and I doubt if they'd be able to afford the trip, whether they knew the lady or not."

"Is Hope an ESP member?"

"No. But I'm trying to get her to meditate. She could use some peace of mind." This time he did meet my eyes and his smile was personal.

I smiled back. "So you met Nina more than once?"

"Yeah, a couple times. She was a nice lady and a good influence on Hope. It didn't seem right that she should die such a violent death." Neither of us said anything for several moments. "It was her karma, though, or it wouldn't have happened that way."

When he met my eyes again it was almost a shock to see pity in his face. It brought out the lines around his eyes and mouth. "Her next lifetime will be better," he said with absolute conviction. "She suffered what she had to suffer to pay her debts."

I took the hint, dropped a dollar in the tip jar, and was about to leave when he turned away to put my cup and saucer in the sink behind him. As he bent over, his t-shirt rode up, revealing a hunting knife in a sheath at the back of his belt.

Chapter Thirteen

I stopped to buy groceries to replenish Maxine's supply, wandered into the discount pet supply store next door, and came out staggering under the weight of a basic cat survival kit.

Maxine must have needed fresh air as much as I did. Back at the apartment the only sign of her was a note saying she would be back around dinner time and would I please call Andy Stack to find out about the speaker at the memorial service. She also asked me if I could tell Mulligan the time and place of the service.

Groucho greeted me by rushing at the bars of his cage and biting them repeatedly before returning to twirling around on his perch. Raoul had settled down with his head resting on his forepaws on the back of the sofa a few feet away from the cage. I had to admire his strategy for preserving his credentials as a predator as Groucho strained through the bars, but ready for retreat if the huge bird should suddenly achieve a jailbreak.

I unpacked my purchases from the pet store, and Raoul thumped down from the sofa and prowled after me to supervise as I set up an official litter box and disposed of the cardboard makeshift I had put together the day before. I poured some cat food into his new bowl and left him crunching happily.

I wandered into the kitchen and poured myself a glass of water. Sitting at the kitchen table, I toyed with Maxine's note for several minutes before I picked up the phone. I didn't like Andy Stack and didn't particularly want to talk to him. But Nina must have liked him, and after all it was her funeral. I couldn't believe I had actually said that, even in my own mind. I dialed the number on his business card. The receptionist immediately put me on hold. Even the musical interlude sounded like an aerobic routine. I was relieved to learn that Andy truly was unavailable, so I just left Maxine's message and number along with the time and location of the funeral.

It was now the middle of the afternoon. I decided that I could get through the Cascades before dark, book a room at a motel off I-90, and go looking for the mysterious Crains the next day. But before I hit the road for Twila, I had to notify Mulligan about when and where the funeral was. With notebook and pen in my pocket I went downstairs. If he wasn't home, I figured I'd leave a note on his door. It was the middle of the work week and the apartment building had an empty feel about it.

I had never been inside either of the basement apartments. Maxine had described Hope's place as spacious for a one bedroom, but totally below ground—no windows. Coming down the stairs from the first floor I entered the dim hallway. At one end was the door to the storage area where Nina let me keep most of my worldly possessions. At the other end, a faint gleam of light from under the door lit the steps leading up to the backyard but did nothing to lessen the rabbit burrow feeling. Hope's apartment and

Mulligan's had doors a few feet apart on either side of a narrow hallway.

Mulligan answered my knock immediately. I found myself stammering at the impact his size and solidity had on me. Then I saw his eyes were red and nearly swollen shut. He had been crying.

"I miss her too." It was all I knew to say.

He stood aside enough let me walk into the room. Neither of us was small and I had to brush past him to get in. He didn't seem to notice. I steeled myself for twilight chaos, the moss-growing-on-the wall mustiness of basement apartments, particularly in Washington state. But one look at the place shattered my stereotypes about bachelor clutter and disorder.

The man himself might look like an unmade bed but the apartment was brightly lit with white-painted bookshelves on the back wall from floor to ceiling, interrupted by a fold-down desk for a computer, and larger shelves for a sound system and television. The small kitchenette had a clean counter with freshly washed dishes drying on the drain board next to the sink. The next room showed a glimpse of a bed. Unmade.

Mulligan seemed more disoriented than abashed to have been caught weeping. He smelled of bath soap and cinnamon toast. It came home to me for the first time that he had been Nina's lover. Our eyes met and overflowed at once. Before I knew it I was hugging him and we were both crying. I stroked his hair for a few moments, but I made myself pull away before my hand started to explore the back of his neck. It was awkward, comforting a stranger. And dangerous touching a man for whom I had such a sudden, compelling desire.

He led the way to the wood table outside the small galley kitchen. A pile of fishing tackle sat on the table. He opened a metal box and began to put everything back into it. It was a moment before I registered that along with the fishing gear was a hunting knife and a whetstone.

Did every man Nina knew have a knife handy? "Going camping?" I asked.

"Just putting things in order," he said offhandedly. "Thought it would distract me, but it didn't help much."

He wiped his face on his sleeve in a suddenly boyish gesture and looked at me a little shyly. "I had never met anyone like Nina. It seemed as if I'd known her forever. She made me feel I could start over again. Like we could do anything together. Now that she's gone . . ." He fell silent and looked away.

I patted his hand a little awkwardly. "So how did you meet Nina?" I didn't mention that Nina had told me nothing about him. How many other things had she never confessed? Either I had been thoughtlessly selfish, telling Nina all my problems and never thinking to find out what she was going through—or she was careful what she told each person in her life. Come to think of it, both those statements could be true.

"We met when I moved in here. I came to Seattle about two years ago when my marriage broke up and I left Alaska. It took awhile to get over that, I guess. I'd always wanted to live in Alaska since I was stationed there in the Army. My wife seemed to like the idea too. We got some land really cheap and tried to get by with some farming, some hunting, odd jobs in the summer. It was too hard. I guess that kind of thing makes or breaks a marriage. It sure broke ours. She went back to her parents in Idaho. I stayed on awhile, but finally I came here."

"I was in Alaska too, as a kid."

"Oh, yeah? What part?"

"Just outside Fairbanks."

"Right, the big city."

"Well, suburbs of the big city."

We both smiled at the thought of anywhere in Alaska as a big city.

"Anyway," Mulligan concluded. "I came here and got a job with the phone company."

"Right. Joan works there, too. Maxine said that's how you found the apartment. Have you known Joan long?"

He didn't look at me, but said slowly, "I was in the neighborhood on business and I recognized Joan from work, coming out of this building. We're in the same department but different sections, so we got to talking and she mentioned there was an apartment for rent here. I took it. I think Joan might have felt we would get together after that." He shrugged. "I like Joan, but once I met Nina . . ." The sentence trailed off as his eyes focused on the past. "When I first moved in, I'd see Nina in the hall sometimes, or in the laundry room across from Maxine's apartment, and we'd talk a little." He gazed at the wall, smiling as he remembered. "Then one day we talked for so long that it was lunch time, so I took her to lunch and we just kept talking. She was so bright and warm. When the afternoon was gone, she cooked dinner for me and we spent the evening and the night. After that we were together every chance we got."

"Look, uh, Mulligan? I didn't catch your first name . . ."

"Let's leave it at Mulligan."

"Okay. This is awkward, but Eric has mentioned that he heard you and Nina arguing, maybe even fighting a lot. What was that about?"

His head came up and an odd expression lit his eyes. "Eric said that?"

"Well, you know he has the apartment under Nina's. You know the guy . . ."

"Oh, I know Eric. I don't know where he got that idea, though. Nina and I disagreed on some things but we never fought or yelled. She might have been arguing with someone else, though that doesn't sound like her. Maybe Eric mistook some of the sounds we made for fighting." He smiled as memories overtook him. "We were all over the map once we got started."

He glanced up and met my eyes and began to blush, a startling reaction in one so large and gruff, but he was a fair-skinned Viking sort, why shouldn't he blush? I wanted to laugh but I also wanted to run my hands all over his reddened face and neck to see if the skin felt as hot as it looked.

He looked at me a little too long and again we both looked away. The desire that sprang up between us was as clear and painful as the prick of pain when you step on a tack.

I patted his hand again, "Look, it's okay." No use pretending we both didn't feel the same thing. "Everything is all mixed up here. If I'm making it worse, maybe we should talk another time."

"No. Don't go." He leaned across the edge of the table and put a hand on the side of my face to pull me close into a kiss.

From the moment I touched his hand I couldn't have stopped if I had wanted to. And I didn't want to. Somehow the closeness of death made my reaction to Mulligan even sharper.

Before I could bring out the words "we hardly know each other and why are we doing this anyway?" I found myself pulled to my feet and standing to embrace him full length. I couldn't help but sigh at how good that felt. It had been a long lonely time since Griff. This was crazy. But when I half-heartedly pulled back, he simply readjusted his grip and I found I didn't want to move at all. I wanted to stay right there.

He led me to the sofa and onto his lap. I responded with

a soft moan, which did nothing to discourage him. It felt good to be on a man's lap, a rare luxury, because I don't fit on just any man's lap.

Things dissolved into a warm haze from which we were harshly roused by the cold chime of the doorbell. Mulligan pulled back and looked at me with such a guilty expression that I might have laughed if I hadn't suspected my own face looked exactly the same. He looked like a child with a hand caught in the cookie jar.

We got up a little awkwardly, rearranging clothing as we did. He rehooked my bra and I straightened my blouse. I checked his face for lipstick, which evidently hadn't lasted long enough on my lips to be transferred to his. This time I didn't even try to meet his eyes. He took a couple of steps to the bedroom door and kicked it closed on the specter of the unmade bed.

Then he answered the front door.

It was the police.

Chapter Fourteen

Maxine was waiting upstairs. "Did you see the Homicide detectives? They went downstairs to talk to Mulligan."

"Yes. I saw them." I didn't go into any details. Gonick and Lasker had united in politely giving me fish-eyed stares that would have sent me packing even if Gonick hadn't growled that they needed to talk to Mr. Mulligan and could I give them some privacy? And, by the way, was I staying there now?

No, I wasn't staying there.

I desperately needed to be alone. Time to hit the road to Twila. Before I told Maxine where I was going and why, I remembered that she was worried about her daughter. "I saw Hope at the Toy Duck Cafe. She was talking to William who was working behind the counter."

Maxine brightened. "That's good. Marilyn Toy must have taken pity on the kid. I know she's been giving Hope some work off and on. I'll go over and see if William can persuade Hope to come home."

"Okay. Nina's lawyer said her will mentioned a William

Crain. But the man I saw with Hope said his name was William Smith."

Maxine shook her head, "I never caught his last name."

"Did you know he was a member of ESP?"

"No." Maxine frowned at me. "He never mentioned it, but then why should he?"

A car started outside the window. I pushed the curtains aside and caught a glimpse of the two detectives leaving. "They sure didn't spend much time talking to Mulligan. Don't the police always suspect the husband or boyfriend?" I asked with a glibness I didn't feel.

"Well," Maxine raised her plucked eyebrows. She didn't miss much. "He was on a business trip when Nina was killed. Maybe that's where they're going now, to check his alibi."

"Oh, damn! I forgot to tell Mulligan about the funeral."

Maxine said nothing for a moment, then she reached out and pointed to my blouse. "You're buttoned up wrong, hon."

I looked down in some confusion and began to rebutton the blouse. "Maxine, do you mind taking care of the cat overnight while I go down to Twila? Nina's will asked me to notify some people down there who don't have a phone."

Maxine grew quiet. I could see she didn't like the idea. I kept talking. "I should be back tomorrow evening at the latest. If I go now and spend the night in a hotel near there I can get on those mountain back roads during the early part of the day."

"Sure. Sure," she said, throwing up her hands. "I'm not going anywhere. I'll just stay here and make phone calls anyway." As I went to pack I heard her mutter, "This thing for Nina either will get done or it won't."

I pretended not to hear, taking the coward's way out and not even caring. I just had to get out of that apartment building. This leaving town thing really was one of my better-honed skills. I'd miss the cat a little bit, but time off from the macaw was looking better and better.

As I walked through the rain, overnight bag clutched in one hand, umbrella in the other, a black Ford Taurus pulled up beside me. The driver's side door opened and a long arm holding an umbrella emerged from it. The umbrella snapped open and Mrs. Madrone's assistant Ambrose Terrell unfolded himself from the driver's seat, locked the door, and greeted me with his usual reserve.

"Leaving already? I thought your friend's funeral was tomorrow or the next day."

"It's day after tomorrow. I have to go to a little town in the Cascades to see if I can find some old friends she wanted notified."

"Uh huh." He nodded, but he didn't look as if he was buying it.

"I don't think anyone in her hometown even knows she died. If these people cared about her, they might want to come to the funeral." As usual, I quailed a little before his burnished perfection.

"So, who's putting together your memorial service? Mrs. Madrone sent me to help."

"Oh." I was startled. "She did say something about that. She mentioned your maternal qualities."

He laughed. I realized I'd never seen or heard him laugh before. It humanized him considerably. "Here's your mail." He handed me three envelopes and a few fliers.

"Thanks." I stowed it in my shoulder bag without looking at it. I had picked up my mail while reporting to Mrs. Madrone a few days earlier, and a rolling stone gathers very little junk mail.

But Ambrose had not come all this distance simply to drop off the mail. "What else can I do? There must be some details I could help with."

"Well, Maxine in Apartment One is in charge of the memorial service. She's in her sixties, partial to beer and wine and cusses like a Cossack. I'm sure she could use your formidable talents."

"Very well. Introduce me to Maxine in Apartment One." He gestured me backward, raising his umbrella in salutation, and I led the way toward the building. There was no need to point out which building. Ambrose had probably examined the builder's plans and the title abstract before coming over. It was a vast understatement to say the man was thorough. "Don't worry," he said as we walked up the steps. "Ladies of a certain age and a sailor's vocabulary are just my cup of tea."

I rang Maxine's doorbell rather than using the key. When she answered, I introduced Ambrose and started to explain that our employer had sent him to help out, but Maxine had taken his arm and half pulled him inside before I could finish. Ambrose made a face over his shoulder and winked at me. I went back out to the car, with a momentary flicker of amusement at the possibility Maxine and Ambrose would clash in open warfare.

I drove into the twilight, a little relieved to be getting away by myself for awhile. Interstate 90 took me across Lake Washington and on into the Cascades. It was midweek and only a few cars were heading toward the ski lodges and resorts ahead. The traffic was light enough that I began to feel uneasy when I saw in the rearview mirror what appeared to be the same blue pickup truck that had haunted me all day in Seattle. It was dark by the time I took the turnoff for Cle Elum. When I didn't see the truck getting off I felt relieved.

I checked into a motel on First Street. My heart stopped when a truck pulled into the motel driveway behind me, but it was a darker blue and a different model than the one that had dogged me in Seattle and on the road up here. I took a deep breath before getting out of the car. I was getting jumpy. It had to be a coincidence.

When I got to the room and settled in, I took the mail Ambrose had given me out of my shoulder bag. I sat on the bed to go through it. Two bills, two advertising flyers. And a letter. The envelope was the kind of creamy bond paper Nina had used, but there was no return address. I opened it. Nina's handwriting. She hadn't dated it. I picked up the envelope again to look at the postmark. April 24th, the week before she died. It had reached Ambrose after she was dead.

Chapter Fifteen

I ran my fingers across the top of Nina's stationery, her name traced in gold script at the top.

Dear Jo,

I can't wait to I see you to tell you—at 45 I am writing my memoirs. Not that I think my life is over by any stretch of the imagination, although I did make out my will not long ago, just in case. The thing is, Jo, I've reached the point where I have got to get some things off my chest before I can go on.

I waited this long and didn't tell anyone because I wanted to protect some people. But now it seems like the whole truth needs to come out.

I was afraid they would try to stop me. I have to speak out for my own sake. It's too late for some people like Isabelle Zangrilli, but secrets do too much damage. People think things have changed. But if no one remembers how bad it was, we might slip back into the same mistakes. It hurts to talk about these things I have hidden for so long. I want to start by telling you. When you get here we can split a bottle of wine and talk all night. I wish you were here now.

Love,
Nina

The last was too much for me. I brushed away a tear before it could fall on the paper. Nina always wrote with a fountain pen. I might have smeared the ink.

I got ready for bed but couldn't stop wondering about Nina. What could she have been holding back all these years? Who the hell was Isabelle Zangrilli? And what was so terrible that it would tear Nina apart as much to say it as to hide it? I couldn't help wondering if someone else might have discovered that she meant to talk and silenced her before she could tell anyone.

Even after I turned off the lights and tried to sleep the questions wouldn't leave my mind. A sob caught in my throat at the thought of Nina's sadness and how someone had killed her before she could unburden herself. I sat up in the dark and cried in earnest for a few moments before a small, scrabbling sound caught my attention.

I froze in mid-sob and stared at the door. Someone was jiggling the knob, trying to get in. A jolt of energy seized me. Before I quite realized I had moved, I was out of the bed and slammed the flat of my hand up against the door, which caused the cautious scrabble to cease.

"You have the wrong room," I said in a loud, commanding voice. "If you try to come in here again I will shoot you right through that damn door and call the hotel desk so they can call the police to come pick up your miserable corpse."

I suddenly realized the intruder might actually have a gun, and I was only bluffing. I jumped for the phone to carry out my threat. But the sound of retreating footsteps blundered down the hallway and I heard the stairwell door shutting.

I lifted the receiver to call the desk. Then I stopped, not sure what I was going to report. Unless there was another attempt on the door I decided it made no sense to call. It might have been a drunken hotel guest trying the wrong room. I couldn't face the dark again though. I left a light and the television on and lay down with the telephone at hand, in case I had to call for help.

I woke up the next morning with the television and the lights still on. The complimentary coffee in the lobby was not up to Seattle standards but I drank a cup before going back to the room to consider my options. I wasn't going to turn back on the basis of a pickup truck that might not be following me and a potential intruder who might have been a hotel guest trying to get into the wrong room. The incident of the night before made me wish I had a weapon with me, but since I wasn't trained to use one it was hardly worth pursuing. What options did I have for self defense? The best bet looked like a small vial of hair spray, although how I could use that I was not sure. I pictured myself persuading an attacker to stand still so I could spray it right in his eyes.

I decided to proceed with caution. I called Ambrose and told his voicemail my whereabouts and plans for the day and took another cup of terrible coffee for the road. I was not well rested.

The map showed the road to Twila as a combination of paved, gravel, and dirt. The legend at the bottom advised the traveler to "inquire locally before using these roads." The desk clerk said the roads up to Twila were paved, but I should ask there about Turnbow, because sometimes that road was closed even at this time of year.

There was very little traffic but half of it seemed to consist of jeeps and pickup trucks. I felt silly about my anxiety at every blue pickup I saw. The person who had tried to enter my room was no doubt drunkenly snoring in his or her own room even as I headed out of town.

The motel clerk had mentioned that there was a general store, post office, and video rental store in Twila. He didn't mention that all these enterprises were in the same small building ironically named Macy's.

The part of Twila that was visible from the road consisted of a long-closed gas station and a boarded-up cafe on one side of the road. On the other side was Macy's store and a small shack beside it with 'Fishing Equipment' painted on the shuttered door. A sign on the shack informed the world that fishing season started the last Saturday in May and rods, reels, tackle and bait were available at Macy's.

The window of Macy's itself advertised "Liquor, Groceries, Post Office, and Video Rentals." A propane tank sat behind the store, which had a satellite dish on its roof. I wondered if that was how Macy's got the movies they rented out.

The rusty screen door squealed when it opened and thumped heavily behind me as I walked into the dimly lit store. Perched on a high stool behind the counter was a lean woman with granite-colored hair and a set to her mouth that might have been a painful dental condition or wry amusement at the idiots who passed through.

I walked over to the counter. "Are you Macy?"

"Mrs. Macy. Husband's dead now." She said no more and stared.

"Oh, sorry."

"Don't be. It's been fifteen years. Ain't used to it by now I never will be."

I gestured to the abandoned gas station. "It looks like Twila used to be a bigger town."

If there was a right thing to ask, this was not it. "Damn religious cult killed the town."

"Oh, yeah, the Eastways people got the land for their retreat here, didn't they?"

"Stupid. That's what it was. Don't know how people can be so dumb." She shook her head. "Damn fool local girl gave them her parent's farm, then they bought more. There had been a coal mining town up there next to her property, just an old ghost town called Turnbow. They carried on like it was Disneyland and the Statue of Liberty. Tried to turn this place into a boom town. Lots of old local people couldn't stand all that touchy-feely garbage—love the trees and crap in the creek. Most of the looney tunes took off and left—one jump ahead of IRS I heard." She shrugged as if she would like to spit but couldn't find the energy. "California people and New Yorkers."

"Don't they still use the land?"

"Maybe a dozen of 'em live up there now. I say send 'em back where they came from. Maybe they're not welcome there either. Still get people like you asking directions up there. Hippies, Orientals, blacks, all kinds, starry-eyed, drugged or just plain crazy."

She narrowed her eyes to slits and examined me more closely for signs of stars, drugs, or insanity. I realized it was time to buy something. I put a few trail mix bars and a pint of orange juice from the cooler on the counter. "So, do they do much business in Twila?" I refrained from mentioning that hers seemed to be the only business open in Twila.

She snorted. "Every month or so I still get some fool come through here trying to buy tofu or some such non-sense. As if I hadn't lost enough money stocking incense and candles for nothing! Look at the junk I'm still trying to unload." She gestured to a shelf at the back. Sure enough, next to the flashlight batteries and matches was a pile of dusty boxes of Manichiko joss sticks and red-wick candles. They could easily have been on that shelf since Nina moved out of town. The prices seemed way out of line, but as I looked at the batteries I realized everything in the store was priced a good twenty percent higher than in a normal store. I decided to invest in some joss sticks, candles, and new batteries to see if spending cash would pry loose a little more information.

"You ain't one of that crowd, are you?" she asked, eyeing my growing pile of stuff by the cash register.

"No, ma'am. I'm just looking for some people who are going to inherit something from a friend's will. They don't have a phone and the only address they have is one of your postal boxes."

I gestured to the lock boxes that covered one wall of the store, then handed her a sheet of paper on which I had typed Emily Crain, Granger Crain and William Turnbow Crain and their post office box number. She looked at the names. "I can't give out any information about our box-holders."

She started to make change from three twenties, the incense and candles alone came to more than twenty—I had no idea how vastly she was overcharging.

"Oh, keep the change for your trouble." I paused a beat and added another twenty to the change.

She gestured toward a stack of paper bags, but I shook my head and dropped everything in my shoulder bag along with the receipt. She looked at me for a moment as if unsure whether to be insulted or not. Then she shrugged and swept the money off the counter and put it in the back pocket of her jeans.

"They're part of that Eastways group all right. Live in a trailer out on the lot there, next to the ghost town. How'd your friend know 'em?"

"I'm trying to find that out. I know she grew up around here. Her name was Nina. Nina West."

"No, it wasn't," Mrs. Macy snapped right back at me. "Must be Nina Turnbow you're talking about." I wouldn't have thought it possible for Mrs. Macy's face to contract any further, but her eyes beaded down into black points of hostility. "She brought all those freaks down here. She shoulda known better. Her and that little jerk friend of hers, Stack."

"Andrew Stack? A little guy with curly hair?"

The woman's face curved down into a mean smile, "My son says they called him Short Stack in school."

"He was in the Eastways group?"

"Never heard he was. Did hear he got rich. He drops in to see my son now and again on his way to visit his aunt and uncle, down in Yakima. But we don't see him round here spending money. And as for Nina Turnbow, who cares? She changed her name. Rumor was she got knocked up, so why not? She just dumped the weirdos on us and took off. Now you're telling me she's dead?"

"Yes. Last weekend."

"Good. Now get out of here."

"How will I find the Eastways Center?"

"Take the first right fork off the main road out of here. Then take the first gravel road turn-off uphill to the left. Ain't but one. Used to be a sign, but I hear it's been shot down. If you miss it, the road you're on will turn into dirt track and then nothing, so turn around and go back and look again."

She didn't say "don't come back here." But that went without saying. She came to the doorway and watched me start the car and drive off. She did not wave.

Chapter Sixteen

The sign announcing the ESP Center was indeed riddled with bullet holes, but still standing and nearly legible, if you knew what you were looking for. The sign for Old Turnbow, pointing the way to the ghost town was more modest, tacked onto a tree off to the side. It was untouched by bullets either out of respect or poor marksmanship.

The winding gravel road opened into a cleared parking lot where the gravel had worn away in spots. It was bordered by logs laid in the dirt. It could have held a hundred cars, but only two Jeeps and an old sedan were pulled up into the spaces just flanking the walkway to a circular wooden dome with windows at ground level on all sides.

The windows were streaked. No spring cleaning here. The grounds immediately around the dome were roughly mowed, but at the edges of the lawn a crowd of brambles and tall weeds pressed in like a leering gang of toughs, waiting for an unwary few weeks to take back the turf.

At the opposite end of the cleared area from the Center, a crude archway of old logs announced: Historic Old Turnbow. A few cabins could be seen from the path that meandered into the trees. Carved out of old growth forest, the whole area was beginning to slip beneath the re-invasion of brushy second growth. A main street just beyond the cabins revealed a more formal structure of large stones held together with mortar. Three battered house trailers squatted incongruously on the border between the parking lot and the entrance to the ghost town.

I approached the dome. At close quarters, it looked bigger than I'd first estimated—a couple of stories high. Most of the windows were shaded. A yellowed, typed notice fixed by cracked Scotch tape to the inside of the glass door announced meditation sessions on Monday, Wednesday, and Thursday and counseling by appointment, with a handwritten note at the bottom adding, "To buy incense, candles, and books call for appointment." That explained why Mrs. Macy wasn't selling her stock. It wouldn't be hard for this lot to undercut her on prices. They already had her beat by a mile on labor costs.

As I rang the buzzer I heard the sounds of a motor and the crackle of tires over gravel. I turned and saw a blue pickup truck coasting to a stop behind the trailers at the other end of the lot. It was the twin of the one that had seemed to pop up in my rear view mirror so often on the highway. The trailers blocked my vision so I couldn't see who got out but the truck door slammed. For a moment there was no other sound, then one of the trailer doors opened and closed on squeaky hinges. I rang the Eastways buzzer again. Still no answer. I copied down the number and called it on the cell phone. An exceedingly soothing recorded male voice answered and suggested leaving a message for anyone at Eastways. I left a message, but didn't have too many expectations of a return call, even though I used the magical word "inheritance" without giving too many details.

Mrs. Macy had said the Crains lived in the trailers at the

edge of the parking lot. I turned to face the trailers, which showed no further signs of life.

I decided to drive the car across the lot, just in case I needed to make a quick getaway. I got out of its relative safety with a chill that was only partly from the wet weather. I knocked at each trailer door in turn. No one answered. I hadn't heard the trailer door squeak again. Perhaps the driver of the truck was in one of the trailers but didn't feel like talking. I looked the pickup truck over carefully. It was an older model, but it looked as if it had just driven off a new car lot compared to the junkers squatting on blocks next to it. I walked a little closer and looked in its window. No bloody weaponry visible on the dashboard, although half stuffed under the front seat there was a grubby cardboard box filled with empty oil cans, fast food bags, and discarded wax cups. I couldn't decide whether the truck was the one that had been following me from Seattle, and there was no way to tell whether the person who had tried to enter my motel room had arrived in that pickup. Perhaps it was all coincidence. A branch cracked in the woods behind me. I whirled around and looked but saw no one. The forest silence fell again, broken only by occasional bird calls under the leaden sky.

It was damp and chilly enough that I went back to sit in the car to run the heater to get warm again. Then I began to get impatient and anxious to stretch my legs. I walked a few times around the parking lot, peering off into the thick brush, looking for signs of anyone who might live in the trailers. Nothing moved but birds and squirrels.

At last I went through the log gate onto the path that led into the ghost town. Once I rounded the bend onto the town's main street I stopped to take it all in. The fast-growing forest had concealed how extensive the town had been.

I walked through the shell of a main street past a dozen

skeletons of timber frame houses and even more collapsing shacks shuffled in between, some with young trees growing through their ruined walls. The stone and masonry building visible from the parking lot turned out to be a jailhouse, complete with a weathered sign. Two of the walls had fallen, but a rusty, solid steel door stood locked in front.

The air was so still that I easily heard a crash from inside a derelict barn standing tall behind a pile of rubble that had once been a cabin. I froze for a moment, listening for another sound. Perhaps there was a faint cry.

Could someone have gotten into trouble inside that barn?

Stepping quietly and listening intently, I advanced on the structure the noise had come from. The barn was one of the better-repaired buildings. The brush had been cleared around it and a plot of land out behind it had been kept clear of the forest's marauding grip. As I got closer I smelled old hay. Boards had rotted away here and there, but the frame seemed sound. The double barn doors hung open slightly, well over twice my height to accept farm machinery. One side swayed slightly in the breeze.

I had no intention of going in. I tried to stand back from the door, half concerned about helping, half afraid of the collapse of the entire structure. I yanked both doors but the left side stuck. The right side flew open, pushing me back a few steps.

Before I could recover my footing, white-clad arms reached out in a blur of cloth my eyes scarcely registered before the world went dark. I smelled and felt the heavy, blinding weight of canvas covering my head. As I stumbled and fell against the edge of the blocked left barn door, someone pulled me into the darkness by the canvas noose around my head and neck.

I drew a quick breath and swiveled to hammer both fists

at the attacker just south of the arms that pulled me sideways. I felt the blow connect and heard a grunt of pain. I pulled back to twist free, but a sharp yank at the canvas nearly pulled me off my feet. I grabbed blindly. For a moment I caught a handful of cloth, a heavy fabric, and kicked out where I hoped were shins and ankles. The cloth slipped out of my grip, as I was pulled further into the barn, fighting to push away the restraining arms and the musty, smothering canvas.

A snarled word came through, barely audible under the attacker's heavy breathing. It almost sounded like ma or mother.

Fighting for breath, I lashed out again. This time I gasped in pain as my hand struck rusted metal machinery instead of flesh. My knees buckled. An arm went around my throat.

In futile hope I tried to tuck my chin into my collar bone as the cold metal touched my neck. A stunning blow from above was the last thing I felt.

Chapter Seventeen

Someone roughly pulled the canvas from my head and I awoke to see daylight and a mousy little face hovering above mine in the dimness. Dust motes danced in a shaft of sunlight. My head hurt.

"Come on! Come on!" Her voice quavered as she shook my shoulder. "We've got to go. He's coming! Let's go." I was dazed but her urgency got through to me. She helped me sit up. The world whirled dizzily but I managed to clamber to my feet.

"This way!" She pulled my arm. She was a small woman with a ponytail of wispy gray hair, wearing baggy polyester pants and a sweatshirt of uncertain color with many layers of stains and fadings.

I followed her. A tremendous crash at the back of the barn sent up a cloud of dust, puffed the hanging door open and set the walls around us quivering. But we made it out the door. She ran, I followed. She skirted the ruined cabin and ducked into the forest on a narrow path invisible through the trees until you were on it. I crashed into most of the tree branches she ducked under and fought my way through bushes she slipped between. We approached the trailers from behind. She led the way to the middle one, up the shaky steps, and slammed the door behind us. There was a little lock she twisted, but considering the way the trailer shook when we ran in, I didn't have much confidence in its stopping power.

She lay back against the door. I stood watching her. Her weathered face might have seen forty-five or sixty-five cold winters. Both of us were panting from the run, which had put me in a definite aerobic flush. The pain from whatever had hit my head and the adrenalin let loose by the danger combined to create a throbbing in my temples that had the potential to turn into a world class headache. I breathed deeply, willing it away.

"You run okay for a fat girl," she said between puffs of air.

"You ain't so bad yourself for an old lady," I said, recovering enough breath to join her in a laugh. Then we both stopped short, silenced by a sound outside. I went to look out the trailer window. "Was that a car engine?"

She cocked her head to listen. "Loft floor probably gave way under him." she said. "Wouldn't kill him. No such luck. But it might take him longer to get back here, not knowing the short cut."

I relaxed a little but kept one ear tuned to noises outside the trailer. "If you hadn't been there he would have killed me."

She smiled and I saw the gap where she was missing a few teeth. At that moment, I found it endearing. "I go up there by the ladder on the side of the building," she said. "Got to watch where you step because part of the floor up there is rotten. There's a stack of old bales of hay was near the edge of the loft, so when he come in, he didn't see me."

My head was still spinning and much of what she was saying seemed to make little sense, but it sounded like she had been looking down from the loft when I was attacked. God only knew what she was doing up there in the first place.

"He grabbed you, so I scooted round the rotten boards and rolled a bale of hay over the edge. It only hit his shoulder, but it got you straight on. I wasn't sure I could get you up and out when he come on up after me. But," she let out a spidery little laugh, "he used the ladder inside the barn, see? While I went down the outside ladder and come round to get you. Musta hit those rotten boards, though I can't say I stuck around to watch." She laughed again and I joined her a little shakily.

"You saved my life. Thank you." I touched her arm and she nodded. I put a tentative hand up to my throbbing head. I was still dazed from being knocked out but I began to assess our situation, "Do you have a phone?" She shook her head. Like a fool I had left the cell phone in the car. Still, it was better than leaving it in the barn for my attacker.

"There wasn't much time to find out names," I said, "I'm Josephine Fuller. I'm here looking for Emily Crain."

"You found her." She moved away from the door to glance out the window.

"I've got a phone in the car over there. I could run out and call for the police?" I said. "That guy might be coming any minute."

"No!" She slipped past the window to the sleeping area at the back of the trailer and came back with a revolver. "This is just a .22, but we can get him if he comes near the trailer. Then you can go call anyone you want. But I'd rather not risk going out in the open just now."

"What's that?" I heard the roar of an engine starting nearby.

We were both silent. She took a deep breath. "I think he's going now."

I got up and looked out the side of the window, cautious

not to be observed. The blue pickup was pulling out of the weeds and driving through the parking lot.

I took a chance and rushed out the door and around the edge of the trailer to squint through the gray afternoon for the truck's license number. The plate was plastered with mud. I couldn't make out any of it except that it was a Washington state license plate. The truck turned out of the lot and vanished from view. I got the cell phone out of the car and went back to the trailer.

Emily Crain sat at the small patch of table next to the trailer's refrigerator, stove, and sink. Her head was sunk in her hands and the revolver was on the table in front of her. She seemed to be slowly disconnecting from what was going on. I reasoned that the sudden exertion caught up with her. Even for me the adrenalin rush had burned off. As I examined Emily up close, she looked to be in her mid-sixties.

"Does anyone who lives here drive a blue pickup truck?"

She looked up and shook her head wearily. "No. I still have two of Granger's cars. They don't run. The family in the next trailer has the old Dart. But it's totalled. They're staying with relatives till their plumbing gets fixed."

I looked out the window, wondering if the truck would come back. "Is there another road in to this place besides the gravel one into the parking lot?"

"No."

"Okay." I had to think but my head was throbbing. I pulled a kitchen chair up to the table, sat down, and breathed a little easier. "Thank you for rescuing me. But are you all right?" I had to ask.

She looked at me a little vaguely and rubbed her forehead. "Oh," she said uncertainly, "I have headaches from time to time, but I guess I'm all right."

As she said it I realized the headache I had expected had not materialized. "Did you get a good look at the man who tried to kill me?" I asked. "Maybe the police could do a composite sketch."

She shook her head emphatically. "No police. Anyway I didn't see much. His back was to me and he wore a knit cap and a butcher apron."

"My god." It seemed that having my best friend murdered had numbed me to everything, but a close encounter with a knife-wielding man in a butcher apron woke up a host of sensations. I took a deep breath to stave off fear that swept over me like a cold ocean wave. "Uh, Emily, we could use some protection here."

"The local police hate us."

"Okay. But I think I saw a blue pickup following me on the way up from Seattle. He tried to kill me, and now he's seen you and he knows where you live."

"You're not from round here, you don't know. But the police have been nothing but grief for me." Her head tilted cautiously. "Besides, maybe he didn't see me in the loft. I go up there to meditate."

So that's what she was doing up there, I thought.

"No one else ever comes there anymore. When I saw him come in and hide, I was afraid to move. Then I saw that butcher's apron and I knew he was up to no good. We used to butcher our own meat when ESP had a farm here."

I was so astounded by her statement that all I could think to say was, "That doesn't sound like Eastern religion. Aren't you all vegetarians or something?"

Emily didn't seem surprised by my reaction, "Oh, yes that's true in many Eastern religions, but in the old days we had a working farm here. Gordon Bliss told us we were free to eat meat if we butchered our own. Some of us studied Kosher and the old ways of ritual sacrifice. I've seen butcher aprons before. I've even worn them. Eastways encourages moderation."

"Moderation?" As in kill your own entree?

"Once Granger and I got a little older we finally gave up meat. It was too strenuous."

Emily was full of surprises. I twisted uneasily in the kitchen chair. "Is all that part of the ESP practice?" I asked, thinking that a weird cult practicing ritual sacrifice might account for some of the strangeness around Nina's death.

Emily cocked her head sideways to examine me. "You're a city person, aren't you?" I nodded. "Well . . . No matter. A lot of us come from farm families."

I set aside the bizarre cult killing theory, at least for the moment. "Well you must come from good strong stock, climbing up that loft and wrestling around bales of hay at your age."

Emily shrugged, "I raised two daughters and a foster son. If that didn't kill me nothing will. But everything I cared about here is dead or gone. Not even a vegetable garden. Oh, they give lectures over at the center. I never go. Only go for the meditation when they keep their mouths shut. Reverend Bliss left years ago. My daughter in Ellensburg comes by to take me shopping every week."

Her words came slower and her attention seemed to slip away. I decided I'd better get whatever information I could while she was still talking. "That man who attacked me. You say you saw him come in, how long was he there before I came?"

"Seemed like hours. Probably half an hour or less though." Remembering it made her tremble slightly.

I patted her shoulder, "Well, I owe you my life and I have a rental car, so if you feel like shopping say the word."

I was rewarded with a wan smile. "Not now, thanks," she said.

I realized she was still staring at the gun. I cleared my throat. "I came out here to find you because of Nina West, uh Nina Turnbow. Did you know her?"

"Of course I know Nina," Emily nodded. "She was born

and raised here. Her grandpa founded Turnbow back in the last century. She come back when she converted to Eastways and donated her parents' farm. Once the dome over there was built, hundreds of ESP people moved out here. Some lived on the farm. Land was cheap. Some got jobs near here and commuted. In the end most everyone left. It's too isolated and people in town hate ESP members."

"So I discovered. Were you very close to Nina?"

"We were like sisters. It's been a few months since we spoke. She would do all the calling, back when I had a phone." Emily slumped over. I had to lean close to catch her words. "I couldn't get away to call her. She said to let her know if I needed anything." Her hand moved on the table as if brushing off spilled crumbs. "There was nothing anyone could do."

I dreaded the next moment, "Uh, Mrs. Crain, when was the last time you spoke to Nina?"

"Last year on my birthday. It's in December. She called my daughter's. Knew I'd be there."

"Did she mention anything out of the ordinary that was going on in her life?"

"No. Well, maybe she did say she had a new boyfriend and he was younger than her. But she had a lot of boyfriends over the years. I . . . really can't recall what else she said."

"Emily, I don't know any good way to say this. Nina is dead. She was murdered."

"Really?" Emily turned mild brown eyes on me and waited for my next comment.

"You don't seem surprised." Or very upset, I wanted to say, but held off.

"Don't I? I . . . I" she ran a hand over her dry brow and eyes. "Well, you see, my husband died a few months ago. I lost my step-son. Somehow it seems like everyone else goes away or dies."

"Oh my, I'm so sorry. I didn't know."

"Of course you didn't. How could you?"

"Was he very ill for a long time?"

"Well, you could say he was sick, in a way. He was a violent man. Even after years of meditation and guidance in Eastways he still would sometimes beat me and the kids. The kids all left home as soon as they could."

She looked at me as if I had spoken. This was the part where people usually asked, *why didn't you leave*? After spending time at that center for battered women, I knew some of the reasons women didn't leave. She answered anyway.

"He kept trying to change. So I kept giving him another chance. But he would always do it again." She sighed. "I guess I got worn down so I didn't know how to fight or run. Anyway one day last year our boy came home. He'd been going to junior college in Yakima. Granger hit me, in front of the boy." She almost broke down in tears as she met my eyes. "I didn't even know Billy had a gun. He shot his pa."

Billy? "Oh, my." I couldn't think of anything else to say but, "How terrible."

She responded with another heartfelt sigh.

"Um, Mrs. Crain . . .

"Emily."

"Emily, where is your son now?" I asked tentatively, half expecting to hear her say the local cemetery or the name of the nearest federal prison.

"Oh, he's gone. He left right away. The police are still looking for him. They come around and ask if I've heard from him every so often. I did get one postcard. It's from Turkey. Want to see?"

"Please." She was losing ground so fast that I wondered if she could manage to stand and shuffle over to wherever she kept her mementos. But she simply set the revolver down on the table, reached back without looking to the kitchen drawer behind her chair, and pulled out a recipe folder filled with postcards and small envelopes. She held it close to her chest as she thumbed through the folder, selected a postcard, pulled it out and handed it to me.

The scene on the front was a mosque in Istanbul. "May I read it?" I asked, flipping it over for a look at the postmark.

"Read it out loud."

"Dear Mom, I am fine. Hope you are in good health. All my love—WTC." I stopped. "So, his name is William T. Crain?"

"Yes. William Turnbow Crain."

Despite the exotic picture on the front, the card was post-marked "Tacoma, Washington." Six months ago, just down the road from Seattle.

I kept turning the card over. "Are you related to Nina and the Turnbows?"

She looked at me oddly. "My son is. We adopted him, but he was Nina's son, born out of wedlock." She picked up the .22 pistol and released the safety.

Chapter Eighteen

"That's a nice gun," I said sincerely. "Do you get to do much target practice?"

"Lately I have." She lined up the sights on a lamp in the corner but did not fire. "I've been practicing since Billy left it here. Police thought he took it with him but I knew where he used to hide things over in the ghost town when he was little. He had a little hollow place under the back wall of the old jailhouse. Sure enough there it was. Police don't make me feel safe. This does." She rested her arm on the table. Holding the gun up must be tiring. "If I had it with me this afternoon, I could have shot that man."

Or maybe shot me, I thought but didn't say.

She read my mind. "Oh, I might have hit you too, but at least I woulda stopped him. Maybe got him on the second shot." She snapped the safety catch back on. Put the gun down on the table.

I took a deep breath and stared at Emily for a moment, wondering if I was feeling lightheaded because of our strenuous morning. Then I realized I was also very hungry.

I looked at my watch. It was afternoon. No wonder the orange juice and trail mix bars from Macy's had worn off.

"Emily, can I take you out for a meal?"

"No!" she said sharply, "I don't want to go out. Could you heat up some soup? I don't think I had breakfast." She looked pale and drawn. For me the shock of having been attacked was wearing off, but Emily seemed to be slipping away into a trance. She was agile enough and she didn't look all that old, but she worried me there with the trailer so isolated and her nearest neighbors so hostile.

I found a can of vegetable soup in the cupboard and heated it in a pan while I got together some whole wheat bread and butter. Emily listlessly watched me prepare it. She did manage to swallow most of her bowl of soup and a few bites of bread. I wondered if she would have eaten at all if no one had been there to fix it for her.

"Did Nina ever tell you who William's father was?" I asked, as she watched me wash the dishes.

For a moment Emily's eyes refocused, "I always suspected it was Reverend Bliss," she said slowly. "Nina said she wouldn't tell me because it would destroy my faith in our religion."

"That didn't make you even more curious?" I asked, putting away some of the dishes on the drainboard to make space for the ones we had used.

"If I didn't have my religion, I'd be dead now."

"I've heard people say that. What does it mean? What would have killed you?"

"In my case, genetic alcoholism."

I stared at her, startled. She was totally serious.

"I don't drink since I joined Eastways," she continued earnestly. "But I must be an addict. Or just plain crazy, right? To live with a man like Granger after all he did to me and the kids. In the end it was Billy who stopped him. I wonder if I was addicted to Reverend Bliss. He was like a father to us. The leaders now just talk a lot. I can't listen."

I put the last dish to drain and sat down across from Emily. It didn't seem right to leave her alone. Perhaps I could get her to go to that daughter's house in Ellensburg. But first I had to ask, "Does the name Isabelle Zangrilli mean anything to you?"

Emily nodded, smiling sadly. "Heavens, that name takes me back. She's been dead twenty five years. She must have been scarcely out of her teens when she died. She was one of a group of girls including Nina that Reverend Bliss spent extra time with. It never entered my mind at the time that he might be using them for carnal purposes. Now you think I'm crazy for sure. That's the first thing most people would suspect. I guess you could say I was brainwashed. We all were."

It seemed fair to say that.

"You've got to remember," she went on, "to us he was the Pope, Gandhi, and Mohammed all rolled into one."

"I guess a religious leader needs to have higher standards."

"Anyone you trust should have higher standards."

I gave Emily full marks for coming out of her trance enough to make a solid argument. I nudged her back on track. "About Isabelle. Nina mentioned her name in a letter to me. She said she was going to tell the truth about Isabelle Zangrilli. She seemed to think some people wouldn't want it told."

Emily considered this. "I remember that Isabelle was a runaway from somewhere on the East Coast, maybe New Jersey? She was a pretty thing but very troubled and headstrong. She was close to Reverend Bliss. He let runaways stay without asking any questions."

"Especially if they were pretty girls, huh?"

For a moment Emily seemed angry with me. "No, he

took in the boys too if they behaved themselves. We thought it was his kind nature, giving the kids food, shelter, and counseling even though it could have got him in trouble. Isabelle never talked about her family except to say she didn't want them to find her. I don't think they ever did while she was alive. One night in 1967 she just left the farm without a word. A week later she was found dead in a hotel room in Bellingham. Someone said she bled to death from a botched abortion—it was still illegal in those days unless a girl could convince a medical board that she was raped or that she'd kill herself. It was hard to find a doctor to do it on the sly and some of them weren't the best."

"And no one ever officially connected her with ESP?"

"No one. Not the police. Not the family. Bellingham is pretty far away and she was very devoted to ESP. She must not have mentioned the group to anyone."

"How noble of her." I was thinking what an awful way to die—alone and bleeding, separated from your family and deserted by the very group you were trying to protect. Including the man responsible. I asked Emily, "Do you think Reverend Bliss might have gotten Isabelle pregnant?"

"Maybe."

"Do you think Nina might have known?"

"Maybe. I shut my eyes to all that. But since Reverend Bliss left I've thought of it a lot, watching Billy grow up and wondering if Reverend Bliss was his father. I was so thrilled when Nina let us have her little boy. Granger and I thought we could never have kids. The girls were born a few years later. Nina sent us money every month for Billy's expenses so he was never a burden. In fact Nina bought this trailer for us. She visited sometimes. But never for long."

"What happened to Reverend Bliss?"

"He just disappeared a few years after Nina left. His wife and children left the same month. They turned up living in Idaho. From time to time he calls or writes. He sent me a book a few months ago but I don't read much these days. Would you like to see it?"

I nodded. "Please." She reached behind her again to the drawer and pulled out a paperback-sized manila envelope. She handed it to me. It was still sealed. "May I open it?"

She nodded and I took a knife from the silverware drawer. Emily watched me open it as if I were changing a tire on a huge truck. "Want me to read it out loud?" I asked.

She shrugged. "Okay."

I cleared my throat and read:

Dear Emily and Granger,

  Sarah and the kids are doing well here. I hope your brood is fine also.

I noted it was dated a year ago.

  I'm enclosing a curious little book I came across that seems to be about a rather eccentric religious group. The setting is familiar. Do you think one of our flock might have written it?

I blinked at the book cover. Unlike the tome by Reverend Bliss that Hope's boyfriend William had been reading behind the cafe counter, this was a paperback entitled *X-Rated Ashram.* The purple and black cover sported a voluptuous young woman bursting out of a highly abbreviated Eastern robe-like outfit, sitting on a garden wall and receiving what amounted to a gynecological examination from a lusty young man whose lotus posture bloomed in unexpected directions. I put it on the table. Emily looked at it as if it was staining the surface.

"May I borrow this?" I asked a little hesitantly.

"*Take* it," she said flatly. "If Granger had known any man

sent that to our home, he would have hunted him down and killed him, even if it was Reverend Bliss."

"Perhaps it's time we stopped calling him Reverend. It sounds like the title hasn't meant much in a long time."

I put the book and letter back in their envelope and stowed both in my purse.

I looked at the sullen gray sky outside. I wanted to get back to Seattle before it got too dark, but I couldn't leave Emily here unprotected. I asked her again to come with me to the police but she shook her head.

"Emily, what if that man in the pickup comes back? You could be in danger."

The thought made her tremble visibly, but she set her mouth and said "No."

"You'd be safer at your daughter's house. At the very least let me drive you there."

Emily reluctantly agreed. She packed a few items of clothing in a crumbling plastic flight bag and looked around the trailer as if she would never see it again. I had a sudden inspiration and brought out the candles and incense I had bought in Twila. I surreptitiously wiped the dust off them with my sleeve as I handed them to her. She took them wordlessly and walked over to put them next to a candlestick and incense burner arranged on a white doily on a small table near the back of the trailer. She dropped her revolver into her purse, gave the place one lingering look, and closed the door behind her.

Her attitude worried me. "Don't you want to lock the door or something?"

"No."

It was nearing sunset as we set out. I kept scanning the road and the rearview mirror for pickup trucks. None presented itself. We met no cars at all until we got to the highway, and even then the traffic was light until we got near the outskirts of Ellensburg. The drive was in silence until I asked Emily to direct me to her daughter's house. I parked on a quiet street where trees nearly blocked the house from view. Two cars were parked in the driveway.

The woman who answered the door said, "Mom, are you okay?" in a tone that made clear her mother frequently was not.

"May I stay with you tonight, Helen? There's been some trouble."

"Of course." She looked at me and seemed even more distressed. I hadn't looked in a mirror but I suspected the afternoon had taken its toll on me. "Would you like to come in?" she asked, clearly hoping for a refusal.

"Just for a second. I have to get back to Seattle." A vehicle drove past on the quiet street and I whirled to look, uncertain whether it was a pickup truck or not. But it was gone before I could tell. The residential street seemed peaceful.

Turning back to Helen, I explained what had happened, got her phone number, and gave her Maxine's number and my 800 number. "I really think it makes sense to notify the police." I said again. Emily came out of her trance long enough to shake her head. "No."

Helen hugged her mother and her eyes met mine over Emily's shoulder. "Maybe tomorrow by the light of day we could talk about it again," she said. "They haven't been much help to our family in the past."

Emily drifted in and her daughter turned away to shut the door before I'd cleared the front porch.

I drove back to Seattle as quickly as possible but it was dark and drizzling when I reached the floating bridge. For the first time in my life I was glad to see the traffic congestion around the metropolitan area. It seemed safe. It seemed welcoming. Somewhere out there a blue pickup might be waiting for me with a knife-wielding maniac inside. But for the moment I sought safety in numbers.

I parked in front of Maxine's house and sat looking at the dark passage up to the apartment house door. Then I saw the light in Nina's window.

Chapter Nineteen

For one crazy, bruised moment I wondered if it could be Nina herself. I got out of the car, went up the steps, past Maxine's apartment, and up the stairs toward Nina's apartment.

Then I heard footsteps coming down. A door closed on the floor above me. That was the level below Nina's—the one occupied by Eric's apartment on one side, Val and K.C.'s on the other. Could one of them have been in Nina's apartment? If so, there was no sign that anyone had just gone in. I continued upward. Confronting Nina's apartment was very hard, yet some part of me yearned to believe that I would open the door and Nina would welcome me with a hug and explain how the past two days had all been a terrible mistake—a nightmare.

Her door was in front of me. No police seal and no crime scene tape. I put the key in the lock and opened the door. The place was dark, with no sign that anyone had been there. I closed and locked the door without going in. I went back down the stairs thoughtfully. I paused at Eric's door, but then turned and knocked at Val and K.C.'s. They didn't frighten me, but Eric now made me distinctly uneasy.

The door behind me opened. I turned to see Eric, peering around it. "Oh, it's you," he said, rubbing his eyes with his pale knuckles. "Woke me up. Heard the steps upstairs. Then knocking on doors. Thought it might be the police again."

I wasn't sure whether to believe him or not. He wore a plaid shirt, with an incongruous load of pens in the breast pocket, open over a black t-shirt. Maybe it was the same t-shirt he had worn at Maxine's the other evening. Would someone sleep in a shirt like that?

"No. I was just coming in and I saw a light up in Nina's window. Then I heard someone on the stairs." I stopped and waited for him to explain or add that he had or had not heard the same thing.

Eric ran a hand over the straggling hairs on his face—it wouldn't really be accurate to call it a beard or mustache, more like an afterthought. "Come in," he said, turning away and leaving the door standing open behind him.

I hesitated. Eric was definitely on my suspect list, despite his alibi. He would be crazy to kill me in his own apartment. Maxine's apartment was just below, and given the notorious thinness of the floors, she would hear me if I called for help.

"I can't stay long," I said. "Maxine is expecting me back downstairs soon," I added a little lamely.

I stepped in and he went back and shut the door behind me, giving me an annoyed look. It suddenly occurred to me that if he was insane he might not grasp the finer points of self-incrimination. Maybe I was the one not thinking clearly. No one knew I was in his apartment. Hmmm. I didn't like that idea, but it was too late.

Three computers glowered in the room, which was otherwise unlit except by the streetlamp outside that sent bars of light and shadow onto the floor through half-slit window blinds. Once my eyes adjusted to the dimness, I stood gaping at the metal shelving crammed with wires, cables, circuit boards, monitors, and high tech equipment dissected into its component junk form. The computers were stacked on one level, with webs of cabling attaching them to black boxes of unknown utility on adjacent shelves. Real spider webs and a light coating of dust gave the place the air of a deserted storeroom despite the high-priced machinery.

Aside from the metal shelves and electronic bric-a-brac, the room was furnished with cardboard boxes filled with newspapers and thick stacks of computer printouts. Most of the boxes had shipping labels attached. Wooden packing crates, scattered about the hardwood floor at random, served as flat surfaces to collect TV dinner trays, pizza boxes, and cups and glasses containing liquids in all stages of evaporation, crystallization, and green fuzz.

A black-leather ergonomic office chair faced the bank of computers and a brown Barcalounger hulked in front of the giant-screen television set. Considering the monster speakers attached to the TV, I was surprised that Eric could sit that close without severe hearing impairment. An adjacent wall of stereo equipment shared the speakers with the television and it looked like with the computers as well.

I'm not an electronics buff, but my ballpark estimate of the cost of the gear in the room put it into the tens of thousands of dollars. No wonder he had so little furniture. Not that he seemed to mind.

One had to say something. "Impressive equipment," I muttered and instantly regretted my choice of words. Male gadgeteers make an equipment-to-sex-organ correlation in about point oh-oh-one nanoseconds with or without encouragement.

But Eric preened without leering. "Eric's command center," he said in a voice that struggled to stay nonchalant.

I tried to make gadget small talk. "I've never seen anybody use three computers all at once like that. Is that usually how you work?"

Eric shrugged. He did not exactly relax, but a certain offhand assurance crept into his voice. "One's tied up crunching numbers. One's downloading from the Net. The third is a Mac." His tone suggested that its purpose should be self-evident to any thinking person—gotta have a Mac, right? "Just leave 'em on. No sense wearing out the switches."

"So you mostly work at home?"

He nodded. "Contract."

"But you were traveling on business last week?"

His eyes narrowed and his voice tensed. "Trouble shooting. Computer security." He reached into the pocket protector of his shirt, pulled out an incongruously elegant enamel pen, and began to drum it nervously on his palm while watching me as if I were an alien with questionable motives.

I wasn't sure how many questions he would answer, so I asked the most significant one first. "Do you have a pickup truck?"

The pen froze in mid-air. "So what?" he said. But his eyes refused to meet mine. Instead he stared at the floor just in front of me.

"I just wondered if you parked it around here or lent it to someone or . . ."

"It's at my folks." He took a sudden breath and resumed the nervous tattoo of pen on palm. "Just an old rusty pickup. What do you care?"

"My car was broken into. I was just checking on the parking lot situation. The lot behind the building is usually full, right?"

"Yeah. My station wagon is behind the building. And the truck's at my parents' place. Is that all you want to know?" He took a sudden step toward me and I flinched backward instinctively.

"Just wondered." I was angry with myself for having been startled, but my recoiling seemed to please Eric. A sudden ghost of a plan occurred to me. "You think you might want to sell it?"

"Sell what?" He stared at me mistrustfully.

"Your truck."

"Nope. Kid brother's working on it." He edged closer with every question. There was an unwholesome look in his eyes.

This was a new and unwelcome side of Eric. It wasn't until he started moving closer that I realized I preferred him to be cringing away. I cleared my throat. "You said you heard fighting upstairs between Nina and Mulligan."

He paused and stuck out his lower lip. "Yeah. Eric can't help what he hears, you know."

"Did you tell the police?"

"Why make trouble for Mulligan? He's okay. Even if he works for the damn phone company. Came and played computer games once or twice. Not worth lying to the police. Anyway, Mulligan has an alibi just like Eric. Sorry, boys, out of town. Business. Talk to the airlines, if you don't believe it."

"Did you hear someone up in Nina's place just now?" I asked.

Eric took a step closer to me, planted one buttock on the edge of a packing crate overflowing with computer printouts, leaned back, and looked me up and down. He switched to nervously flipping the pen against his thigh. "You think Eric can't hear every step that goes on up there? You were just up there, right? You opened the door but you didn't go in, right?"

"That's right." Eric was the logical candidate to have been up in Nina's apartment, but it could have been someone else. He had said he was sleeping. I wasn't sure how dangerous it would be to contradict him.

Eric nodded in satisfaction. "Told Mulligan you could hear every word down here. Not to mention thumping and moaning and shouting."

"What did he say?"

"Not much. Hah!" A bitter syllable, as if at his own stupidity. His mouth folded into a grim line. "Laughed. Thought it was funny." He looked down at his hands and as if just noticing the black enamel pen, he began to half unscrew the top and screw it back again.

"Any other questions? No." He didn't give me time to speak. "What are you, an amateur cop?" The hostility in his voice gave it a cutting edge. "Think you're smart, huh?"

"Not really." I started backing toward the door, suddenly trying to remember if he had locked it.

He unscrewed the pen completely and looked at me with a suddenly cheerful expression. For the first time I realized there was a serrated steel blade under the cap. It must have been two or three inches long. I felt the door behind me and fumbled for the doorknob.

"You're just like the cops though. Checking my alibi over and over. What do they think, an airline company would lie?"

He stood but didn't follow me. "It isn't Eric Shumacher the cops really want to frame for this murder, you know." His voice began to rise in volume. "It's any ordinary white guy who tries to make something of himself without the help of any damn connections, or affirmative fucking action, or some fat bitch coming around and poking her nose into his business."

I turned my back on him for long enough to turn the doorknob. Not locked, thank God. As I ducked through the door, I turned back to say, "Hey, settle down," but he was close on my heels with the knife in his hand.

Chapter Twenty

I slammed the door behind me and heard him hit it, but no sound of the door opening again. After pounding down the stairs to the next landing without looking back, I paused and listened. No sound of pursuit, fast or slow.

By the time I reached Maxine's door, my panic began to subside as I fumbled with the key she had given me and threw open the door.

For a moment all I saw was a crowd of people. I froze like a night creature who has blundered onto a bank of floodlights. I put a vague hand up to my hair, which I suddenly realized must be a thicket of tangles. The way everyone stared at me confirmed that impression.

After the first blank moment I sorted everyone out. A card table had been set up in the middle of the room and heaped with stacks of papers that were being sorted, folded, assembled, and stapled. Beth, red-haired and lanky, sat at the head of the table carefully folding. At the foot of the table Joan wielded a stapler with Buddha-like serenity. Val sat between them facing me as I came in the door. I remembered his streaked beard. He looked forlorn, assembling folded sheets of paper and passing them to Joan, then taking back stapled booklets to put in a box in front of him. There was no sign of his beautiful boyfriend.

I could see from across the room the words "NINA WEST MEMORIAL" on the booklets. Maxine sat on her sofa checking something on a clipboard with Ambrose, who had settled in next to her, nudging her shoulder as if he had known her forever. Groucho greeted my arrival by swinging upside down from his perch inside his cage, cackling and tilting his head to see better.

Mulligan stood looking out the front window. He was fiddling with the curtains but otherwise he didn't seem to be doing anything at all. The window faced on the street where I had parked. I wondered if he had seen me come in.

Everyone stopped what they were doing and stared at me. Maxine started to rise, but Ambrose was up in an instant, pressing her back down with a hand on her shoulder. "Just a moment, Maxi, dear, let me have a word with Jo before I release her for general consumption."

He drew me into the hall. "Jo. Sweetie, there's lipstick on your collar," he pulled the collar of my blouse aside and looked closer. "No, it's blood. You've been cut. No one's even cleaned this, let alone disinfected it." The mocking went out of his tone. "Do you want an infection? Are you shaky? You want me or Maxine to wash that for you?"

"I didn't realize I'd been cut," I said, wondering more at the gentleness in his manner than at any possible injury. But his tone was kind, and when I met his eyes I saw they were full of genuine concern. I turned aside to keep from losing my composure. "I'm okay. I'll just wash up."

He patted me on the shoulder. "Fine. Go. I'll have a good stiff brandy waiting for you, or what do you drink? I know Maxine has brandy. Is that okay?"

"Sure." I couldn't help looking back at him in puzzlement. "Did you know Maxine before?"

"Well, no. But Val's mentioned her, of course. And when I've come here to visit I heard the parrot—excuse me the macaw. I mean, you can probably hear him on the other side of Puget Sound. I knew a zoologist once who kept a parrot, so we had something to talk about." His lip twitched in a smile. "Go. Wash."

I closed the bathroom door and looked in the mirror. Ambrose was right. A trickle of blood had dried along my neck where the skin had been cut and it had printed on the collar of my blouse as if marked by a kiss. The knife had cut right through the doubled fabric of the collar and pressed the edges of the cloth into my skin.

The cut hadn't bled much. A little sharper knife or a slower reaction from Emily in dropping that bale of hay and I would be lying on the floor of that barn in a pool of blood.

I pushed away thoughts of Nina's body . . . Her throat gaping, blood blanketing her and sinking into the mattress. I turned on the cold water and wet my hands. They were sore and blotched red with swollen knuckles where I'd connected with the steel farm machinery. Bruises were rising up through the skin. Judging by how I felt when I moved, there would be bruises on my body as well, but nature's padding had protected me from major damage or broken bones. I drenched my face and brushed my hair until I looked, if not calm, at least clean and neat. I poured a little hydrogen peroxide from Maxine's bathroom cabinet onto a tissue and dabbed it on my cut. Then I buttoned my blouse up to the throat and opened the door.

Mulligan pressed me back into the bathroom. "Wait, I've got to ask you something."

"Please, I can't take much more. I've had a really rotten day."

"Josephine, listen, I'm sorry about what happened yesterday at my place."

Our eyes met for a flicker of an instant. The rush of sexual energy swept my exhaustion and aching body onto a distant back burner. It was more difficult not to touch him, having touched him once.

I looked away. "It was my fault too," I said. What was it about him that exploded my hormones like popcorn in a hot pan? I even liked his taking the blame. But I didn't like the thought of this sudden wild pull toward the lover of my best friend—especially since she literally was not yet in her grave. The suddenness of the way he had turned to me made me wonder if Mulligan had lied, and Eric had been right about the fighting he said he had heard from the apartment above. If my radar on Mulligan was fouled up by hormonal interference he might have been lying to me about not being involved with Joan as well.

"I don't know what came over me." He was apologizing but pushing closer to me in the small bathroom, we were both conscious of how our bodies were not quite touching. "All I can say is please forgive me. I really need your help."

I glanced up at him and once our eyes met, I was incapable of looking away. "My help?" I said slowly, as if language were new to me.

He nodded. "I don't know if you're aware that Nina had been talking to Hope and her friend William about some trouble he's in. Hope asked me to tell you that William wants to talk to you."

"William Turnbow Crain? Is this the same man who was working at the Toy Duck Cafe, who said his name was Smith?"

"Yes, Hope told me that. He's in trouble with the law. But I heard you went to Twila today. If you talked to his mother then you know about William's situation."

"Yes. And *you* must know that you're an accessory after the fact by concealing his whereabouts."

"I don't know where he is. I don't think Hope knows either. But he does call her every day or so, and she said he needs to talk to you."

"She sure has changed her mind, because the last two times I saw her, she ran like hell."

"She's been trying to protect the guy, but I think I've managed to get through to both of them that he can't run from this forever. And he's going to need more help than she can give."

"And just exactly what do they think I could do?" I asked, though I had a suspicion.

"I don't know. But they seem to think you're the only one who can help."

I wanted to say no. It might even be dangerous, but I thought of Emily. She had saved my life with no questions asked. The very least I could do was see her stepson, help however I could short of breaking the law, and report back to her how he was. Maybe I owed it to Nina as well.

All I said was, "So how do I reach William?"

"Hope said she'll be at the funeral tomorrow and she could take us to meet William. Someplace where we can talk."

"Okay. Nina would want me to talk to her son." I watched his face. "Did you know William was Nina's son?"

He nodded, "Yeah. She told me. What a mess." He ran his hand over his face. "Nina would have hated this. We've got to see if we can help straighten it out."

"Why me? You seem to be getting along fine with both the kids."

"Yeah. Well so far they won't listen to me alone, but maybe between the two of us we can convince William that he'd better turn himself in as soon as possible."

"I sure agree with that. I've got to tell you I have no way of knowing he wasn't the one who tried to kill me today."

"What?" He looked at me and for the first time seemed to notice the spot of blood on my collar.

He reached out a hand that almost touched my neck when someone tapped on the door tentatively. It was the only bathroom in the apartment. I pushed Mulligan out ahead of me.

Beth watched us come out together and raised one cinnamon-colored eyebrow. "Okay," she said, with an ironic downturn to her mouth. "Whatever gets you through the night."

"Someone tried to *kill* you?" Mulligan whispered, after moving aside so Beth could get into the bathroom.

"It's too complicated. I'll tell you tomorrow."

It was clear that Ambrose had smoothly taken most of the organizing off Maxine's shoulders and helped out wherever needed. The programs were folded and packed in a box to take to the funeral home. Now Ambrose was exchanging warm hugs with Joan and Val. Why had he been so frosty to me for so long? I wondered if I was jealous of how instantly he had won the hearts of so many of Nina's friends. More than usual I felt like an outsider.

Maxine came up to me with a short, squarish glass that sent up a halo of brandy when she swirled it under my nose.

"Here, this is for you, Jo. Sit." When I was seated she handed me the glass. "Now, drink."

"What kind of car does Eric have?" I asked Maxine, sure she would know.

She stared meaningfully at my glass, so I sipped the brandy and felt it burn my throat and warm my stomach. "I think he has two. A station wagon and a pickup truck."

"A blue pickup truck?"

"It might be blue. Usually he uses the station wagon in town. He keeps the pickup at his parents' place in Renton. Eric is a strange bird, but then he is a computer genius. That kind of says it all, doesn't it?"

I couldn't argue with such a sweeping, and frequently

true, perception. Anyway, I was more interested in the pickup truck census. "What about the other tenants? Cars or trucks?" I pulled out my pad and pen.

Maxine looked at me strangely. "Just a minute, sweetie, finish that brandy. I'll see the others out and we can talk about cars all you want."

She bustled over to say goodnight to Joan. Beth took that moment to leave as well. When the door opened, I noticed Ambrose hugging Maxine goodbye. Val went upstairs. Beth went across the hall while Joan and Ambrose headed for the front door.

I don't remember finishing the brandy, but at some point I noticed Mulligan bending over me and gently removing the empty glass from my hand. I was too tired to react at all. When I woke again I was alone in the living room. The lights had been dimmed and someone had put a blanket over me. Groucho's cage was shrouded and for once, he was silent too.

Chapter Twenty-One

The next morning I woke with a sore neck. Then I opened my eyes and remembered. I had wandered in from the front room and crawled under the covers without undressing. I still couldn't quite believe that Nina was dead. But today was the day of her funeral.

Something shifted against my legs. I looked down to see Raoul pinning the blanket to me with his fluffy yet formidable bulk. "I didn't see you last night," I told him, rubbing his ears, barely visible in his blue-gray mane. He yawned and purred loudly. It wasn't news to him that he could fade like a puff of smoke when confronted by a crowd of strangers. He turned his head to let me scratch under his chin. I lay back and stared at the ceiling.

Raoul rose, stretched, and thudded to the floor. He began pace back and forth. I made the mistake of meeting his round orange eyes. He meowed. "This has something to do with your breakfast, right?" I said. He reared back with featherweight grace that seemed impossible in such a large cat and put his front paws on the edge of the bed, eyeball to eyeball, purring suggestively either at the very word breakfast or to underline a simple concept which he'd finally gotten across to a mentally challenged human.

In the front room Groucho squawked from his covered cage. There was no way to hide from the day. Raoul led the way meowing continuously as I shuffled into the kitchen. A can of cat food quieted him instantly. I got into the shower. I heard the doorbell as I was dressing back in the cramped guest room, gingerly lifting my hair away from the cut on my neck. Then Groucho began to make happier chuckling sounds and I heard Maxine talking. A lower, male voice answered hers.

I put on a beautiful black silk dress Nina had sewn for me. I wrapped one of her hand-painted gold and red scarves around my wounded throat. The voices were in the kitchen by the time I came out. Maxine was sitting in her dressing gown at the table. Mulligan stood next to her rummaging through a pink bakery box. He was scarcely recognizable, his thick neck looking raw, trapped in a white collar and a dark gray suit that must have been tailored. When I saw the elegant maroon and gold-striped tie with a narrow brown border inside the gold that echoed the color in his eyes, I couldn't help wondering if Nina had picked it out for him. He sat down and refused to meet my eyes.

I felt suddenly shy as well. "Morning," I said, heading for the coffee machine. I poured a cup and narrowly missed stepping on Raoul, who had abandoned his food bowl to follow me the moment I picked up the container of half and half. The cat hissed and retreated despite my apologies.

Mulligan held out the box of donuts. I selected a chocolate cake donut with as much dignity as I could muster and sat down to dunk it in my coffee before I said anything more.

"Poor Raoul," I said, watching him grudgingly slink to the food bowl, keeping a weather eye on the clumsy humans. The donut and coffee revived me somewhat. "Gosh, he must have been there through everything. He went crazy when I picked him up, almost as if the guy was still there."

Maxine and Mulligan were both looking at me as if I were seriously deranged. This was the wrong time to discuss it, but I was suddenly putting it together for the first time, I needed to say it out loud so I wouldn't lose the thread. "My god, I kept hearing the floor creaking when I was in the apartment getting the cat. Then a couple minutes later someone drove away in a pickup truck."

I put the donut down and took a few deep breaths. I must have turned pale because their expressions of dismay gave way to concern. "Sorry, I'm a little shaky." I pushed my hair away from my face. "This crazy guy came after me with a knife yesterday. When he got interrupted, he drove away in a pickup truck just like the one that seems to be following me." Suddenly it sounded like a bizarre delusion.

Mulligan stared at me, shaking his head, "So that's what you meant last night about being cut," he said. "I had no idea."

Maxine came over "Let me see it, dear." She said. "Ambrose mentioned an injury." she murmured, her face furrowed as she bent over to peer at my neck.

I shrugged and unpinned the scarf to show the wound, which was neither long nor deep—it was the thought that counted, and the intent in this case had been clear. Mulligan craned his neck to look. "Everyone sure hit it off with Ambrose," I said, a little jealously.

"Isn't he great?" Maxine straightened up after inspecting my cut and brightened at the thought of Ambrose.

"That's not the word I would have used until yesterday, but you may be right," I admitted.

I started to put the scarf back, but Mulligan stood up.

"Wait. Let me see," he said.

He put his donut on a napkin on the table, rinsed his hands at the sink, and came close to examine the cut. He bent over me and put a finger on my chin. "Turn your head so I can see."

I heard the rush of his breathing and felt solid presence next to me, but his fingertips came near without touching my throat.

"That's right," he murmured, as if to himself. "Could be from a straight-edge razor or even a sharp hunting knife. Whoever jumped you was going for the carotid artery. Lots of muscles round there. You got lucky. Maybe he slipped. Maybe his blade wasn't sharp enough. How'd you get away? You fight him off?"

"No, you were right the first time. I got lucky. I looked in the door of an old ruined barn. He threw a canvas cloth over my head. I was saved by an old woman who lives on the property who'd been up in the hayloft when the guy came into the barn. She saw him attack me, and rolled a bale of hay over the edge of the loft down onto him and me. It knocked me out for a minute. He left me there and climbed up to the loft to chase her, but fell through some rotten flooring. She came down to get me and we both ran to hide. Fortunately he drove off instead of following us further."

Mulligan whistled. "Yeah, you were lucky all right. And of course you went straight to the nearest police station and reported the attack."

"No. Emily, the woman who saved me, refused to go to the police. It was all I could do to get her to go to her daughter's house in case he came back." I turned back defiantly to meet his brown eyes. This was the man who wanted me to meet and confer with a fugitive from the law. I didn't say anything more to avoid upsetting Maxine.

Mulligan straightened, the better to look down at me. For the first time I felt no rush of lust. For his part he was staring at me with the cautious amazement of a farmer who has walked into a stand of corn and encountered an alien spacecraft.

"Anyway," I concluded lamely, "the guy drove off in a pickup truck."

"That's why you asked about the tenants' cars!" Maxine exclaimed.

Mulligan continued to stare. I couldn't be sure he was disapproving of me, but if he was, I perfectly willing to return the favor. "Did you get the license plate number?"

"No. I ran out to look when the truck drove off, but I couldn't make out the number. I think he covered it with mud on purpose."

"Are you sure it was a man who attacked you?" Maxine said, her elbows on the table. Hearing about my afternoon's encounter seemed to be distracting her from thoughts of the funeral and Hope's absence.

Mulligan snorted, "You want equal opportunity killers now, Maxine?"

I shrugged, "I couldn't see the person who attacked me. The driver of the pickup was either a man, or a woman with very short hair and square shoulders. Whoever dragged me into the barn was taller than I am and strong, but not much taller or much heavier." I realized with some relief that I had just ruled out Mulligan. "What do you think?" I asked him, "Could a woman have done that to me physically?"

Mulligan shrugged, selecting another jelly donut and holding a napkin under it to shield his suit as he bit into it. "A strong woman might have." A shadow came over his face and he swallowed with difficulty. "A woman could have killed Nina too, and in some ways that makes sense because of how she was found." He put down his donut and went to the sink. Again, he rinsed his hands under the tap.

With his back to us I noticed he put his hands on the side of the sink and took a few deep breaths. In a moment he turned back to face us. Maxine's face was creased with sympathy. "Hell," he said, "I've been wondering who she would have trusted enough to talk to in her bedroom in a nightgown." He dried his hands on a paper towel, wiped his mouth, swept up the rest of the uneaten jelly donut and dropped it in the trash under the sink.

He moved to the doorway, as if anxious to get going. "Still, it would take some special instruction in where and how to cut," he concluded. "Strength, training and a sharp blade."

"Where would someone learn how to cut throats?" I gulped a little at the question, my fingers instinctively shielding my throat.

"Oh, you could join a street gang, practice with switchblades and razor blades set in sticks," Mulligan said, racing through the list as if hoping to get past the entire subject. He sighed. "The Army and the Marines give hand-to-hand training—not the Air Force or Navy."

"What about livestock?" I asked a little giddily.

"Oh, they don't let them in the Army or the Marines," Maxine said with a gravelly chuckle.

Mulligan didn't even glance at her. His eyes were grave. I wondered if he had been under the illusion that I was like Nina and now realized I was not. I pushed the thought away, fighting to get a rational hold on the moment.

"No, I mean like on a farm." I continued, struggling. "Couldn't a farm kid learn to slaughter animals that way?"

"Yeah," Mulligan said.

"Andy Stack grew up on a farm and served in the Army as well."

"Yeah, well, I told you before I was in the Army," Mulligan said.

"No one's suspecting you, dear," Maxine said gently, sending me a warning look.

But I couldn't help going on. Maybe it was the way he was looking at me, I hate disappointing people. "I don't know about Eric, but William's mother told me they learned to slaughter their own meat on the Eastways Farm."

"Is this the same William that Hope has been seeing?" Maxine asked, new fears of danger for Hope dawning in her eyes. "You're saying he could be a murderer?"

Mulligan shook his head slightly. It was too late to shut up, I had to talk my way out the other side of this mess. "No, I don't exactly suspect William, because Emily would have recognized her own son. But she told me the man who tried to kill me wore a butcher's apron."

Mulligan brushed a few phantom crumbs from his suit. "You need to talk to Seattle Homicide about what happened to you, the sooner the better. It might tie in with the Captain Ahab thing."

"Hey, I agree. In fact I'm going to call Emily before we go today and see if I can get her to talk to the police. After all, she saw the guy."

"Meanwhile, watch out and don't do anything else stupid like going off alone. Whoever came to kill you came prepared. And if it's Captain Ahab, he's gotten away with it so far."

I accepted the lecture in silence. It was a tough day for all of us. Maybe Mulligan was disillusioned with me, and now he seemed to be getting all self-righteous on me, but it didn't stop him from using me for his little encounter with Hope and William, whatever that was about.

I hoped that appointment could be kept without arousing Maxine's suspicions. No sense raising her expectations in case Hope didn't show up. I also wasn't sure just how close to breaking the law it would be to talk to William.

Mulligan half turned away from us, restless now. "You'd better get ready to go, Maxine."

I stood up. "I'll call William's stepmother Emily and maybe convince her to talk to the police this morning."

"You can use my phone," Maxine said. "I'll go get dressed, but maybe Mulligan can help you persuade her."

I looked at Mulligan, who shrugged. I went to get my address book and used the extension on the kitchen wall to call Emily's daughter's house.

A man answered. Gruff but cautious.

"Hello, I'm the woman who brought Emily Crain to her daughter's last night, I was wondering if I could speak to Emily.

"She's not available right now. Can I get your name and number?"

I gave him Maxine's number and my 800-number, which seemed to startle him. "Is Emily all right? We're going to a funeral in a few minutes. But some guy with a knife attacked us yesterday and I was worried—"

"Wait, stay on the line. Just a minute." He conferred with someone in the room.

Another man's voice came on the line and now I could hear sounds of people moving, voices in the background, and the buzz of static from a two-way radio. "Excuse me Miss . . . Fuller is it?"

"Yes."

"There's been an incident. Mrs. Crain was attacked."

"Oh, no," my hand went to my own throat, "Was she . . . was she cut?"

"Yes, ma'am, her throat was cut. She died almost instantaneously. Look, if you have any information—"

"When?"

"It must have been last night. Her daughter found the body in the spare bedroom not long ago."

I couldn't speak. I handed the phone to Mulligan.

Chapter Twenty-Two

I looked out the front window at the street below and tried to make my mind a total blank. The alternative was to think about how I had led a killer to that old lady's door. After she saved my life, he had taken hers. The doorbell rang. I went to the door.

A delivery man stood holding flowers. He said something, I wasn't sure what, but I stood aside and watched him bring in half a dozen wreaths and baskets of flowers.

"Hey, Josie." Mulligan appeared in the doorway to the kitchen and gestured to me urgently, "Get back on the phone. The man has a few questions for you."

That was an understatement. They wanted to know all about the previous day's encounter. I gave them the short-form version, but I could tell it wasn't enough. They wanted to know anything and everything I remembered about the attack.

Finally I said, "Look, officer, a woman who was a dear friend of Emily's was killed here in Seattle and possibly by the same killer. You need to talk to Gonick or Lasker of Seattle homicide." I read the numbers off the card I had.

"I'll be talking to them tomorrow. If you want to come over and they don't mind, I have no objection to talking to you then. But just now you're going to have to let me go to my friend's funeral."

Mulligan watched the delivery man place the last basket with sprays of bright magenta gladioli, hand him a slip of paper and leave. As the delivery person went out the open door, Eric came down the stairwell and stood in the hall, looking horribly uncomfortable in a narrow, knitted tie and a suit jacket that was a size too large for him, with the "Goodwill" sticker still stapled to the hem. In his own way Eric had gone to great lengths to honor Nina. He glanced in my direction but didn't make eye contact. Instead he inventoried me from the toes up to the neck and focused on my red scarf. I knew he was shy and I should make it a little easier on him, but I was so stunned at the news of Emily's murder that I could barely whisper, "Hello."

Eric's reply was equally inaudible as he turned with visible relief to Mulligan. A moment later Beth came down the hall with a loose-jointed energy that didn't fit with her sober gray dress.

The phone rang. "It's Ambrose calling from the funeral parlor," Maxine reported, standing in the doorway and stepping into high-heeled shoes. She turned her attention back to the phone. "He wants to know why all the flowers haven't come there. Because they screwed up and sent them here, that's why. No. I can't tell the delivery people to take them, damn it, because the delivery people already left."

As Groucho let out a shriek and Maxine began to condemn delivery people in general and specific, I realized I was mentally examining the prospect of strangling them both. Instead I said, "I could take a couple of the baskets, maybe in the back seat."

Eric piped up. "Eric has a station wagon. The rest should fit in there."

They didn't quite. We hauled all the flower arrangements out to where the cars were parked, put Beth in the front seat, and stuffed most of the larger arrangements into the back of Eric's station wagon. There were still three baskets of flowers left on the sidewalk, destined for the back seat, assuming we left room for Mulligan and me in the front seat of my rental car.

Mulligan was cramming in the second, a huge basket of tiger lilies, orchids, and out-of-season chrysanthemums when Andy and Susan drove up in a silver Rolls Royce. Andy wore an impeccably tailored black suit. Susan, who seemed almost sullen today, wore a sleeveless black silk jumpsuit covered by a cloak that fell open to revealing the highly defined muscles in her arms and shoulders. *She must lift weights,* I thought. For all her slenderness she looked as if she could easily bench press Andy Stack and then beat him at arm wrestling. It was hard to imagine such a contest though, since he seemed to control her every movement with a snap of his fingers. Now Andy was snapping his sharp little eyes at Maxine, Mulligan, and me. "You folks need a ride?" he called out.

"Don't do it," Mulligan muttered to me. He was so close I could feel the heat of him and some of my earlier desire rode back in on the smell of his Old Spice aftershave. I felt like a whiplash victim. "Let me ride with you, my car is in the shop. I'll drive, if you want."

"No. I'll drive," I hissed back. I called out to Andy, "I'd better take my car. I'll need it later, thanks." What was it about Mulligan that made me feel I was conspiring with him?

Maxine volunteered. "I've never in my life ridden in a Rolls," she said, stepping up to the back door Andy held open. "So, if you'll excuse me . . ."

"Here, take this last flower basket," Mulligan said. Once Maxine had settled in, he put it on the floor next to her feet.

In a few moments we were strapped in and following behind the Rolls Royce, which Andy drove at a slow and stately pace, as if he were following a nonexistent hearse. More likely he was talking with Maxine in the backseat. I still hadn't seen him say much to Susan except simple commands.

"So, your truck is in the shop. A pickup truck?" I asked Mulligan after a long silence.

He tilted his head to look at me oddly. "Yeah, it's a Ford pickup. Blew an axle. I had to get it fixed."

"What color is it?" As far as I could recall I hadn't told him the color of the pickup that had followed me.

"It's green." I could see him about to tell me to give that topic a rest, but he thought better of it.

As I drove in the uncomfortable silence, I wondered about Emily. The shock on top of the previous day's attack had frozen my mental processes for a moment but now my mind was racing. Unfortunately, it seemed to be racing in circles.

Could the same person who killed Emily have killed Nina? From all accounts this so-called Captain Ahab specialized in killing large women, but Emily hadn't been much bigger than your average jockey. The killer must have seen her and thought she could identify him. I followed the Rolls into the parking lot at the funeral parlor.

"Hope said she'd meet us here. After the funeral we could go talk to William. Is that still okay with you?"

"I guess so," I said grudgingly, turning off the engine. I didn't trust anyone today. Nina had trusted everyone and look what had happened to her.

I hadn't thought ahead to what Nina's funeral would be like. I had sat with the women planning it but the memory of that day was a blur. Of course, now that Ambrose was involved, the thing should run like Austrian clockwork, but don't those things always have a cuckoo popping out when you least expect it?

Mulligan pulled the two baskets from the backseat for me and went over to help Eric with the masses of flowers stuffed into his station wagon. He and Beth each took one in each hand and headed for the building. Eric was lugging a floral basket across the parking lot in one hand with his tape player in the other. I grabbed a basket of tiger lilies and orchids and a fan of roses and calla lilies and followed the crowd.

Ambrose must have been watching out for us because he held the side door to the building open and motioned us all in that way. It was an old building with wood paneling and frosted, tulip-shaped lamps hung by wrought-iron molding. A few stained-glass windows turned blind eyes on the gray morning outside. Once the doors closed, the entrance area down to an eternally fireside coziness—I guess that was the parlor part of a funeral parlor. Somewhere organ music was playing, but so very faintly that it seemed to fade the instant I heard it. When we followed Ambrose bringing the flowers into the room where the service was to be held, the sound faded entirely.

At one end of the room was a casket. I stopped dead. Okay. I had forgotten that part. Flashbacks of my mother's funeral when I was thirteen came in a rush of scattered fragments. The rain. The sweet, chilly breath of the flowers. Numbness and fear. Open casket.

I forced myself to walk up and look. It looked like Nina. The blood had been washed off of course. Whoever made her up had somehow made her look even younger, or maybe I had just never seen her asleep. She did look peaceful, closer to twenty-five than forty-five.

But my old friend's total stillness made its own brutal statement. The silk lining and pillows in the casket were not for her comfort. They made the same helpless yearning statement as the rose petals and pollen at a prehistoric grave site. The fact was, Nina had gone to where I could not reach her. The fleeting beauty of the flowers and bright silks gave us something to hold onto while we stood in front of the coffin.

The delicate white and gold embroidered scarf around Nina's wounded neck was one of her own design. One of the women's group must have brought it.

My knees felt weak. I started to turn to look for a seat when someone touched my elbow. I jumped forward and knocked into the side of Nina's coffin. It didn't budge, but I turned in fury to see Hope.

"Give me a ride home will you? Mulligan said you'd come with us. You know—to see *him*."

"Okay. Fine." I could hardly say more. My rage at the girlish conceit that her boyfriend was the center of the universe gave way to the realization that, in this case, he was William, Nina's son. And he couldn't even come to his own mother's funeral. Maxine bustled up the aisle to Hope, took her arm, and with a nod to Nina in the casket, as if asking permission, dragged her daughter off to a corner for a little motherly, "Where the hell have you been?" chat.

The entryway seemed suddenly full of people. I saw Joan Leti, despite her voluminous trench coat, looking oddly small beside two Samoan men. She introduced me to her brother and cousin, who were both close to seven feet tall and broad in every dimension. When Mulligan approached to shake hands he looked delicate by comparison.

I covertly examined Joan and Mulligan for any signs of involvement. It was hard to tell. They were talking to each other with familiarity, but there didn't seem to be that arc of electricity that arose when Mulligan came near me. I turned away to keep from staring.

Eric backed out of the room where Nina lay. He huddled

against the wall with his tape player in both arms. The mortuary had a mahogany lectern by the door with an open guest book on it. People signed it and went in.

Joan left her relatives for a moment to join Scar, Cora, and Patrice, who had made a circle around Eric and began to speak softly. His eyes kept bouncing from one to another as if looking for an opening to run away. But then he nodded and began unwinding the electric cord from the back of the tape player. They all went back into the room where Nina lay among the flowers. I guess we were going to hear some music Nina liked. I should know all this from the funeral planning meeting, but my mind was blank.

Scar lingered for a moment watching Hope wither under Maxine's whispered rebuke, then she turned and went in with the rest. I followed. Joan, Cora, and Patrice sat together and kept their raincoats on, even though glints of gold thread and brightly colored cloth glittered at the collars. If they were wearing clothes Nina had made, why not let them shine?

A diverse crowd began to fill the chapel pews. Some were sober business types. I nodded to Sam Foley and his wife, Bonnie. Some familiar faces looked as if they had thrown on their quilted jackets and come over directly from the produce stands or warehouses of Pikes' Market. The homicide detectives Gonick and Lasker were there. They made a point of greeting me as they came in. Gonick told me they expected to see me tomorrow. I got the impression that if I didn't willingly show up in the next day or so, they would come find me.

Marilyn Toy arrived wearing a black beret and wool dress, looking very sophisticated in contrast to her roommate, an intense-looking woman in a blue suit, whose name I had forgotten, although I did remember that she taught high school math.

A small stir went through the crowd as Ambrose made

way for Mrs. Madrone's wheelchair, pushed by one of her nurses. The funeral director followed in her wake, instructing assistants to remove a couple of folding chairs to make a space for her. He hovered until she was installed and murmured a few words to Ambrose, who dislodged him with a gesture similar to one scraping gum from furniture. I hesitated for a moment, thinking I would pay my respects to Mrs. Madrone, but Ambrose arrested me with a look. I went back to sit numbly up front in the row with the women from Nina's group, Mulligan, Andy Stack, and Stack's girlfriend Susan, who fidgeted in her chair.

A hush came over the room. Almost everyone who was coming seemed to have arrived. Andy Stack rose and walked to the lectern next to Nina's casket.

"I've asked an old friend who knew Nina as a teenager to come here and speak. I know she would have wanted it that way. The Reverend Gordon Bliss."

I was startled at the name. I still had his porno book in my shoulder bag. A husky, gray-suited man in his fifties approached the lectern. I heard a gasp from the back of the hall. Maxine had been whispering urgently to Hope, but now she fell silent and fixed the man with an implacable glare of hatred. I hadn't known she was acquainted with the Reverend Bliss. Now I had a few new questions for Maxine.

Gordon Bliss straightened his stack of index cards on the lectern with the practiced air of a frequent speaker. He was not the sort of man you would pick out of a crowd. He wore his graying blond hair in a short crew cut. The hair and the coke-bottle-thick glasses combined to lend him an unborn baby rabbit look which gave me a twinge of unease. A devious person who looked that innocent had to be dangerous as well.

Before he had uttered a word, Bliss was already making me a little queasy. Whatever had possessed Andy Stack to invite him? Bliss turned away from the crowd to stand over

Nina's casket for a second. All we saw of him was his back as he bent forward as if believing Nina might whisper a few last words. Or perhaps he had a last message to deliver to her. Then he faced us and bowed to the mourners with the gravity of a martial artist greeting his opponent.

"I haven't seen Nina West in twenty-five years," he said. "But she was such a light in all of our lives that I kept hearing about what she was doing, even in another state. I felt as if I talked to her just yesterday. She was that kind of person. Even as a young woman she made you feel good because she was comfortable with herself and it rubbed off on the people around her."

He was slick, I had to grant him that. He radiated an aura of innocent goodwill. He was pond scum so far as I was concerned, but he was pond scum that glowed when the light hit it just right.

I glanced back to find that Maxine and Hope had disappeared. Although I was sitting in the first row, I didn't think Nina would mind if I turned my back on Mr. Bliss and went to find Maxine. She was in the entry area of the funeral home, clutching a handkerchief to her eyes. Ambrose was standing quietly by her with one hand on her shoulder. I had really misjudged Ambrose.

I went to embrace Maxine, but she drew back like a cobra about to strike. When she brought the handkerchief down, her face was twisted with rage. She was shaking with emotion. "What is that bastard doing here?"

A moment later Mulligan joined us. Poor Nina was the only one who couldn't get up and leave.

"Get him out of there or I'll do it myself!" Maxine hadn't lowered her voice. I could see through the glass pane in the door that a couple of people in the back rows had turned to look.

Ambrose patted Maxine's shoulder gently and cast me a rueful look. "Come on Jo, introduce the women."

"What women?"

He tilted his head to one side Groucho fashion, "Hellooo. You haven't been tracking, have you? Just push the Reverend off and say the women from the newsletter have come to honor Nina's last request. They'll do the rest."

"Okay." I shook my head all the way up the aisle.

Then suddenly I reached the microphone and stood next to the Reverend Bliss, who broke off, mid-sentence, as surprised to see me there as I was to be there.

What the hell. "Excuse me, Reverend." I moved in front of him to the microphone. He was forced to back up or I would have either stepped on his feet or shoved him out of the way. He gazed at me in bewilderment, as if expecting me to announce that a red Toyota Tercel had its lights on in the parking lot.

"I'm sorry to interrupt, we all appreciate your coming such a distance to pay your last respects to Nina—" I said to him, nodding politely, "But, Reverend, um," I thought fast, "Reverend, you have an urgent phone call in the lobby." I gave him a little shove and he walked reluctantly down the aisle toward the door, his best lines still unspoken.

With a mental shrug I continued, "We're all here to honor Nina and what she meant to us. She had one request for her funeral, and her friends from the newsletter are here now to honor it."

I met Ambrose's eyes and he gave me a thumbs up sign. Eric punched a button on his boom box and a Middle Eastern wail arose from it. Unintelligible lyrics and a light but persistent drum beat underneath.

"Wow." My exclamation was amplified. I hadn't seen them take off their coats but suddenly Joan, Cora, and Patrice were gliding gracefully up the aisle in glittering belly dance outfits. I went to my seat as they reached the slightly raised dias.

The crowd seemed to take in breath at the same moment. I couldn't help smiling. Nina might have scored a Seattle first here. Not that she would have cared who was first to have bellydancers at their funeral. The important thing to her would be that the women who danced at her funeral be large and uninhibited. They were all of that and more. Those who had gasped, let the air out again with a sigh.

Now that I watched, I did recall something in one of the newsletters about a bellydancing class, but I had no idea these women were so accomplished. As they shook and undulated, with limber spines and agile hips, the flesh in their ample bellies and thighs trembled with a power that caused a hush to descend over the place—part shock, part admiration.

Their faces were serene and solemn, and with every graceful move they pushed away the myth that flesh on a woman is ugly or clumsy. Each woman was offering a personal tribute to a fallen sister. The dance concluded with linked hands across Nina's casket—Joan at the head, Cora on the far side with Patrice almost concealing her in front—her massive backside daring the crowd to disapprove. I felt like a heel to have suspected Joan of any involvement in Nina's death.

The music died away. Eric, standing open-mouthed in the back, gulped and jumped to click off his tape recorder. Mulligan was smiling and nodding. Andy and Susan were conferring in what I took to be a slightly distracted way. In the collective hush that followed the music, I had no idea what would come next.

Reverend Bliss had returned to the front row. He began to rise, eager to forgive my interruption and resume his speech. But Maxine had taken a seat two rows behind him and from the way her whole body was clenched, she might have physically assaulted him if given the slightest excuse. I wondered if she knew what he had done to Nina. I was dying to ask her how she knew him, but not at Nina's funeral.

I leaped up to beat the Reverend to the microphone. He

sat back down with growing irritation. I cleared my throat. "Um, Nina was my best friend and I hadn't planned to say anything. I understand why Joan, Patrice, and Cora chose to dance, because it's hard to find any words for this kind of situation. Even though we lost Nina, at least we had her for awhile and I'm glad for that. I would still be lost if I hadn't met her when I did. She had such an unusual gift for bringing out the best in people. There's no one on this earth I could miss more." My voice trembled. I swallowed and took a deep breath. A few people in the audience wiped away tears as well. "I hope a little of what she had stayed with me and you and all of us, because it would be terrible for it to be lost. It won't be easy without her. But what she did give me was like a strong sword to cut through the . . . uh-" Why did I have to talk about cutting? For all I knew someone here at this very moment had a knife, the knife that had killed Nina. "Er, ah, to cut through the negativity and to stand up for what I believe in." I turned away from the crowd and toward the casket. "My dear friend, wherever you are, thank you. Until we meet again."

Instead of walking back to my seat I stared strongly at Ambrose and he met me in mid-aisle. "Make sure that damn Reverend doesn't talk again, can you?" I hissed.

"Okay." He squeezed my arm supportively and passed. He whispered to Andy Stack, who went to the microphone and announced that the cremation would take place later in the day and the ashes would be disposed of privately. He invited everyone to come to his house afterward. "It's only a ten-minute drive. I've left a stack of sheets with directions next to the sign-in book at the door." He then nodded to Eric, who pressed a button. The tape player clicked and this time played a Beethoven string quartet, a favorite of Nina's.

Most people left after spending a minute or so staring

down into the casket. I had seen this viewing ritual in newsreels and films. I watched everyone else do it before I got the nerve to go up myself. Mulligan, Maxine, and Hope were lingering there.

It was odd to look down at Nina like that. To see no animation. The strangeness of it and the overpowering sweetness of the flowers, had begun to make me dizzy, but I couldn't tear myself away. I knew this was the last time to see Nina in the flesh, even though her life force no longer inhabited that body. There was a small scattering of notes and cards and keepsakes people had tucked into her arms.

Maxine must have seen me swaying a little because she tugged at my elbow. "Come on, Jo, you'll make yourself sick. You need to eat something. I'm going with Andy and Susan. Do you want to follow us?"

"I'll come in a minute. I'll bring Hope and Mulligan. We'll get a map. Don't worry."

"Okay. See you there." She left by the side door. As the door closed behind Maxine I felt a slight puff of air from outside. I looked down at Nina and saw something move. It was one of the scraps of paper turned over by the wind. But instead of love or thank you, the block letters on the white scrap of paper read: "KILL THE WHALES!"

Chapter
Twenty-Three

The killer had been there. Had walked up to Nina's casket and casually delivered that ugly message.

"Do you see that?" I whispered. My voice came out strangled.

Mulligan leaned over to look. "I'll go get one of the cops. You stay here. Don't let anyone touch that paper."

Detective Gonick hadn't left yet. He secured the note in an envelope and said he would log it in as evidence and have it tested for prints. He said we could go on ahead to Andy's. A few feet down the aisle, I stopped and looked back. "I hate to leave her here," I said.

"You can't hate it more than I do," Mulligan said softly. "But she's gone. We can't bring her back."

"And William can only wait a short time. He has to keep moving," Hope said softly, her eyes on Maxine, who was walking between Andy and Susan toward the Rolls.

I wanted to slap Hope for that thoughtless comment but I contented myself with a very nasty look. "Don't get on my bad side, Hope." I muttered. "I'm seeing William out of respect for the people he's lost." I managed not to say that I wasn't sure I cared whether William got caught or not.

Maxine looked back over her shoulder at Hope, who waved. I raised my hand as well, which seemed to reassure Maxine that Mulligan and I could be trusted to keep an eye on Hope and bring her safely to Andy's. Hope put her arm through Mulligan's. They seemed to know each other awfully well. "Can't you see?" she said to me softly. "If the killer left that note, it *couldn't* have been William. He wasn't even here today." *Unless you put it there for him, Hope,* I thought but didn't say.

We passed the Reverend Bliss getting into a cab. I had a few questions to ask him, but this was not the time. I also knew he was another person who had an opportunity to put that paper in Nina's coffin—that moment when he bowed to Nina before speaking.

I asked Hope if she would sit in the front seat to direct me. Packing the three of us into the car took effort. Mulligan got into the back seat without a complaint, but I had to avert my eyes when I found myself examining his backside too intently as he jackknifed himself in.

I got in the car and took a deep breath. I had better ask Hope a few questions before she ran off again. As I put the key in the ignition I asked her, "What kind of knife does William have? Don't tell me he doesn't have one. I saw it on his belt at the Toy Duck Cafe."

Hope let her seat belt snap back into the roller with a jerk. "It's just a plain old knife from the Army-Navy store," she said, narrowing her eyes at me. "He gets a lot of stuff at surplus stores. You know he's been living rough since he left home. He didn't kill Nina. Okay?"

Mulligan spoke up from the back seat, "If owning a knife meant killing someone, you'd have to suspect me and every hunter and camper in town as well."

I couldn't answer that. It was true that Mulligan was too

tall and bulky to have been the attacker who had pulled me into that barn. I badly wanted to trust Mulligan. But I certainly hadn't ruled out William and most of the people in Nina's building.

I started the motor.

A few blocks away from the funeral home Hope pulled a bright yellow scarf from her shoulder bag and waved it out the window. A moment later a motorcyclist exited a supermarket parking lot and roared up behind us. He passed us on the right, then moved in front of us.

"Follow him," Hope said.

"Is that William?"

"Yes. He said he didn't think it was safe to come in."

The sadness of it all struck me. Waiting outside at his mother's funeral—afraid to come in. Did he even know that the man who was probably his father, Gordon Bliss, was there as well? I wasn't looking forward to telling him the news about his stepmother Emily's death last night. Another thought pushed out the first—perhaps young William was responsible not only for the death of his stepfather Granger, but of his birth mother and stepmother as well. If he had done that he might have also killed several women whose only crime was being the same size as Nina.

We followed the motorcycle to a nearly deserted parking lot with a greasy spoon restaurant lighting up the overcast day. He had parked his bike and gone in before Mulligan managed to maneuver his bulk and long legs out of the back seat. We joined him at a booth in the back near the door where he could glance out the window every minute or two.

Hope came up and slipped in to sit next to him. He leaned down and kissed her. I mistrust booths because they frequently attack me at the midriff. Simply fitting in behind the table can be a problem, let alone being comfortable.

Fortunately, this one had a table that wasn't bolted down, so I pushed it toward Hope and William before slipping into the booth with relative ease. I let Mulligan take the one chair outside the booth. The table didn't actually squash my stomach but Mulligan with endearing delicacy moved it even farther toward Hope and William to give me room to breathe. I wondered if Mulligan had always been sensitive to other people's needs or if Nina had taught him that. Either way I thanked him and cast him an appreciative smile. I took a deep breath, realizing that the worst part of the day was over. Hope ordered a Coke and William got a pot of tea while Mulligan and I had coffee.

"So how was the service?" William asked, looking down at the table and meeting no one's eyes.

"Who wants to know?" I asked pointedly. "William Smith? Or Nina's son, William T. Crain?"

Hope shot me a hostile look and put her hand over William's on the table as if to shelter him. But he lifted his head and met my eyes steadily. "Yeah, I lied to you last time I talked to you, I am William Turnbow Crain." He looked at me defiantly. "Nina was my mother, even though she never raised me. I saw her maybe once a year."

I examined his tanned face. He had circles under his eyes and tense lines around his mouth, but he still looked more like a college kid who has been staying up studying for finals than like a killer. Hope stared at him with passionate intensity. Despite her many-colored hair and skin-piercing jewelry she and William looked oddly alike. Two young, blond people with tense expressions.

Mulligan's bulldog features twitched in something resembling a smile, "I think Nina would have liked the funeral today." I had to agree. "Well, most of it. . . ." I turned to William to fill him in, "The Reverend Bliss came to speak."

William nodded, as if not surprised, "He's a legend in

ESP, and he's been known to show up at the funerals of old time members." He squeezed the last tea out of the bag and poured in a generous amount of sugar and cream.

"Have you ever met him?"

William restrained a snort of irritation, "Couldn't help it. He's living out of state but they dragged me to see him whenever he came to town to speak. He was like God incarnate to my parents. They really should have known better. It's not about idolizing a person."

If William knew the rumor about Bliss being his biological father he wasn't letting on. We were all silent for a minute, then William asked, "Who contacted Bliss?"

"Andy Stack."

"Never heard of him."

Mulligan continued, "The Reverend began to talk but was interrupted in mid-speech."

"My mom wanted to take that Bliss guy apart," Hope said with glee at her mother's ferocity. "She came within a heartbeat of cleaning his clock."

"Let's see," I picked up the story, "Then there was belly dancing. Then the formalities were cut short—"

"You forgot to say that you spoke," Mulligan interrupted, covering my hand with his and squeezing it briefly. The touch was unexpected and so electric that I very nearly jumped. But he let go before I had time to react. Hope and William exchanged a glance. "Nina would have liked that part," Mulligan concluded.

"I hope so," I said. Everyone was quiet for a moment. "Well, she's being cremated rather than buried. Just a few of us will scatter her ashes on the Sound next week. After the funeral everyone went off to Andy Stack's." I looked at my watch. "Which is where we're going very shortly, so you'd better get to your point, William." I took a deep breath. "What can I do for you?" William pushed his tea cup away and swallowed convulsively. Hope looked at him with concern and ran her fingers along his knuckles, as if to give him courage. I expected him to ask me for money. I wasn't disappointed.

"I need a lawyer. Nina said she would help me pay for one when we talked, before . . . Before she was killed." He fell silent as the waitress came back with the check and Mulligan paid for everything. I wondered if William had asked him for money before getting around to me.

William glanced around uneasily to make sure the waitress was out of earshot. "I told her I would pay her back, no matter how long it took. You met my stepmother. She must have told you what kind of trouble I'm in."

His stepmother. I would have to tell him about her murder—but not yet. "So you came to Nina when you were in trouble?"

William looked into his tea cup as if it contained the answer to some riddle. At last he sighed. "Yeah. I knew where to find her. She sent money and came to visit sometimes, but she wasn't there every day like mom and dad—" he looked up as if to be certain I understood. "Emily Crain is my real mother. And as bad as he treated us sometimes, Granger was all I had for a dad."

"You never thought to ask Nina for help when Granger was beating you and your sisters and Emily?"

"No." He shook his head. "I didn't expect her to help. I felt awkward with her. She was more like an aunt that visits sometimes. I know she sent money, but, I . . . hell, she'd already rejected me once. It wasn't like I could bring my sisters there to stay with her. She never wanted me around when I was little, why should she . . .?" He stopped and drained the last of his tea. It must have been cold. My coffee was.

"Even after I killed my step-dad I didn't call Nina. I

wasn't sure how I felt about her or whether the cops would know to check with her. I hung around getting up the courage to talk to her. That's when I got to know Hope."

He glanced at Hope and smiled briefly. Hope squeezed his hand. "Hope told me Nina was sure to help. When I did talk to her she said she'd get a lawyer for me. Then the next time I called, there was no answer on her telephone. She must have been dead already."

I sat still for a moment. There was no choice. Nina had made her intentions clear. "I'll try to help you. You are supposed to inherit some property under the will and I'll talk to Nina's lawyer." I got out my notebook and copied Sam Foley's number onto one of my cards. "I can always be reached at the 800 number and here's the lawyer's number. Talk to him. He may not represent you himself, but he'll know who to recommend. You'll be better off turning yourself in. As soon as possible."

We all took a deep breath at the same time. The relief on William's and Hope's faces was like a sudden sharpening of focus. But I wasn't finished. "You said about Nina that it was her karma to die that way."

He nodded. "I believe that."

"Well, then you must believe it's karma that you did this, and you're better off facing your karmic debts, because it sounds like the kind you take with you everywhere you go."

"Yeah, okay, you're right." He started to get up, but I found myself reaching across to touch his sleeve. "Wait." He sat back down. I took a deep breath. "William, when was the last time you spoke with Emily?"

"I sent her a post card. Called my step-sister in Ellensburg last week, but she hadn't talked to Mom in a couple days."

Was he lying? His feeling for Emily seemed to run deep

and true. "I hate to have to tell you this, William. There's no good way to say it. Your stepmother was killed last night."

"What!" William looked at me as if I had hit him with a large blunt instrument. For a moment he couldn't seem to make sense out of the words. Then he leaned over the table as if he was about to leap across it. "How? What happened?"

Before I could say anything, Mulligan briefly explained.

William's mouth twisted in a futile effort to hold back a sob. At that moment he looked closer to twelve than twenty. He put a hand over his face and stood up, pushing Hope's comforting arms away. "Look, I've got . . . I've got to be alone for awhile." His voice was thick with tears. "Hope, I'll call you later, okay?" He stumbled from the restaurant, dragging his backpack after him awkwardly and bumping into one patron's chair in the process.

Hope started to rise to go after him, but Mulligan caught her arm. "Don't do that. He knows how to reach you. When he says he needs time alone, listen to him."

I was starting to respect Mulligan in action. He let go of Hope's arm when she sat down, still staring over her shoulder at William's retreating back.

I didn't know where to look. Hope turned back to the table and fastened on me. "Did you have to tell him like that?"

"Hope, we couldn't keep it from him. He had a right to know."

Hope sighed. "Okay, but can't you see? I never met Emily Crain, but she's William's real mother, the one who raised him. He shot his stepfather to protect her. Now he must think it's his fault she was left alone to become a victim of this killer. I only hope he doesn't do something desperate."

Mulligan patted her arm, "Look, Hope, the kid doesn't

have anywhere else to go or anyone else to help him, does he?"

"No." Hope looked up at him, reluctant to be persuaded.

"Believe me, he'll be in touch. Drink the rest of your Coke and let's go to Andy Stack's place. Your mother will be missing you."

I stared at Mulligan. Just when I got adjusted to his doing nothing, he would suddenly develop a take-charge attitude. It was hard to predict the man.

"Was that true about Nina's will?" he asked me.

"Yes. Except for a couple of cash and property gifts and some sentimental bequests. Nina owned the apartment house and William is supposed to split the income with me."

"Son of a gun," Mulligan said reflectively.

"And you didn't explain it to William!" Hope said accusingly.

"When he calls the lawyer, he'll hear about it. Of course if I die within forty-five days of Nina's death, William would get it all."

"And someone tried to make that happen yesterday," Mulligan said thoughtfully. I felt a twinge of resentment that he could contemplate my death so calmly. Of course, we were all still numb from Nina's death. Or was I seeing a cold-blooded side of Mulligan?

"What if William should die within forty-five days, would you inherit the whole thing?" Hope asked, her lower lip pushed out resentfully.

"I think so."

Hope looked from me to Mulligan. "Everyone *close* to William has died. How do we know this isn't aimed at framing him? If he's in jail for murdering Nina he can't inherit. That way you get the whole thing."

I took a deep breath, reminding myself that Hope was just a child. "Believe me, Hope, Nina meant a lot more to me than any damn property. Besides, it hardly makes sense to kill Nina just to frame William. He's already wanted for murder. All anyone would have had to do is tell the police where he's been seen recently and with whom. They could just follow you till they found him. But I haven't done that. So far. I'd like to give him a chance to turn himself in first."

"My mother told me you were cut by the man who killed Emily. You could be lying. Maybe Emily cut you trying to defend herself, while you were killing her."

"Okay, let's look at the times involved." I was quickly losing patience with Hope. "I dropped Emily off at her daughter's house late in the afternoon. Her daughter will vouch for that. I was at Maxine's within a few hours. Mulligan, you saw the cut on my neck."

He nodded. I continued. "Emily was still alive at that point. She was killed in the spare bedroom of her daughter's house probably after everyone had gone to bed. Which brings up the question of where William was last night."

Hope looked at the table sullenly. "I don't know. I was staying at Scar's house. But William doesn't have a car. He just borrowed that motorcycle."

"Does he have any friends who have trucks he could borrow?" I asked.

Hope shrugged. Mulligan rolled his eyes. "Again with the trucks. He borrowed my truck last week, but it threw a rod. Had to go pick him up in Bellevue. He was doing some kind of gardening, yard work. Odd jobs like filling in shifts at Marilyn Toy's cafe."

"Mulligan, just out of curiosity, where were you last night?"

"I don't have any witnesses. You were fast asleep in the armchair when I left Maxine's. I went downstairs to my apartment. I didn't see anyone else the rest of the night." He looked at me without amusement. He didn't like being a suspect.

"No witnesses to your whereabouts?"

"Like several other people, I spent the night alone. Are you asking them as well?"

"I intend to."

"Then let's go on to Andy Stack's. You can interrogate lots of people there. If nothing else it will keep the Homicide detectives amused."

We walked to the car in silence.

Chapter Twenty-Four

The crowd from the funeral home had filtered down to about twenty people forlornly wandering through Andy Stack's house on Queen Anne Hill. Of course, we were late, some might have come and gone already. The house had been built into the hillside on three levels. The living room looked out over Lake Union both from the main floor and from windows off a balcony that ran around three sides of the room.

The caterer had set up tables across from the picture window with enough food to feed several times as many people as the room now held. Andy greeted Hope and me with hugs and nodded at Mulligan, intoning his name. Mulligan nodded back and growled something I couldn't make out. Hope waved vaguely and went to talk to Scar, who was petting a carousel horse in an alcove.

I let Andy drag me up the stairway to show me the view from the balcony. "Both this room and the kitchen were featured in *Architectural Digest*,' he told me. 'We're quite proud of them.'

Speaking of "us" I asked, "Where is Susan?"

"Oh, something with the caterers ... " Andy said vaguely, his hands straying up to tug at his already frazzled hair.

Mulligan trailed along behind us but he was not in a talkative mood. He kept glancing down at the knots of people on the main floor below and then up and out at the cloud cover over Lake Union.

Now Andy was pointing out something on the other side of the main room. I had to squint a bit to take in the far wall—I've seen gymnasiums smaller than his living room. We dutifully followed Andy back down the staircase to look at his art treasures. Lined up along the wall under the balcony were groups of antique china cabinets and display shelves, each holding dramatically lit blue and brown glass bottles and quaintly lithographed boxes. Andy obviously adored and collected old-fashioned patent remedies. I couldn't tell if this represented the rudiments of an elaborate sense of humor in Andy Stack or whether he was trying to legitimize snake oil as an art form. There was no pinning him down to answer questions—he was in perpetual motion mode. The doorbell rang and Andy ushered us toward the wet bar and was off to answer it.

"You want some wine or beer or something?" Mulligan asked, as we approached the bar. "I can drive home if you want."

"Ha. You just want to get in the front seat."

"I won't argue with that," he said with a faint smile. "My knees are still recovering."

"Well, you can sit in front but I think I'll stay the designated driver. Anyway, I'm not even thirsty after what we had in the cafe. I want to look around a little first."

"Okay. In that case *I'll* get a beer," he said. He went toward the bar. Seeing Stack's home made me wonder why, even in his own living room, he was still selling so hard. I wandered along the wall full of antique advertisements. In one framed sequence, the world-famous 98-pound weakling suffered from sand kicked in his face until he sent for the product and quickly sprouted muscles, causing women to chase him and bullies to run. A little further on "Before and After" pictures stared numbly from tasteful frames. I always liked the before pictures better, even during my early dieting years. A glass-fronted cabinet near the bar was full of shaving mugs, brushes and razors. When at last I reached the bar, there was no sign of Mulligan.

"You know, a barber shop with a wet bar might do a roaring business," I said to the bartender, who wore a barbershop quartet style uniform.

"That would confuse the customers," he said, adding another level to the stack of empty bottles of beer and designer water piled on a wheeled cart behind him, "Barbers talk. Bartenders listen." He winked. "What'll it be?"

I opted for a glass of apple juice.

Mulligan emerged from behind a tall exhibit case that displayed medicine balls, weathered Indian clubs, and what must have been the oldest set of dumbbells in the western hemisphere. He came up and put a hand on my shoulder. His possessive gesture startled me.

"Thanks for what you did for the kid."

"It's what Nina wanted done."

"I think he'll end up doing what's right. Otherwise . . . "

"Otherwise you'll turn him in?"

His face hardened. He took a swallow of beer and with constant pressure on my shoulder, moved us away from the bartender. "Sooner or later."

"Look, I'm sorry if I offended you with all my questions about pickup trucks and all. Seeing what happened to Nina—oh, I don't know." I gritted my teeth. "It makes me crazy not to know who killed her."

"Crazy is right," he said. "But, of course, I understand. I feel the same way myself, I just don't seem to have your delusion that I can actually do it."

"I don't know why I feel this way. But I've got to say,

almost getting killed really pisses me off and I'll be damned if I'll let it stop me."

Mulligan favored me with an inscrutable bulldog stare. "You're a strange one, Jo Fuller."

"Why do you say that?"

"You'd be surprised how few people, when attacked like that, would immediately start snooping around again. Are you always like this?"

"Like what? You think I suffered a head injury when I was knocked out?"

"That might explain it."

I shrugged. "I don't know. Nobody's ever tried to kill me before. One thing I did learn traveling all over with my ex-husband is that you never know how you'll react in a crisis till you get in one."

He grunted noncommittally, looking more like a bulldog than ever.

"Hell, I don't know. I have to find a way to live without jumping at shadows. I don't trust anybody, but I don't really suspect you . . . "

"Thank you."

"Don't thank me. You're too tall and broad to have been the person who attacked me. But someone could have borrowed your pickup truck. Like young William."

"Except that my pickup truck is still in the shop."

I didn't say anything.

"Well, I'm not offended." Again he put his hand on my shoulder. I liked it a little too much. "I'd like to know who killed Nina. But nothing will bring her back."

I drank some more juice. "So do you have a first name?" I inquired of Mulligan.

He took his arm away. Wrong question. "Another time, okay?" He surveyed the glass case full of shaving mugs and old-time toiletries. "Hey, get a load of all the swastikas—" he tapped the glass. "See that red leather case in there."

I looked and sure enough gold swastikas were stamped on the dark-red binding. Mulligan must have raised his voice because Andy came out of the hallway that led off to the kitchen.

"You have a good eye, sir. You found the cornerstone of my collection," he said smoothly.

"What is it?" I asked

"My uncle brought it back from Germany after World War II. He gave it to me when I turned twenty-one. It's a set of straight razors. Here, I'll show you."

He pulled a key ring from his vest pocket. The smallest key on it opened the sliding door on one side of the display case. He lifted out the morocco-bound case, not quite as large as a ring binder. He flipped it open and revealed a row of seven ivory handles resting in seven pockets in the lining.

"One for each day of the week."

Black Gothic script read Montag, Dienstag, Mittwoch, Donnerstag, Freitag, Samstag, Sonntag. A small pocket on the side held a piece of stone, I pointed at it, "What's that?"

"Carborundum to take off the rough edge."

"They don't look rusty, do you sharpen them yourself?" I asked, fiddling with my scarf, hating to show my curiosity.

"Oh, every few months to keep the rust off. I have a professional cleaning staff in to dust the antiques. But these remind me of my Uncle George. Of course the original owner would use the razor strap on the outside to sharpen the blade of the day."

"Did you ever use them to shave with?" Mulligan asked.

"Once." Andy rubbed his face with a grimace. "I still have the scar. Ever since then I've wondered about those so-called dueling scars." He closed the case carefully, restored it to its shelf and locked the glass cabinet.

Mulligan and I exchanged a look while Andy was replacing the razors.

"Come on, Beth wanted to see the garden out back. I'm hoping if I send them home with a bunch of cuttings, I can get Maxine to forgive me for inviting the Reverend Bliss. I had no idea she even knew him. Obviously they aren't on very good terms."

"Andy, how did you know Reverend Bliss?"

His mellow expression drained away like water from a cracked glass. He ran his hands through his hair. "I don't. Know him that is. Look, don't you hate it at funerals when the clergyman hasn't even met the guest of honor?"

"Yes, but why Bliss?"

Stack was decidedly uncomfortable. "I've told this to Maxine and she's forgiven me, now don't you start. Nina and I grew up together. After her parents died there was a time when all she could talk about was this wonderful Reverend Bliss. Eventually she left that religious group, but I know she still meditated." He shrugged. "I thought she would have approved. Hell, after high school, Nina had some money from her parents so she went off looking for the meaning of life and found the Reverend Bliss. Me, I joined the Army one step ahead of the draft. Just for the record, if you want to invite my old Army chaplain to *my* funeral, I won't be offended."

Andy kept talking, but I took a deep breath and made a mental note that, as Mulligan had pointed out, the Army was one of the places that teach killing with a knife.

"I tracked down Gordon Bliss in Idaho. He remembered Nina vividly and he was happy to come and speak. I had no idea Maxine knew him."

Something in his explanation rang false but I couldn't tell what, and wasn't quite sure how to question a man's truthfulness while standing in his living room, sipping his catered apple juice. "So you never knew any of Nina's friends who were Eastways members? I asked.

"No. She's the only one from back home I kept in touch

with here. We were friends—allies really—the short boy and the fat girl. She was my best friend. When we grew up we didn't always agree but we never let that get between us." He wiped away a tear and turned aside to grind his knuckles angrily into his eyes. "Sorry."

Mulligan turned on his heel and walked away without a word.

"Do you think he's jealous of my relationship with Nina?"

"Should he be?"

"I don't see why. After all I have Susan. If Nina and I were going to be together, it would have happened a long time ago."

"So you and Nina were never lovers?"

I saw an odd gleam come into Stack's eye. "Look at Susan. What do you think?" I thought he hadn't answered my question. And by the way, where the hell was Susan?

Stack snagged my sleeve and started to pull. "Come on, I want to show you the flower garden. One corner of the place is all greenhouse. Maxine, Hope! Come on, Jo."

I stood stock still and pulled my sleeve out of his grip. "No thanks, I need to eat something."

Stack shrugged and went off to round up the group for his next guided tour. I went over and studied the buffet. Frosty pink cans of his Stack Shakes and trays of Stack Snacks sat scarcely touched on special platters with little cards identifying them and giving a complete nutritional run-down. None of the other food had such labels on it, so that in itself was the message—if it didn't have a label, it was probably bad for you.

I contemplated this while I ate smoked salmon on some excellent crackers. Then I judiciously filled a plate with prosciutto and melon, spinach quiche, a couple of sandwiches with crusts cut off, and a raspberry tart.

I settled down on a straight backed chair to enjoy the lot

when I heard Maxine's voice rise about the hushed crowd. "A well-scrubbed colon is a happy colon," she pronounced while gesturing at the buffet table and draining the last of a martini, which I suspect did not contain any dietary fiber.

My appetite wavered a bit. I finished most of the plate and put it aside, not so much satisfied as refueled. No doubt Susan had hired Seattle's best caterers and they had done a fine job, but Andy Stack's home was not meant to be a place where food was enjoyed.

Marilyn Toy and her roommate were greeting Ambrose, who said a few more words over his shoulder to them but nodded at Val, whom he led toward the exit. Val looked even more miserable than the last time I saw him. Still no sign of the beautiful K. C., which might account for Val's discomfort. His white-streaked gray beard was a little ratty around the edges and his eyes were bloodshot. Ambrose saw me and raised his eyebrows, then he steered Val my way.

I went to meet them, "Ambrose, thank you so much for pulling everything together."

"I was glad to be of service." He actually beamed under the praise. I was so used to thinking of Ambrose as one of life's stinging nettles that I had to marvel at how badly I had misjudged him.

"I noticed that Mrs. Madrone left early," I said. "It was a great honor to have her there."

"She liked everything she heard about Nina. She said she wished she could have met her."

"And you, Ambrose, have been indispensable."

"My dear, that's what they'll put on my tombstone." He gave a final glance round as if writing off Andy's house in toto. "Now." He turned to Val with a stern schoolmaster quality that did seem more like the familiar tyrant of expense accounts and office equipment interrogations. Val winced. "Val, you need to talk to someone about what K. C.

told you." Val nodded but said nothing. "I think Jo is a good person to start with," Ambrose said.

Val sighed, eyeing the exit longingly. "Ambrose," he said in a pleading tone, "I'm getting a terrific headache and this isn't the time or place. Josie, could you come talk to me at the apartment, say tomorrow?"

"I'm free in the afternoon," I said, remembering my morning interview with the homicide detectives.

"I'll make a point of being there from twelve on," Val said, glancing at Ambrose, who although a decade younger was doing an excellent imitation of a stern parent. I told them I'd try to make it by 1:00 p.m.

Ambrose nodded. "I'll be there too."

It was as much a threat as a promise. As the two men headed for the exit I realized that the old Ambrose was back, or perhaps he had never gone away, just turned his laser drill gaze on inefficient florists and underachieving funeral directors. Whatever it was K.C. had seen, Ambrose would make sure Val told me. But why was Val so reluctant to talk about it?

Chapter Twenty-Five

I handed in my empty juice glass. "Do you have any bottled water?" I asked the man behind the bar.

He shook his head. "Just going back to the kitchen to get some more."

"I'll come along if you don't mind and get my own."

I followed him down the hall, through a formal dining room, into a pantry. Beyond that was the kitchen—a long, narrow t-shaped room with a refectory table running along its length. A butcher-block island just beyond the end of the table separated the working, cooking area. A stove the size of a Volvo hunkered against the back wall and pans on hooks dangled from a strip of metal above the island. Susan sat at the head of the table, the pots and kitchen equipment behind her like a backdrop. She was reading.

The caterer took a Calistoga bottle from a case and gave it to me with a glass. He would have sliced a lemon to go with it, but I waved him on.

Susan looked up when we came in but returned her eyes to her book. Blue tinted glasses shielded her eyes. I brought my glass over to stand next to her.

She must have hurried straight in here from the funeral because her cloak hung over the back of the chair next to her. It was warm in the kitchen and she didn't seem uncomfortable in the sleeveless black silk, but her breathing was a little rapid from the stress of grimly ignoring me. Her blond hair was twisted up, anchored with pearl clips. She reached in front of her, poured tea from a pot into a cup, and took a sip without ever acknowledging that I was there. She pointedly ignored the caterer as well. He picked up a carrying case of drinks and left.

From where Susan sat at the head of the table, most of the kitchen tools were in easy reach. Decorated with bright tiles, the kitchen island behind her held bulk supplies below and an arsenal of kitchen tools on shelves. The formidable knife block just above her shoulder within arm's reach might as well have been a decorative statue. The forest of braided garlic, chili peppers and bay leaves that hung down in garlands over the spice rack at the other end of the island might have been wallpaper.

I continued to stand a few feet away from her and wait. From the stiffness of her averted gaze and the blotches of emotion on her cheeks, she was only pretending to read, hoping I would go away.

"Close your eyes and think of England," I said.

"What?" she looked up at me in annoyance. I was not going away.

I pulled out a stool near her but not too near. "That's another way of saying it will be over soon. It's very nice of you to have this gathering in your house."

She shrugged. "It's Andy's house," she said reluctantly closing the book, marking her place with a bay leaf. Her voice grew even softer, barely audible, "But it's okay with me." She still hadn't met my eyes.

"What are you reading?"

She opened the book. Whatever it was, she had used it

to hide a magazine on bodybuilding. She lowered her glasses and her unshielded eyes met mine. For a moment I thought she had bruises around both eyes, then I realized her make-up had worn off and I was seeing the deep circles under her eyes.

After a moment of shocked silence, I managed to ask, "So, you lift weights, do you go to a gym or work out at home?"

"Both." She nearly smiled, took a long shivery breath. She suddenly reminded me of Nina's cat, Raoul, and how he had clung to me with his claws the minute I rescued him from the linen closet.

"I used to do it at home but there's a complete gym at Stack Attack Central. So I go there now. It's good to get out, you know. I like living with Andy but sometimes I need to get out on my own so I don't feel like a . . . a prisoner?" Her voice rose questioningly. "Oh, I'm not ungrateful. Andy shares everything, well . . . most everything, but . . . "

"Oh, I know. I just got divorced last year, so believe me, I understand about how marriage can be, uh, confining."

"Do you think so?" She looked at me worriedly. "Even after you're married? We're not married yet, but we set the date for July 4th. That's Andy's birthday, so he won't forget our anniversary." She smiled a little. An often-heard joke.

I smiled back encouragingly, hiding a wince. But hell, I didn't even like Andy. Susan was the one who felt she had to marry him. "So how did you two meet?"

She smiled a little more surely now. "I was his secretary about two years ago. He moved me from being another guy's secretary because he decided to *mold* me."

I stifled a laugh, turned it into a cough. She was totally serious. "How did he mold you? Really, Susan, you look absolutely perfect to me."

"Well, of course *now*. I'm not perfect but I've made a lot of improvements. But no one is ever perfect, you know?"

She was starting to look at me with that speculative, this-can-be-fixed gaze that I know so well. I hastened to forestall her. I didn't want to have to slap her down verbally. And I knew I would have to do that very thing if she started in on me. If she thought she was feeling bad now, she couldn't even begin to imagine.

I took a deep breath and asked, "So what was the program, how were you molded?"

"First Andy wanted me to lose sixty pounds. You look shocked."

"No. I'm not shocked. He's in the weight loss business. I'm sure he says that to all the girls."

Susan examined my face to see if I was making fun of her. I wasn't. But I wanted her to understand that I easily could and it wouldn't be wise to push me. I felt a fresh burst of anger at Andy. True, it was hardly an unusual request. And how many women like Susan think their man will love them after they lose that sixty pounds? But even in the unlikely event that she never regained any of that weight, I would bet money that the sixty pounds was only the first on a long list of demands.

"Well, I really was overweight. And I felt bad about it. Not like you." She looked at me cautiously. Even taking her anxiousness into account, Susan seemed almost feverishly intense. She wouldn't have had those hollows in her cheeks sixty pounds ago. But then Susan probably liked the hollows in her cheeks. "I totally agreed with Andy but I didn't know how to go about it. So he helped me start working out, eating right, but that wasn't enough, you know?"

"How well I know. What did he want then?"

"He wanted to start body sculpting with me. Now he's trying to train my mind, teach me stuff about manners."

Without warning she pulled her magazine out of the book and whipped the book across the room, hitting the tiled wall across from us with a broken-crockery clatter.

I flinched back way too late. Even though it had been aimed a good foot way from my head, I felt the whoosh of air past my ear. Turning, I saw the book had grazed a pile of sandwiches the caterers had set on the drainboard and smacked a decorative hanging plate of a windmill into the mosaic wall behind it. The plate broke in half and fell together with the book onto the sandwiches.

"Whooa—good arm," I said, a little breathlessly. I didn't like her impulsiveness a bit. If she'd wanted to hit me with that book, I'd be down on the floor in a bad way by now. "Where'd you learn to throw?"

"Five brothers. I grew up on a farm. Sometimes Andy treats me like I'm a dumb hick. He grew up on a farm too, y'know. He wanted me to help out this afternoon. He and Nina used to be lovers, you know. How could he! How could anyone expect me to go along and hostess her damn wake?"

"Very insensitive of him." So, Andy and Nina had been lovers. Somehow I believed Susan, while I hadn't believed Andy.

"Oh, sheesh, the sandwiches are all mushed." She got up. I followed her over to the drainboard to inspect the tray with its dented, plastic-shrouded pile.

"I think only the top layer is ruined," I said, undoing the plastic and wondering how close the top of my head had come to the sandwiches' fate. "If you have some more plastic wrap we could just get rid of those and wrap the others back up."

She nodded, and went to get a roll of plastic from a cupboard.

"So you grew up on a farm?" I asked, watching warily to make sure she wasn't getting ready to heave another missile in my direction.

"In Idaho."

"And you played a lot of softball?"

"You kidding? With my brothers! Baseball." She came back with the plastic wrap and we both relaxed a little as we sorted out sandwiches. "Want one?"

"Sure." I had one. "Not bad. Chicken salad. It probably only got mushed because they cut the crusts off."

She looked at me a little in awe, then looked at the sandwich. "I guess I'll have one," she said without conviction.

"If you want." I kept my voice neutral. She seemed to be asking permission. But hell, this was her house, her body, and her sandwich.

She put the whole thing in her mouth and swallowed it in haste, as if she hadn't had food in a month. She took a deep breath, wolfed a second sandwich, sighed, took a third sandwich and ate it more slowly. "My brothers don't talk to me anymore. None of my family does," she said, licking the mayonnaise off her fingers.

I had another sandwich myself. "Good bread." I remarked. "Why won't they talk to you?"

"Because I'm immoral." She took another sandwich and nibbled at it. "They stopped talking to me when I moved in with Andy."

"Old fashioned, huh?"

"Oh, yeah. When I wanted to move to Seattle they warned me I'd become corrupt. I guess they think I have." She swallowed the last of the sandwich in hand and looked at the plate speculatively.

"Will they come to the wedding?"

"Oh, sure, they'll come to the *wedding*. But they don't believe it's really going to happen. My mother says why buy a cow, when you can get the milk for free? My oldest brother offered to come and bring his shotgun." She smiled wistfully. "Like that would help."

"Well, you can't exactly whip out a gun to solve every little difference of opinion."

"Exactly. So they said they'll believe it when they see it.

Do you think having a minister and a marriage license will make Andy treat me better?"

Boy, that was an easy question to answer with a resounding "NO." But Susan didn't want to hear it. "You know, Susan, you can't change people—" I began.

"Sure you can. Andy changed me."

"Well, yes, but . . . " I sighed. "Gee, Susan, if you have that kind of doubts, maybe—"

"Look!" She held out her slender left hand. For a moment I thought I was going to see bruises, as in "look what he did to me." But I realized she was showing off the immense diamond on her engagement ring.

"Impressive."

"Andy had the ring made just slightly too small, you know. So if I gain weight, I'll know right away . . . "

"Susan, that's terrible! Are you sure you want to live like this?"

She glared at me with a grim set to her jaw. She grabbed another sandwich and bit into it so fiercely that I only hoped she didn't bite humans. "This is the only thing that will make it all right," she said.

I sighed again. With Andy's set of razors I wondered if gaining weight around this man could prove fatal. "Do you feel safe with Andy?"

"Sure. As long as I don't gain weight." She looked at me coldly as if wondering if my condition could be catching. Then suddenly she seemed to notice the sandwich in her hand for the first time. She dropped it down the drain as if it had burned her, reached over and turned on the garbage disposal.

Then, as she looked up and over my shoulder, Susan squeaked in terror.

Chapter Twenty-Six

I snapped around to follow Susan's gaze. Andy Stack stood in the doorway behind me.

"Sweetheart, you should be out talking to our guests." He came into the room. Maxine and Beth followed close on his heels, murmuring small admiring comments about the kitchen.

"Oh, all right," Susan said indifferently. She put the book she had thrown into a wall-mounted shelf by the door that held a raft of cookbooks and went to where she had left her teacup and magazine. She set the cup in the sink but took the magazine with her, snatching it out of reach and glaring in defiance when Andy made a grab for it.

I made sure I was the last one out of the room and looked at the book she had just reshelved. It was *The Carnivorous Chef—Cooking, Carving, Curing*. Hmmm.

We all left soon after that. As I rounded up Maxine and Hope, Beth pulled me aside.

"Would you mind if I ask Mulligan to ride along with me in Eric's car. Eric alone is more than one woman should have to take."

I looked at her in surprise. "It's okay with me. You don't need my permission."

"I guess not," Beth said, with an arch tone to her voice that irritated me.

The rest of the afternoon and evening at Maxine's passed in such a blur that it was hard to remember what happened, except that Hope seemed reluctant to go to her own apartment, and the television was on most of the evening. I couldn't have told you what we watched.

The next morning I was up and out before anyone called. I dutifully drove to the Seattle Police Department to talk to Detectives Gonick and Lasker. Before they could say anything, I asked if the note in Nina's coffin might have come from the killer who wrote on her wall. Gonick and Lasker exchanged cynical glances.

"It will be weeks before we get those kind of results," Gonick muttered, as soft-spoken and windburned as ever. Lasker blinked through his orange-tinted shades, gripped his ballpoint pen with long pale fingers, and scribbled on his note pad without comment.

When I showed them the letter from Nina, it was Gonick who took it, carefully, by the edges–even his fingers were chapped. He turned it over to Lasker, who went off to photocopy it. We waited in silence until he returned.

Lasker came back with several copies and the original in a plastic bag. He handed me a copy of a letter and made out a receipt for the original.

Gonick explained, "Sorry, but we have to keep the original for evidence. We'll also need your prints later to eliminate them. It's not likely the suspect left prints on the letter or the envelope, but we have to be sure."

The two detectives studied their copies of the letter intently. Finally Gonick said, almost too softly to hear, "This part here."

I waited this long and didn't tell anyone because I wanted to protect some people. But now it seems like the whole truth needs to come out.

I was afraid they would try to stop me.

"What does that mean to you?"

"I guess it might have something to do with the East-ways religious organization."

"Those crazies over in Twila?" Gonick asked. "William Crain is part of that group isn't he? The kid who killed his father." Gonick massaged his sunburned chin.

"Right. That's how Nina knew the Crains. They were all part of the same group."

"The kid kills his father, takes off, and his mother just turned up dead yesterday," Gonick observed. "Did the mother know where her son was?"

I shook my head. I wasn't about to get into William's parentage. One can of worms at a time. "She said she hadn't heard from him in months."

Lasker looked at me over his glasses.

Gonick gave me a look that had a growl in it. "You wouldn't happen to know where he is, would you?"

I swallowed. But I told them the truth when I said, "I have no idea where he is."

"And you never heard of this Isabelle Zangrilli before you read this." He tapped a wind-chafed finger on the copy of the letter.

"Nina never mentioned her. I asked Emily and all she could remember is that she was an ESP member who died twenty-five years ago, in Bellevue, probably from an ille-gal abortion."

Lasker noted this on his tablet.

Gonick leaned forward, "And you say Nina West's law-yer sent you to talk to these people in Twila?"

"I volunteered."

"Why? If you didn't even know them."

"Nina's will requested that I inform them personally. It made sense. I wanted to go because they were her friends. The least I could do was let them know what had happened—besides they had no telephone. It's not exactly cheap to hire a lawyer to drive up to a little town in the Cascades to scout around for someone whose only address is a post office box."

"But you managed to find this Emily Crain and speak to her."

"It's a pretty small town. It took a few hours."

"And you say someone attacked you. Do you think Emily Crain recognized that person?"

"You think it was William?"

"We don't have enough evidence to think anything yet. For example, you show up on Nina West's doorstep and she's dead. You go over to Twila to visit Emily Crain and she winds up dead."

They both stared at me. I had to say something. "Does this mean you're not inviting me home to meet the wife and kids?"

Gonick snorted in disgust and Lasker rolled his eyes— obviously we had mismatched senses of humor. Gonick leaned forward and muttered hoarsely, "You're in this up to your neck. But, you've got a point about William Crain. Nine times out of ten it is a friend or a family member. We really need to talk to William. Have you seen him?"

"I didn't even know he existed until a few days ago." I wondered if he noticed I was dancing around the question. If so, he let it pass.

"If you do see him, let us know immediately. It's in your best interest. And be very careful. You've already attracted this killer's attention. It might be the Crain kid. We don't know enough about what makes him tick but no one is disputing that he killed his father. Why not his mother and an old family friend? Why not you?"

My hand went to my injured throat. I swallowed convulsively. "Thank you. I appreciate your concern. But I have one question."

"Yes?" Gonick sat back, his eyebrows raised as if surprised that something could surprise him. Lasker raised his pen.

"Do you think whoever killed Nina is this Captain Ahab or just a copycat?"

Gonick and Lasker looked at each other. What the hell, it was worth a try. "That just about wraps it up for now," Gonick said with a shadow of a smile, "Unless you got any questions, Lasker?" Lasker shook his head.

For a few happy moments, I thought the interview was over. But then the detectives from Ellensburg came in and talked to me about Emily, the attack in Twila, and all the same things Gonick and Lasker had asked me.

That gave the Seattle team some new ideas, so Gonick and Lasker came back and asked me about my relationship with Nina, with Mulligan, with Emily, and basically with everyone I had ever known since high school. I was surprised that they could think of so many questions to ask. The crime scene tape alone was worth about fifteen minutes of repeated questions. At last both teams seemed to have run out of steam, either that or they were getting bored with my answers.

"You can go now Ms. Fuller," Gonick said, "But let us know if you plan to leave town."

They did give me permission to go back into Nina's apartment. I promised to call them if I found anything that might have given anyone a reason to kill Nina, but they didn't seem too optimistic. They finished the interview by taking my fingerprints.

It seemed to have taken the whole day, but the sun was

still dazzling the rain-weary town when I walked out of the Seattle Police Department. Getting into the car, I realized I'd forgotten to tell them about Andy Stack's razor collection. Was he even a suspect? He hadn't seemed reluctant to show them to us. If they were murder weapons he could have taken them down long before we got there. Of course, if they had been part of his living room decor, it might have seemed suspicious to suddenly take them down after there had been a slashing death.

I didn't feel like any more questions, so I decided to tell the homicide detectives about it later. Maybe I could get Mulligan to tell them. He'd seen the same demonstration I had.

Ambrose and Val weren't expecting me until one. I headed for Maxine's to call Sam Foley and let him know he would be hearing from William. All the questions and police warnings had put me on edge. I kept glancing in the rearview mirror, wondering if there was a car, a truck, or even a motorcycle following me.

By the time I arrived back at Maxine's I was very nervous. I came in through the back yard and noticed that the door to the basement was open.

Chapter
Twenty-Seven

I went to the door, keeping well out of range of anyone who might be lurking inside with a burlap sack and knife. "Anybody there?" I called.

Hope's voice floated up from the basement but I couldn't hear the words. A moment later Mulligan came slowly up the stairs into the sun. He smiled at me. I smiled back.

"Maxine decided this back door wasn't secure enough," he said, stretching in the sun. "So I'm helping them reinforce it."

"I see. If you're helping—what part do they do?"

He laughed in surprise and I took a deep breath, realizing my words had came out harsher than I had expected.

"Let's see," Mulligan said, putting down a battered toolbox on the cement step outside the back door. "They've bought the parts and now Maxine is watching Hope cook lunch." He lowered his voice. "Hope doesn't want to leave the phone in case William calls, and Maxine doesn't want to let Hope out of her sight for fear she'll take off again."

"I see. So how do you reinforce the door?"

"First we sink a hole into the door frame." He pointed to

a freshly-drilled hole. "Then we'll drop an I-bolt down there. Once the bolt's in place someone would have to take the frame apart to get in. Of course now no one can come in from the backyard with a key once the bolt is shot, but that wasn't a good idea anyway." He straightened up and looked at me oddly. "Maxine approved all this as the manager, but I just realized I'm talking to the new owner. Do you have any objections?"

Oh, great. Now I was his landlady. "I can see why Nina didn't let anyone know she owned the place," I said ruefully. "Believe me, I'm in favor of every security measure. But Maxine has done a great job for twenty years. I have no intention of second-guessing her."

"Good." He seemed relieved.

"Mulligan, I'm surprised you should think I would do that. Obviously Nina thought Maxine was great, because her will specified no changes be made and no tenants be disturbed."

Mulligan studied the metal toolbox for a moment, then looked up a little shyly, "Yeah. You're right. This is rough for all of us. I don't know you, that's all. The whole thing is . . . Hell, I don't know."

Our eyes met. This time I looked away, muttering something. Even I didn't know what.

"Did you call your lawyer?"

"Right. I'm on my way to do that now." I moved toward the door and he stood back to give me room. It seemed to be clear to both of us that if I brushed past him, neither of us would be responsible for what might happen. I went down the stairs past the basement apartments.

Maxine stuck her head out of Hope's open doorway and called down the corridor, "Jo, are you coming for lunch?"

"Okay. Do you want me to bring anything down from your place?"

"Yes. Bring a six-pack of Corona."

I went on up the stairwell.

At Maxine's, Groucho and Raoul continued to threaten each other. Just as I got Sam Foley on the line Groucho let out an ear-piercing shriek.

"I won't keep you on the phone, that sound hurt my ears from halfway across town," Foley said when I explained what I wanted. I stopped short of saying I had actually met William. "And, Jo, here are the names and numbers of a couple of good criminal lawyers. Just in case you should run into young William. Refinancing the building to put up the money won't be a problem. I'll get started on the paperwork and send you the information and the name of the bank officer we worked with before. You may want to get some other offers."

"Okay. I trust you," I said, wondering if it was true.

After I got off the phone, as I put my address book back in my purse, my hand touched the package Emily had given me.

Was this evidence of something? I hadn't even thought to mention it to Gonick and Lasker. The prospect of pulling out a pornographic novel in the hallowed halls of homicide didn't have much appeal. I would have ended up blushing redder than the wind-braised Gonick.

In the calm of Maxine's apartment, I took out the envelope and extracted the paperback Gordon Bliss had sent to Emily Crain. Without really planning to, I settled down on the sofa and started to read.

X-Rated Ashram was, as the Supreme Court used to say, not totally without redeeming social value. Set in the 60's in a settlement of religious seekers, it sketched a very brief and nostalgic picture of the ashram and its rainbow of cultures and races, living in harmony, praying for peace, and happily straying into carnal encounters at every turn.

The hero was the pure-hearted, but weak-willed leader. Before, during, and after meditation sessions, the fellow couldn't seem to keep his robes in place, what with all the hard-panting acolytes laying siege to his holy implements.

I had been prepared to dislike the Reverend Bliss because of the suffering his self-righteous seductions had caused. I wasn't sure what connection he had with Nina and Emily's deaths but the idea of Bliss sitting up in Idaho playing with his self-inflated fantasies compounded the insult.

In spite of all that, on paper I had to grant that Bliss at least had a goofy sense of humor. From all reports it sounded as if he had manipulated brainwashed young women in real life. But his fictional guru was the befuddled object of his followers' determined lust. I wondered if poor old Gordon had deluded himself into believing that was what actually had happened.

A more serious-minded feminist might have sneered or howled with righteous rage, but I must confess that my sense of humor is such that if I hadn't known that someone might have died because of the randy reverend, I would have found the book amusing. The heroic guru kept trying to be good until some nubile follower dropped her harem pants and then it was off to the races.

The moment the bumbling saint stumbled, of course, the primary focus of the book narrowed down to penises the size of intercontinental ballistic missiles and target orifices erupting like volcanoes.

I skipped the heavy breathing—well, most of it—and was halfway through the admittedly thin volume when I heard the door open. I sat shaking my head over the pursuit of the straying guru by a hot-blooded widow with coppery curls. When Maxine came in, I looked up.

"You didn't show up with the beer, so I thought I'd make sure you hadn't fallen victim to another axe murder. Oh my God." Her face fell when she realized what she had said. "I didn't mean it that way, I was trying to joke, but I was worried."

"Sorry. I got to reading."

"What are you reading?" I held up the book. "Josephine! Dirty novels, at your age." But then she zeroed in on the detail of the cover art. Her smile evaporated. "Let me see that. Where did you get it?"

"It says Anonymous but it looks like Gordon Bliss wrote it. He sent it to Emily Crain and she gave it to me. I don't know why he'd be sending her this kind of book unless he wrote it himself. She hadn't even opened the envelope. She seemed too tired to read much when I talked to her."

Maxine scanned the page I had been reading when she came in. She looked close to having a coronary.

"Are you okay, Maxine? Can I get you something? Water? Saltpeter?"

She lowered the book and sat down heavily in the armchair nearest her. Then she looked straight past the bird cage where Groucho was preening and chuckling for her benefit. But she didn't seem to notice the bird or me or anything else, the book still clutched, forgotten in her hand.

"Did you know that Hope was born three years after my husband died?" The look on her face made me gulp.

"No." I didn't know what else to say. She was telling me her daughter was illegitimate. It didn't seem to have much to do with anything.

"Well, it's true. Come on, I could use a beer."

We went into the kitchen. She pulled the six pack of Coronas out of the fridge and put them on the kitchen table. Maxine looked at the paperback in her hand. She put it down next to the six-pack, pulled out a beer, opened it, and drank off nearly half the bottle.

I sat across from her and took a bottle too. I opened it, sipped it and waited for her to speak.

"My husband died from injuries in an auto accident, but he spent a few weeks in intensive care. The shock and the hospital bills nearly killed me. I was grieving, broke, and desperate. I thought my life was over at thirty-six. This was in California. I met a woman who brought me to an East-ways meeting. All their talk about life and death and karma helped me bear the pain and keep going, and within a year I was a dedicated member. The group helped me find a job. They became my closest friends.

"Then Gordon Bliss blew through town. They treated him like a movie star. He wasn't bad looking in those days, but of course he was married and his wife traveled with him. I realize now she didn't trust him. Somehow when I met him, he saw something in me that made him offer me a job. He asked me to move up to Washington state. He promised he would personally make sure I had everything I needed.

"I can't express to you the amazing honor it was for me to be offered a job working for ESP Headquarters. It was everyone's dream within the organization. I mean, most of us were devoting all our free time doing ESP volunteer work anyway, the idea of being paid to work for them was the highest achievement of all. You can probably imagine what the Reverend Bliss had in mind. I feel stupid not to have been able to see it myself. All I can say is, it was a more innocent time. In those days . . . I'd been an old maid at thirty when my husband married me. I was sure no man would ever look at me again."

I started to say something, but Maxine waved me into silence. "Let me finish. I hate to admit it, but I was lonely and flattered, and at first I thought it was a love affair. I thought I was the only one. I was too blinded by my religious faith to realize that Gordon Bliss had singled me out simply because he wanted at least one woman totally under his control."

She swallowed the last of her beer. I noticed tears pooling in the corners of her eyes and running down her cheeks. "It took several months to realize that Gordon intended to use me any way he could. He tried to convince me that it was part of the religion and counseled me never to tell anyone. I finally said I couldn't go on and then he told me if I tried to leave he'd give me such a bad reference I'd never find a job. After all, he was my boss at the only job I'd had in years."

She stopped, put aside her empty bottle, and let out a ragged sigh, "He wasn't just after sex without complications. I think he got a thrill out of controlling people. Women were toys for him. His idea was that when he was tired of me, he'd pass me on to some deserving subordinate. It was a kind of slavery.

"He thought he'd put me into such a helpless position that I wouldn't dare risk my job, my home, my living. Well, he was wrong. I just walked out. Took the clothes on my back, whatever I could fit in a suitcase. I had cash from my paycheck in my purse. One of the other women helped me. Then I got to Seattle and found out I was pregnant. Another woman friend introduced me to Nina. I never knew Nina when she was in the organization. She left before I moved up to Twila. But she treated me like a long-lost sister. She helped me with everything. I never told her or anyone here in Seattle how long my husband had been dead. I've never told Hope."

"Maybe Nina knew all along. Did you know what had happened to her?"

Maxine shook her head.

I told her about Nina's illegitimate child. William. Clearly, it did nothing to ease Maxine's mind. Considering the relationship between Hope and William, I could see why not.

I took another long swallow of beer. "Well, now it makes

sense that you wouldn't exactly warm to seeing Gordon Bliss yesterday. Have you talked to him at all since those days?"

She laughed. A single cracked syllable. "Hell, no. After twenty years I'm sure he didn't even recognize me."

"Does he even know Hope exists?"

"No. And he never will." Her eyes narrowed in hatred. I edged the book out of her reach. She looked capable of ripping it up and I wasn't sure yet whether I would be able to use it somehow to get to Gordon Bliss.

"Don't you think someone should tell Hope? I mean, doesn't she have a right to know who her father is—especially if William . . . um, has the same father?"

Maxine just stared at me. Then she went to the refrigerator and selected two more bottles to put in place of the two beers we had taken from the six-pack.

"Maybe we should go down to lunch," I said. She still said nothing. With my half-finished bottle in one hand and the six-pack in the other I headed for the door. After a moment, she followed.

Chapter
Twenty-Eight

Surprisingly the lunch itself went smoothly. Hope made salmon patties with a salad and garlic bread from her mother's recipe. Maxine told her cheerfully that fresh basil seemed to improve the salmon. The beer helped. I was still working on the bottle I had brought from upstairs. Hope and Mulligan each had one. Maxine finished the last four. Her mood improved to the point where she ate several carrot sticks and made explanatory drawings diagraming the journey that dietary fiber takes through the intestinal tract.

Mulligan got up to go finish reinforcing the back door.

"The police gave me permission to go into Nina's apartment," I said. "I'll check it out today and start to get an idea about cleaning up."

"Take your time. There's no rush," Maxine said, putting the last empty bottle in the cardboard holder. "We'll have at least the next month or two to clear things out. Then they'll repaint before renting it again. The realty company said they'd talk to the owner, but I haven't heard yet."

"They didn't tell you who the owner was?" I felt awkward. Maxine shook her head. "No, it's a big secret. I know it's owned by a woman, though, because the people at the realty company refer to the owner as 'she.' Why?"

"Nina owned the building."

Maxine stared at me. "I don't believe you."

"It's true. Her lawyer told me that William Crain and I will inherit it."

"But, Ma, this is good. It's just what William needs." Hope clasped her hands in excitement, thinking only of William's chances to fund a lawyer and get out of fugitive mode.

Maxine turned to Hope. "You're telling me *your* William is the one who profits by this? Unless, of course, he killed Nina. You can't inherit something from someone you murdered?"

The cordial mood of lunch was sinking fast along with the salmon patty in my stomach.

Mulligan stepped in. "Nina was talking to William about helping him with his problems before she died." I noticed he didn't bring to Maxine's attention exactly why William was in so much trouble.

"This just came out after Nina died," I explained, watching Maxine grow paler by the second. Maxine's mouth was now pressed into a thin line, the lips invisible. The more I talked the worse it seemed to make things. "But her will specified that no changes be made and the present tenants wouldn't be forced out," I concluded lamely.

"So this makes you my boss?" Maxine's already deep voice grew hoarse with anger. "You knew!" she rounded on Mulligan like a small angry carnivore.

He took a step backward, shaking his head. Although she was more than a foot shorter, and less than half his weight, she looked ready to do him severe bodily damage. He put up a hand to ward her off.

She turned back to me with a hunted look in her eyes. "Here I sit spilling my guts out, invite you into my home, and suddenly you say you've known all along you have the power to fire me and you never even mentioned it."

"That's not fair, Maxine," I protested. "I didn't know about the will when I accepted your offer to stay here. I only found out after I talked to Nina's lawyer—"

"All I can say is, fuck you!" She stomped out, slamming the door.

I turned back to Hope and Mulligan. "She's got a lot of stamina and an up-to-date vocabulary for one of her years."

We all laughed, partly from the sudden relaxation of tension in the room.

Hope smiled at me. That was a first. "Don't worry," she said. "Ma will take a nap and sleep it off and then she'll be stiff and formal for a few days. You can come down and stay with me if you don't want to be around her for awhile."

Mulligan smiled at me too, "I'd make the same offer but I don't think it would be wise."

I smiled back at both of them, but shook my head. "Thanks. But I think the time has come for me to find a hotel. I'll get my stuff later this afternoon. Val needs to talk to me about something. Then I guess I'll go up and look at Nina's apartment."

They both nodded. Hope went to wash the dishes. Mulligan returned to his door. I caught up with him on the way there and asked him to call homicide and tell them about Andy Stack's razors. He nodded thoughtfully and agreed.

I turned and trudged up to knock on Val's door, across from Eric's apartment.

Chapter Twenty-Nine

Ambrose opened the door and let me in almost as soon as I knocked. I wasn't surprised when he hugged me, although the thought of hugging Ambrose would have astounded me a month earlier. Hugging relative strangers was part of the grieving process, I guess. Actually it did help, just now it felt very comforting. I hugged Val too and the three of us sat down at a white marble slab of a table.

While Ambrose and I watched Val fidget in silence for a few minutes, I glanced around the apartment. The floor plan was identical to Nina's, but the furniture was all black leather and chromium angles. The curtains, pleated back from the windows, wore gray and yellow stripes. Huge-leafed plants in white buckets were the only visible things not copied from someone's geometry homework.

As Ambrose sat patiently and Val worked himself up into talking, I realized the apartment did complement Val's black hair, with its white streaks, his brown eyes, and ivory coloring.

On the other hand, the sharp wrought iron sculptures displayed on shelves and the ebony and chrome end tables looked as if they could be used as weapons. I blinked. I was seeing cutting edges everywhere and I had to tell myself how highly unlikely it was that Val or his boyfriend had killed Nina because they disagreed with some of her decorating choices.

"I don't blame him," Val said at last.

"Okay," I nodded encouragingly, totally mystified but ready for more information.

"You see, I have a very demanding job in advertising and I have to get up too early in the morning by K.C.'s standards. So why shouldn't he go out at night on his own if he needs to let off steam?"

Ambrose raised his chin. I was getting to know him well enough to see that he sometimes had as much trouble restraining sardonic remarks as I did. "Letting off steam might be acceptable," he said carefully, 'if you have that kind of relationship. But staying out all night?'

Val sighed and massaged his temples, "Last week Sunday night, Monday morning—"

"The morning after Nina's body was discovered," Ambrose put in.

"Right. K. C. came in at five minutes to four. I know, I was watching the clock. I couldn't sleep waiting for him."

"Where is K. C. now?" I asked.

"He's off cruising."

Ambrose smothered a snort of laughter.

"Oh, shut up, Ambrose. You know what I mean." He turned to me. "K. C. works as a waiter on a cruise line. He goes off for a week at a time, sometimes two weeks. He should be in Glacier Bay right now."

"I think I only met K. C. that one time," I said. "The day we found Nina, you two had just got back from camping."

"Yes. Nina's death upset him. He needed to get out. It was that same night."

Val began to warm to telling his story. The faintly plaintive tone suggested that he would really like to take this occasion to complain, if Ambrose would allow it, which he clearly would not. "I had to work the next day. He always asks if I want to go, so it's my fault if he has to go alone. We have a weekend of hiking around, bonding to beat the band, and he leaves me to unpack the gear and goes out dancing till all hours."

"Bonding elsewhere," Ambrose said, leaning back and crossing his long legs.

Val regarded Ambrose severely, but he resumed, "I tossed and turned for hours although I was dead tired," he heard the word and shuddered. "The trip wore me out and then hearing about Nina, and K. C. gone. Finally, I got up to heat some milk, hoping to get even a few hours sleep, when K. C. came in. It was 4:15. He was terrified." He paused for dramatic effect.

"Why?" I asked.

"He saw someone breaking into a parked car in front of the building. A white rental car. K. C. ducked behind some bushes the minute he saw what was happening. But after the person drove off, K. C. went over and looked at the car. I checked later and that white rental car was the one you were driving."

"You're right. I thought someone had broken in there, but I wasn't totally sure because nothing was taken."

"Did he see the person—was it a man or a woman?"

Ambrose leaned forward, "Val, this could be very important, did K. C. recognize the person breaking into the car? Would he have known if it was someone who lived in the building?"

"I don't know. I assumed it was a man because K. C. said 'he' drove off in a pickup truck. I didn't pay a lot of attention because, frankly, I had a few questions on another subject to put to the lad."

"A pickup truck. It might have been the killer. Did K. C.

tell the police?" The minute I asked, I knew the answer was no.

Val looked steadily at the floor. "K. C.'s not too keen on talking to the police. He had a little problem several years ago." Val sat up as if suddenly realizing this could reflect on him. "He's pulled his life together a lot since then."

Ambrose patted his shoulder. His mouth was twitching with unspoken comments but he said nothing.

"Seriously, Val," I said. "If the man breaking into the car saw him, K. C. could be in danger." I explained what had happened to me in the barn and to Emily in Ellensburg. "This killer doesn't like to leave witnesses."

Ambrose nodded, "Maybe you should call K. C. on the ship, or send him a fax."

Val hunched his shoulders, clearly miserable. "I'll try. But he's a willful boy. Just because I say to do something, he might just as easily do the opposite. Anyway he'll be home day after tomorrow."

"Look, Val, could we try now? Just in case K. C. is in danger. He should know before he comes back. Do you have a number where you could reach him?" I asked. After what had happened with Emily, I was unwilling to let another person become a potential target.

Val looked helplessly at Ambrose. "What if he refuses to come back at all?"

Ambrose patted Val's shoulder. "Would you rather see him dead?"

Val did have an emergency number. Ambrose and I waited while he talked to the receptionist and then a company official.

When he set down the phone, his face was deathly pale. "K. C. doesn't work there anymore. They say he quit three months ago."

"And he's been going off regularly, pretending to work all along?" Ambrose was irate.

I thanked Val, but he looked so dazed I'm not sure he heard me. He looked like he was in for a rough couple of days. Ambrose patted his shoulder with the air of someone who is going to listen to some major league complaining. Somehow I didn't think K. C. would turn up for awhile.

Chapter Thirty

Once inside I took a deep breath. The smell of blood and death was still present. I opened the windows. The heavy, wet air was clean, if cold. It helped. I got a jacket from the hall closet and draped it over my shoulders—Nina had been shorter than I, although rounder and not as broad shouldered.

I sat down at Nina's small desk, pressed into a corner with a file cabinet on one side and a computer on the other. I turned on the computer. It beeped. The chair was an old oak office chair with a worn Paisley cushion. I hesitated to sit there, but when I did it felt comfortable.

I pulled a pad of lined paper from the stack on one corner of the desk. Pretty paper. Nina would naturally have pale blue lined tablets with marbled strips holding the paper together at the top. I took a pen from a flock of lavender ones in a gold-flecked ceramic jar. I smiled at the pens. They all had the name of Nina's store—Lunar Moth Fashions.

My first note was to get a cleaning service to clean the place thoroughly. I couldn't face the bloodstains in the bedroom and I wasn't about to ask any of her friends for help on that. When it came time to sort out Nina's belongings, her friends could come in to select mementos. I thought of Mulligan and the strong emotion that brought up made me feel very uncomfortable sitting in Nina's chair thinking about her boyfriend. Not here. Not now.

I opened the deepest desk drawer. It contained account books from her store and old dressmaking clients that went back ten years. I saw entries for clothing she had made for me. I wondered where she kept the older records. I tried the file cabinets. Locked.

I got up and wandered through the room, looking through her bookcases with a different eye than I had before. I had always browsed through her fiction or the feminist literature, or the big art books on fashion and design. She also had several rows of cookbooks in the bookcase nearest the kitchen. I had never before noticed how many books she had on psychology, philosophy, and mysticism.

The Eastways books occupied their own little shelf with a candle and a Japanese round bell sitting on a cushion on top of a little stand. For the first time I noticed that the low cushioned chair next to that bookshelf turned it into a sort of inconspicuous meditation area. I sat on the chair and took up the stick that sat like a spoon in a mixing bowl. The bell let out a faint tone as the stick touched it on the way out. I hit it a little harder with the suede-wrapped end of the stick and a sweet tone filled the room then vibrated into silence. I didn't light the candle, but I looked where Nina would have looked if she had been sitting there. A slice of blank white wall.

The phone rang and I flinched in surprise. *Very brave, Jo,* I scolded myself as I went to the desk in the next room and picked up the receiver.

"Hello."

"Jo? It's me, Mulligan."

I let out a breath of relief. "Thank God it's you. The phone scared me," I found myself blurting out. "I was afraid someone was calling who didn't know. Or, hell, I don't know, maybe someone who did know."

"You mean the killer."

"Yeah, I keep thinking someone could be watching my every move."

"That's quite possible. So stay on guard. Make sure you're not alone with anyone. Well, except maybe the women. As I said, they're pretty sure the killer was a man or a very strong woman. But, get this, Detective Gonick told me right off the bat that Andy Stack's razors couldn't have killed Nina or any of Captain Ahab's victims."

"They can tell that sort of thing?"

"Once he pointed it out, I understood. Remember how those straight razors fold out on a hinge?"

"Yeah."

"Well, the hinge makes it give when you have it open, that's how it can adjust to the contours of a man's face when he shaves. It doesn't stay fixed the way a hunting knife or even a switchblade would. So if you try to cut through something that resists, a straight razor makes a wobbly cut because it keeps getting caught and bending at the hinge, even if you hold it straight with your hand. But if you used it to slash someone, it would be highly unlikely to stay straight in your hand."

"Okay, okay I get it," I said, wincing at his clinical tone and the thought of those razors wobbling along cutting wiggly lines. "Do you think maybe Andy Stack knew that and was trying to throw us off the track?"

"Maybe. Or maybe he's only guilty of collecting old German razor kits."

"And the bad taste to show them off at the wake of someone who was killed by a slasher."

Mulligan sighed. "Yeah. Anyway, I'm sure there are other

things about the murder weapon they're not saying. They have to keep some things back so they can rule out fake confessions."

"You think they're ruling out Stack because of the razors?"

"I don't think they've exactly ruled anyone out. But Stack's girlfriend backed up his alibi that they'd been together driving down to the Columbia River. Why should she lie?"

"She wants to marry him. We talked about that at the wake. She's really determined to marry the guy."

"Okay." I could tell from the sound of his voice that he wasn't impressed.

"Mulligan, I think Susan is afraid of Andy. Do you think he gets violent?"

"It's hard to imagine. Nina never talked much about him. Until this week I thought he was just the owner of the building where she rented the storefront. He does look pretty scrawny compared to Susan, though. Why should she be afraid of him?"

"I don't know, but he seems to control her every move."

"I'll never understand women. So, you're moving out and going to a hotel?"

"Yes." I asked for his number and gave him my 800-number in the meantime.

We both said goodbye. After I hung up the phone, I sat at Nina's desk playing with the pencils in their holder.

For some reason the whole mess reminded me of my mother's bobby pins. She had long hair, which she set in pin curls. She kept the pins in a mass like a heap of black ants in a round bowl with a lid. They always stuck to each other and I had to resist mightily the urge to dump them all out and separate them when I saw them.

I turned over another leaf on the tablet and dumped out the pins—metaphorically speaking.

I picked up the pen and printed the name of each person I suspected and why. That helped when I tried to figure out what a group needed and whether they met Mrs. Madrone's strict standards. The categories were a little different here, of course: suspects, weapons, alibis. After half an hour I had a few pages for each name. Of course, they were small pages. It was a small tablet.

I looked at each one in turn.

Mulligan. What the hell was his first name anyway? That alone was a little weird. Maybe he and Nina weren't on such good terms as he reported. He sure had been quick enough to jump on me. Of course, I hadn't exactly beaten him off with a stick either. I decided to put it down to temporary mutual insanity. Still, if Mulligan was prone to bouts of temporary insanity, maybe he could have killed Nina during one. I wasn't sure what Mulligan's relationship with Hope was. I put the matter of Joan aside. She deserved her own sheet of paper. Could Mulligan have had arguments with Nina over his interest in Hope or Joan? Maybe he was one of those men with a short attention span.

He also owned a hunting knife. But he had been out of town until the day after Nina was killed. If that hadn't checked out the police would have arrested him by now. Besides, he was too big to have been the one who dragged me into the barn.

I turned the page.

William Crain. Another man with a hunting knife. He might have secretly hated Nina for abandoning him. But he was in so much trouble already, and Hope confirmed that Nina had been willing to help. It didn't make sense for him to kill someone who was about to help him. Unless the secret Nina was going to talk about sent him into some kind of tailspin. As Detective Gonick had pointed out, William had killed Granger Crain. Perhaps he was still thinking like a predator.

I took a moment to fervently wish that Maxine would tell Hope about who her father—and William's father—was. Who knows what that would mean to a couple of kids in the 90s. Maybe nothing. Besides, unless they felt like getting a DNA test, they had only Maxine's word and Emily's suspicions that they were half brother and sister. But it didn't seem fair not to tell them. Could that have something to do with Nina's murder? Even Hope couldn't vouch for where William had been when Nina was killed.

Although William was about the right height and weight to have been the person who assaulted me in the barn, it was hard for me to imagine him killing Emily. The news of her death seemed to have devastated him. Although the police certainly suspected William, I wasn't so sure.

Another page. Eric Shumacher. He was out of town on business when Nina was killed. Just as Mulligan had been. They hadn't arrested Eric or Mulligan. So, I reasoned that the airlines must have verified the flight information to the police.

Still, Eric was a very weird person. He was the right height to have been the one who attacked me. Perhaps he was down in his apartment just below this one, listening to every step I took. That thought made me feel a little creepy though he might be harmless. He had one knife I had seen. I had no idea what else he might have in the way of knives. And how I could find out without endangering myself?

I turned the page. Andy Stack. Okay, so his razors could not have been murder weapons. Did he have some less openly displayed knives? He was involved with Nina long ago, but they seemed to have settled into a friendship. Why kill her now?

Andy Stack and Susan Dryden had alibied each other. Would Susan lie for him? The only motive for Andy to kill that I could imagine would be that he had slipped off the track of rational profitmaking. After raking in the dough reducing women for fun and profit, he had decided to do it with knives. If he was that crazy, Susan would be a fool to defend him. Still, what I had seen at the battered women's shelter had taught me that women can destroy themselves for love. No. Love is not the right word. Women destroy themselves clinging to the fantasy that the magic of the right man will solve their problems.

The end of the page on Andy Stack led to the page on Susan Dryden. Andy might be too short and wiry to be the one who attacked me in the barn, but Susan was about the right height and certainly muscular enough. She couldn't be ruled out. Perhaps the murder weapon was resting in the knife block within arm's reach of her kitchen island. Same problem as with Andy Stack's alibi, if one of them was involved the other must be involved. Susan's jealousy over Andy's relationship with Nina might be a reason for her to kill him. But Andy was so outspoken about his disgust with fat women. Hell, it was his life's work. How could Susan be jealous of someone Andy found repulsive?

For a moment I considered Sam Foley. I gave him a page on the tablet, but I didn't see him as a very likely suspect. I couldn't imagine him killing Nina unless maybe he was secretly siphoning off funds from her estate. I made a note to get a full accounting. He didn't strike me as the type to do anything unless there was some profit in it.

I saved Joan for last because I just couldn't see her killing Nina. At six feet and four hundred pounds, she could have overpowered Nina, and she wasn't too tall to have been my assailant, although I remembered more of an angular feeling than Joan's soft curves would have provided. Unless Joan had a well-hidden crazy streak under her mellow exterior I couldn't see her killing Nina simply to have Mulligan for herself. However, if she was that crazy she was as dangerous as a rabid animal. I made it a point to remind myself not to get caught alone with her just in case.

I dumped my figurative bobby pins back in their figurative bowl, where they looked only a little less confused than before. The pretty little tablet I was writing on was halfway used up.

Wait a minute. I had once seen Nina retrieve an extra set of keys to her apartment. I went to the driftwood sculpture and pulled it slightly away from the wall. Sure enough, the lowest piece had been hollowed out. When the sculpture was raised, I could put my finger inside and extract a small embroidered purse. It contained the apartment keys. Suddenly I realized I hadn't asked whether Mulligan had a set.

Okay. Settle down now, Jo. The smallest keys fit the two file cabinets. I opened the drawers and looked at her tidy, color-coded folders. The records were very detailed, including invoices for purchases of fabric and payroll records of the women who sewed for her. In the bottom drawer I found checkbooks from very old accounts which she had marked "Dead" in black magic marker.

The earliest one, at the bottom of the heap was labeled "Trans-Atlantis Fashions"—a business ledger from the early 70s. I didn't remember her little shop as having a name, but it could have been called that. Thumbing through the old account book, I wondered if I would find any record of the earliest things I bought from Nina.

Wearing the clothes Nina sewed had made me feel like a real person for the first time since I had graduated from the "Chubbettes" section to the Women's Department, where the only colors were black, navy and aqua and the only designs were Tent Dress and Senior Citizen Pantsuit topped by a vest with no buttons and patch pockets. The wine-colored skirt and blouse I bought from Nina that first day suddenly made me feel like a sensuous young woman. It was like in *The Wizard of Oz* when the black and white of Kansas turns into Technicolor Oz. I sighed thinking about it.

I opened another folder. Nina had listed the outfits by item and selling price as she sold them. I found the year and the month. Another sheet in the same folder showed the deposit she had made to the Trans-Atlantis account.

Running my finger down the list of what she had sold I was surprised to find several sales of Burgundy Skirt and Blouse. But the real shock was that blouse and skirt were each listed as selling for $85. Even in those days a blouse in an upscale boutique or department store might fetch $85, but not from most fifteen-year-old girls. I had a small allowance and an occasional after-school job helping my aunt clean apartments for her rental agency. But never until recent years had I paid anything like $85 for a skirt or blouse. I would have remembered if Nina's prices had been outrageous. She must have given me a break on the prices. But my memory was that all her prices had been low.

I looked at the deposit ledger for the Trans-Atlantis account. It matched the sales totals. I noticed that the account itself was closed out abruptly when the entire amount of $56,500 was withdrawn. The next old bankbook was for a business called "Lunar Moth Dreams." It started with a $6,500 deposit the same day the first account was closed. Had the $50,000 gone for the down payment on this building?

I looked through the other folders in the drawer. One was titled "Tenant's Ref." It was a stack of rental applications. Evidently Nina had to approve the tenants before an apartment was leased. There were only a few in the stack. I looked for anyone I knew. There was one for Maxine. One for Val, but not for K. C. Val's roommate was listed as "Dave Park"—not even from Kansas City. Several people I didn't know. Then one for Mulligan, who was recommended by Joan. Interesting.

Most of these applications were recommended by Margaret Toy. Mulligan was an exception. So was Eric Shumacher, who had listed his parents' house in Renton as his only previous address. In the case of Maxine and a couple of other tenants I didn't recognize, the notation "ESP."

I locked up everything in the file cabinet and decided to take the keys with me. So far nothing anywhere in Nina's apartment had mentioned Isabelle Zangrilli.

I looked at the computer, noticing at last that it had not properly started. I tried to soft boot it with the old three-finger salute control-alt-delete. The machine obediently beeped, the screen went dark and lit up again, but no prompt told me it was ready to go.

I opened up the caddy that held her diskettes and pulled out one that looked like it should boot the system, slid it into the drive, and got the machine going. I asked for a list of files stored on the C drive, where the operating system should have been. It was blank. Someone had wiped it clean. No memory. Nothing. No wonder it hadn't started properly. It had amnesia. Was the person who killed Nina the one who erased her computer's memory?

Chapter Thirty-One

I flipped through the diskette caddy more slowly. According to the labels, the few diskettes left were all commercial software. Strange. None with data. Would Nina have confided the secret she had held for so long to a computer file? If so, it was gone.

I stood up and turned off the computer. There was no proof that whoever had tampered with it had killed Nina. But she had been prevented from speaking out. I couldn't see why someone would kill Nina over the money she had funneled into her early clothing business and used to buy the building. That was decades ago. But there might have been some other skeletons in someone else's closet

As I walked downstairs and passed Eric's apartment, I imagined his three computers glowing in the dimness. I wondered if the police considered whether Eric was talented enough to hack into an airplane reservation computer to add his name to a passenger list? I wasn't sure that was possible. He certainly knew enough about computers to erase the computer's memory and probably very efficiently too. He had also demonstrated that he owned a knife and kept it close at hand.

I pushed the thought aside and headed for the rental car. I knew Eric owned a pickup truck, which was conveniently out of the way. And since I happened to have his parents' address, I decided that before I stopped and thought about it long enough to get scared again I was going to track down at least one of those elusive pickup trucks.

No one followed me as far as I could tell. At the time of his rental application, Eric's parents had lived in Renton. I found the address without any trouble. It was a working class neighborhood with enough trees and bushes to blur the barrenness of the small houses. A pickup truck did sit on blocks in the Shumachers' driveway. No other derelict vehicles were visible. The battered orange Volkswagen bug parked behind the pickup would probably be running long after my new rental car was scrapped.

I approached. Only then did I see the skinny kid sitting on milk crate next to the truck. It was clearly Eric's brother. He stared down at an oil-dripping piece of metal whose function I could not begin to guess. He didn't look like he was much more informed than I was. Several other bits of auto anatomy sat on a greasy drop cloth next to him.

I couldn't tell if the truck was the one that had been following me. It had the same shape as the one I had seen outside of Emily's trailer. But it was solid primer gray.

"Is this truck for sale? I think I may have seen it over at Eric's last week before he brought it back for you to work on."

The kid looked up at me as if surfacing from under water. For a moment I thought he hadn't understood me. But he squinted skeptically and said at last. "No way, lady. This truck's been on blocks since New Years."

"But it used to be blue, didn't it? Before you painted it."

"Nope. Um, red."

"When did you paint it with the primer?"

"Couple months back."

"Your parents home?"

He shrugged, glancing at the VW bug. The bumper was thick with what appeared to be several layers of ecology-oriented bumper stickers. Someone had done a poor job of scraping off some of them. Fresh ones were plastered over the half-removed stickers. The basic message was that of someone who usually felt strongly about saving the planet, but occasionally said to hell with it.

As I passed the truck I surreptitiously ran a fingernail along the side of it and, sure enough, got a crust of half-dried primer under my fingernail. The paint underneath was blue.

I was knocking at the front door when a late model Toyota Corolla drove up and a tall, thin man emerged.

"Hi, are you Mr. Shumacher?" I called out.

The man frowned and stood outside the Toyota. He slammed the door and said nothing. The skinny kid turned on his box to watch. I had a feeling he also went out of his way to see dogfights and roadkill.

I ignored the kid's smirking interest and the man's flat stare. I folded my fingers with the half-dried primer on them and took a deep breath to go into my routine about buying the truck. Shumacher turned on his heel and headed for the house. I followed. "You know my son, Eric?" he said over his shoulder.

"I'm a neighbor."

He turned back and stopped dead so suddenly that I nearly ran into him. He frowned at me, looking me up and down with a hostile glare that would have caused me to leave or instantly go for his jugular if I hadn't wanted more information. "You aren't Eric's girlfriend are you?"

I almost laughed, but managed to turn it into a cough. "No. We're . . . just acquaintances."

Shumacher senior stared a little longer before turning back to go into the house. He left the door half open so I followed him in.

A short, round-figured woman in her fifties came out of the kitchen. "What you doing back there, Lucille? Are you eating?" He said in the aggrieved tone that was evidently his normal conversational mode.

"I just put a casserole in for your dinner, Harry. There's a salad and dessert in the fridge. Just take it all out when the timer rings in half an hour. Now, Harry, who is this?"

"Hell, I don't know. One of Eric's neighbors. Thought it was someone from your diet group come to mooch a ride. I knew it couldn't be one of those 'Save the Sea Otter' people, not after what I did to the last one." He laughed casually as if his rudeness were amusing. He went on back to the kitchen.

I smiled uncertainly at Mrs. Shumacher. She held out her hand and I introduced myself.

"I'm sorry I can't stay long, I have a, uh meeting to get to."

"Lucille!" In the kitchen Harry had found something he didn't like already. "What the hell is this?" The door smacked against the wall with the force of his re-entry and he held a crumpled poster in his hand. All I could see was a word and a half along the ripped edges "gered Species."

Lucille's bee-stung lips took on a firmness that surprised me. "Now, Harry, I put that up over the sink so I could look at it while I did dishes. I don't see where it's any of your business what I have there. It's not like you've ever washed a single dish in your life."

Harry never glanced my way. Both of them seemed perfectly willing to quarrel in front of a total stranger. "I use the kitchen. I even have to get my own dinner tonight. Not that I don't support your efforts to lose weight, Lucille.

Now this meeting," he approached her and stood over her in a way that set off alarm bells for me, but she stood her ground and didn't tremble. If he was physically as well as verbally abusive she seemed to be past caring. "I want you to go to this meeting. OA or whatever the hell it is. But don't think that means I'll let you put up this weeping dolphin kind of crap on the walls of my house! Do you hear me?"

The whole block could probably hear him. I had to admire Lucille for not backing down. It didn't seem healthy to cross Harry. Clearly she was cautious about how she did it. "Just give me the poster Harry," she said.

Harry tossed it at her and retreated back to the kitchen. At the door he turned back to snarl something incoherent about seals eating the fish that fed their family and didn't they know his father had been a fisherman.

"I'm going now, Harry. You—come with me," Lucille had forgotten my name but I followed her with alacrity. I was not about to get trapped with her husband. In fact, he stood glaring at us in the kitchen doorway. Before we reached the front door his eyes lit on me again.

"You say you know my son Eric. Are you sure you aren't a girlfriend, coming around spying on his family?" Harry bellowed as a parting pleasantry.

Although we were almost out the front door I turned back to say, "Look, I just came because I heard his pickup was for sale." I didn't want any more talk with him, but I didn't like exposing my back to him as I went through the door either.

I should have kept my mouth shut. Harry followed us out to the front porch.

"It's not a woman's kind of car—what kind of woman are you anyway, to want a car like that?" As I followed Lucille down the walk, Harry stood on the porch shaking his head, as if dimly aware that if he accused me of lesbianism, he couldn't accuse me of pursuing his son. He let it go. "Besides, our younger son is using the truck."

I noticed that the younger son had packed up his gear and left. That must happen a lot when Harry arrives at a place.

We had now reached the front yard and Harry revved up the volume, noticing an elderly neighbor standing with a pair of garden shears across the street. "You stay away from my boy. I've seen him once with a fat girl and I never let him hear the end of it. Damn fool should be lucky he turned out like me and not his mother. You think you're picking out a nice healthy farm girl with big tits, and the bitch explodes in front of your eyes like a goddamn Zodiac life raft after you pull the plug. Happened to me. It could happen to him."

I looked at Harry in exasperation, remembering why I don't carry firearms. Surrendering to the overwhelming temptation to shoot such a sorry excuse for a man would seriously disrupt my schedule for months if not years. Suddenly I saw a deadly similarity between Harry's prejudices and the killer Captain Ahab's. I took a step toward him. "What do you do for a living Mr. Shumacher?"

He halted his charge a moment, slightly derailed by my question and the fact that I wasn't retreating anymore. "I sell fishing tackle, why?"

"You don't much seem to like big women. I wondered if the police had questioned you yet about the serial killings." I nodded to the neighbor who was listening with no pretense of using his garden shears. "This Captain Ahab expressed opinions just like yours. I think the police will be very interested to talk to you, if they haven't already."

To my surprise he laughed raucously. "Captain Ahab! The fat-lady killer. You better be good on your diet, Lucille, or he might come and get you." He laughed again and went back into the house chuckling to himself.

I looked at Lucille, who was getting into her car to drive away. I went to speak to her but she started the engine and waved me off. Without really planning to I ran over to my rental car, fished the key out of my purse, and dove in. With a little luck and the age of the VW bug it would take her long enough to get underway that I could follow her. It did and I did.

Chapter Thirty-Two

I didn't try to hide the fact that I was tailing her. She looked back a few times in the mirror. I wondered if the driver of the blue pickup truck had noticed when I checked my mirror and saw him behind me.

I don't know where I expected Lucille Shumacher to go, some office with an awning that advertised a diet program, even Andy Stack's headquarters. But she drove out to a more upscale residential part of Renton, turning into an apartment complex. A private security patrolman sat in a radio car parked in front of the manager's office. Lucille Shumacher swung the VW into a visitor's parking place and for a moment I thought she was going to summon the security guard to warn me off. But she got out of the car and gestured me into the adjoining visitor's slot.

When I had got out she said, "For your sake I hope you told the truth that you aren't seeing Eric romantically."

Ah, the concerned mother. "No, ma'am, I was interested in the truck though. Eric was driving it over in Seattle until a few days ago, wasn't he?"

"That's right," she said, "We've only had it back since Wednesday." So much for the kid's lie.

"I'm sorry Harry was so rude to you," she said evenly. "It's just his way. Harry's worst fear was that our boys would turn out to be heavy like me. Luckily the boys escaped that. But Eric was a disappointment anyway. Harry scared the boy so badly he hardly ever came out of his room. Once he discovered computers he even stopped coming out for meals. We were so thrilled when he got a summer job down at the meat plant, because it seemed like he was getting out, making a salary and meeting people. But then he took the whole summer's savings and bought a computer. I never would have believed it possible. Not even a car, a computer."

"I understand he's a genius with computers," I said

She snorted in disbelief. "He's not as smart as he seems. Did you know that boy didn't even finish high school?"

"That would seem to argue that he's even smarter—to have taught himself enough to work in the computer field."

She shrugged, "You say you're not his girlfriend?"

"No."

"Well, that's good. When he was a teenager he went out with a heavyset girl once and his father like to have killed him."

"Excuse me, Mrs. Shumacher, your husband, does he ever get physical with his abuse?"

She shook her head, gazing off into the distance for a second, then her eyes met mine. "I have to be going. I'd invite you for the meeting but this is a committee. Still, if you'd like to stop by for a moment to get some literature and a cup of tea, you may. We're meeting in the rec room here."

"What group is this?"

"Oh our environmental group of course. Today we're putting together some material on toxic waste dump sites. My children have to live on here."

"What does Eric think of your groups?

"Eric? I doubt he knows what planet he's on, let alone caring about saving it." She looked at her watch, "I've got to get going, you want to come or not?"

"Just for a minute maybe." I followed her down the cement path to the recreation building. "But, wait, what about Harry, doesn't he ever guess that you're not on a diet?"

She turned back and looked me straight in the eye again. I realized that she was one of those steel-fist-in-the-oven-mit older women. Soft and shy but not to be crossed once she had set her mind. "Between you and me, do you think those diets work?"

"I know they don't," I replied. "True, people lose weight, but ninety-five percent gain it back within five years, or gain it back with interest."

"Well, I figured that out on my own. You've met Harry. I've given up trying to convince him that dieting is a waste of my time. But, you know, somewhere deep inside, I think he knows that. It's just easier to live with him if he thinks I'm trying. So I just tell him I'm going to my OA meeting, and I take a few dollars and I give it to my groups." She shrugged and went on in to the meeting.

Half an hour later, I drove away with a fistful of literature on toxic waste, ground water, and endangered species in the area. I had knocked on enough doors for one day. I didn't know if Eric or his father hated fat women enough to kill, but I couldn't imagine falling asleep under that roof again. The place was starting to give me the creeps. I decided to find a hotel.

Maxine was snoring when I came in and started to assemble my suitcases, garment bag, and computer paraphernalia. Raoul came out and watched as I strapped my luggage onto the little wheeled cart that I had rolled through so many airports the past year. I looked at his gray-ruffed face and realized I'd miss him. I didn't think it would be quite so easy to find a hotel that included him as a guest.

"Poor guy," I said, stopping to scratch his ears, "Everybody's leaving you. I know how that feels. I'll come back and get you, I promise."

The snoring ceased and a few minutes later Maxine came in. I was sitting at the kitchen table writing a note to her asking her to look after Raoul for another day or so until I could sort it all out. Raoul was spread out over my lap as I wrote, purring and hanging his front paws off one knee, kneading the air in polite rapture. He followed Maxine with his eyes but didn't raise his head.

"Oh, you don't have to get out, Jo. I didn't mean it." She rubbed her forehead with her hand and held the door frame.

"It's okay, Maxine. I need some time alone anyway. There's no need to worry about the building. Nina's will requested no changes and that makes total sense to me."

"She was such a sweetheart," Maxine wiped her eyes, "but she played her cards so close to the vest. I had no idea she owned this place."

"I know what you mean. I'm finding out there were a lot of sides to her we didn't see. Look, I was just writing you this note to ask if you could keep this big fuzzball for another couple of days?" Sensing rejection, Raoul slipped down off my lap in one smooth motion and disappeared into the front room without a backward look.

"Sure."

"I've got to run round and talk to a lot of people, but I promise I won't park him on you forever. Unless you fall in love with him . . . "

"Don't worry, I won't."

"By the way, do you have Marilyn Toy's number?"

"Sure." She walked a little unsteadily into the front room and came back with an address book. "Why?"

"Was she the one who recommended this apartment building to you?"

Maxine put the book down on the table in front of me. "Why did you ask me if you already know?"

Here came the down side of drunk again. I got the number and wheeled my awkward way out of the place. "I'll call you as soon as I get checked in someplace." I thanked her and made my escape.

Chapter Thirty-Three

I booked a week at the Chancellor Hotel and found myself, as I so frequently had in the past year, sitting on the bed, calling to let Ambrose know where I was. He didn't like it.

"The Foundation keeps a courtesy suite at the Waverly Arms. Let me put you in there."

"Ambrose, Mrs. Madrone has been wonderful and you have been a true pillar of strength to me, but I had better start standing on my own now. Besides, I may need to ask favors in the future and I don't want use up my account all at once."

"Well, your credit is good. In any event, I have a personal stake in keeping my friend's landlady happy."

I hesitated, "You have to be more specific on that one."

"I know you're inheriting the building Val lives in."

"Half the building. How do you find these things out?"

Ambrose chuckled fiendishly. "Connections, dear. It's that international conspiracy of personal assistants that executives everywhere have been so justly worried about." He cleared his throat. "And, if you buy out the other, ahem, heir so he can pay for a lawyer, then you will indeed own the entire building."

"You've been talking to that lawyer Sam's wife, Bonny."

"Sorry, can't reveal sources. But I'm serious, Jo. Val has trouble enough in his life dealing with the little airheads like K. C. I don't want him to have problems with the building management as well."

"You surprise me, Ambrose."

"Just looking out for myself. I'll never get any rest if I'm listening to Val complain all the time."

"Well, considering your incredibly thorough research, I'm surprised you didn't hear that the terms of the will include keeping the current tenants."

"Oh, that. Consider if anything were to happen to you. With the boy in jail, and you know he's going to jail at least for awhile, the place could wind up sold to a developer—probably some friend of the lawyer. Who knows what could happen? Anyway, you're much more useful for my purposes alive than dead and the fact is we could provide a more secure environment at the Waverly."

"Security. That rings a bell. Were you ever in the military, Ambrose?"

"I hope you're not auditioning me as a suspect. The military! I don't think I would have survived that experience. But the cold war fact of the matter is my father worked for the same outfit your father worked for."

"That explains a lot."

"If nothing else it explains the singular lack of roots we share in common, no?"

"Yes. But I'm not checking into the Waverly. I appreciate your concern but I'll stay here."

"All right, but keep your eyes open."

"Just don't tell anyone where I am."

"You're expecting someone to ask me?"

I sighed.

"No really, Jo, if those kind of people want to know where you are, they'll find out."

"I don't think I was followed, so no one else will know where I'm going."

Another eloquent Ambrose pause. "All right, have it your way."

"By the way, you aren't an old Eastways member are you. Or Val?"

"Not I. Val neither."

"Do you know how he happened to find that apartment?"

"Yes. Marilyn Toy recommended the place. You know, Marilyn? She owns a cafe, the Toy Duck—"

"I know Marilyn."

My next call was to Marilyn Toy. She seemed surprised to hear from me so soon after the funeral, but she said she would be glad to see an old friend and reminisce about Nina.

"Can you come for dinner? I could throw together a few things from the fridge. You know my place in Bellevue, don't you?"

A few hours later, after getting stuck in traffic on the floating bridge and lost in the maze of Bellevue streets, I was sitting in a cozy cottage on a tree-fringed cul-de-sac watching Marilyn chop carrots, green onions and bok choy, while I sipped a glass of carbonated water and blackberry juice. She seemed even smaller and more slight in blue jeans and a fisherman's sweater, and I noticed new white streaks in the long black hair she kept in a coil at the back of her neck. "Reba was sorry she couldn't join us," Marilyn said as she chopped. "She's teaching a night school class this semester."

I had met Marilyn's roommate on my last visit with Nina and had seen her again at the funeral. Until this moment I hadn't realized she and Marilyn were a couple and probably knew Val through the gay community. I felt naive not having put that together before, but I had always thought of Marilyn in terms of her café.

"Maxine told me you were the one who steered her to Nina," I asked at last. "Were you an ESP member yourself?"

"Oh yes." Marilyn was comfortable with the question. "That's where I met Maxine—at ESP in San Francisco."

"Did you ever live at the retreat in Twila?"

"No. Reba and I have been together since college. I always worked a full-time job and we wanted our own place. I wasn't about to give up my lover simply because Gordon Bliss thought lesbians could be cured." She looked around at me and winked.

"So, did Gordon Bliss try to cure you himself?" I asked.

Marilyn threw back her head and laughed. "I never let him get that close." Then she returned to the can of water chestnuts she had been opening. "It's hard to describe it now, but before Gordon Bliss went bonkers, ESP was actually spiritual. I guess I was trying to get back to my Asian roots. I may look totally Chinese to the world, but I'm just a regular California girl inside."

She dumped shrimp into the sizzling wok and begin to stir earnestly. "ESP had seminars by religious leaders from all parts of the Far East and the Near East as well. Back then it seemed like a small United Nations to us."

She shook her head. "Hand me those bowls please. Thank you. It was the 60s, what can I say? We were naive, idealistic, arrogant—and we really thought we could make world peace happen in twenty years." She sighed and expertly scooped rice out of a rice cooker.

"Anyway, about Maxine." She put a spoon and fork as well as chopsticks, napkins, and soy sauce in front of me. "We had our own underground network of women from

ESP who helped each other. Maxine needed a place to stay so I introduced her to Nina and she ended up managing the building."

"You knew that Nina owned the building?"

"Oh, yes. Nina knew I could keep a secret. She could too. Here's your shrimp."

We ate at the table in her kitchen. The food was worth our undivided attention. When we had eaten all the shrimp and vegetables and most of the rice, I asked, "So. Nina had a kind of half-way house for Eastways refugees?"

Marilyn laughed again. "Not exactly. But I used to kid her that it was the ESP Hotel back then. The organization doesn't really exist any more—it's just a little so-called non-profit family business for Gordon in exile in Idaho and a few hard-core followers."

"You seem cynical. Do you still do that stuff, whatever it is?"

"That weird meditation? Yeah. I still do it to keep my inner bitch in check. Ask Reba if you don't believe me. She won't talk to me about anything serious until after I finish my meditation, says we have fewer fights that way and she's right. Nina and I talked about that sometimes, why we kept on doing it even though Gordon Bliss was such a jerk."

"You know, Marilyn . . . " I found myself lacing my hands together in anguish.

She saw my distress and got up and began to clear the dishes. "Go ahead. Shall I make coffee? Tea? Wine? Beer? Sorry I can't offer you any valium."

I laughed. "Okay, coffee is fine, thanks. The more I find out about Nina, the more I feel like I never knew her."

"How so?"

"Well, she belonged to this cult, excuse me, but that's what it looks like to me." Marilyn nodded. "I had no idea she had done that and now I learn she was involved with this total asshole who makes millions selling diet products."

"Andy Stack."

"Right. She never mentioned they were lovers. It's so hard to believe."

"What else?" asked Marilyn.

"Well, the baby. You knew she got pregnant by Gordon Bliss." Marilyn nodded. "Well, she forced him to pay her some kind of settlement by threats of a paternity suit."

"I didn't know about the paternity suit thing," Marilyn said, "but good for her!"

"Nina gave the baby to a couple in Eastways." I gave Marilyn a questioning look.

She nodded. "Yes. I heard that."

"It turned out that the man was violent. He beat his wife and kids. Did you know about that? Did Nina?"

"No." She shook her head. "How sad. I knew Nina sent money back to care for the baby and she visited. But I never knew about the violence. I'm sure she didn't know, Jo."

"It's just so hard to reconcile with my picture of her. She seemed so self-confident, so loving."

"There were no legal abortions in those days. And the illegal ones were very risky. Would you have felt better if she had kept the baby and maybe gone on welfare instead of working? There wasn't much day care in 1968—not that there's all that much now. She shouldn't have let herself get seduced by Gordon Bliss, but since she did and she got pregnant, do you think she should have faded away like a nice little victim instead of forcing him to pay?"

"Well, no, of course not. I guess I just pictured Nina as knowing how to stand up for herself."

"She wasn't born knowing that. You can't learn without making mistakes. She had to remind herself every day until the day she died that she was worth standing up for."

"You mean that positive self-image that seemed so natural wasn't real for her?" I couldn't keep a faint hysterical edge from my voice.

Marilyn took a deep breath. "No. I just mean it was a daily struggle. Cut her some slack, Jo. You know what the world is like for anyone who's just a little different. It's constantly beating us up."

I nodded, unable to trust my voice.

"One thing Nina knew, and I know, is that if you build your self-respect day by day, one brick at a time, you own it. No one can take it from you. But you can never just sit back and not work on it. It's like a house, it demands some upkeep."

"Yes, but if she had that strength, why was she vulnerable to a killer like that? How could she let a hateful person into her bedroom?"

"Whatever her destiny was, at least Nina was strong enough to face it. She wasn't stabbed in the back running away."

"Do you think she had a choice about how she would die?"

Marilyn smiled sadly, "We make choices every moment by what we do. But why Nina had to die that way is a question we can't answer with hard evidence—not on this side of death anyway. I'm still trying to understand what her death means for me, and it will mean something different to you."

We both sat quietly awhile. "Nina wrote to me that she was writing her memoirs," I said finally. "Did you know about that?"

"No, but it would be on her computer. Have you looked at what's there?"

"I tried but most of her diskettes were missing and someone had wiped her hard drive."

"The police might have taken the diskettes."

"I'll ask." I wasn't sure they'd checked out the computer at all. I paused. "Did you know Isabelle Zangrilli? Nina mentioned her name in her letter to me."

Marilyn paused for several seconds before replying. "Anything involving her is too dangerous. I don't think you should get involved." For the first time since we started talking, she seemed actively worried, perhaps even a little agitated.

"Marilyn, do you think Nina was killed because of what she knew about Isabelle's abortion, and how she died?"

"Maybe. Dr. Morton probably performed the abortion and he was killed in 1969. That's a matter of public record. I really don't think we should be talking about this. Be very careful who you tell, that's all I have to say."

Marilyn was still polite and cordial, but a curtain had fallen between us. Fear had come into the room. I left soon after.

Chapter Thirty-Four

When I got back to the hotel I called to leave a message for Ambrose. He startled me by answering the phone. "It's nearly eleven, don't you ever go home and get some R and R?"

"R and R happen to be my middle name, and I am home. Call forwarding. What are you doing?"

"Remember Gordon Bliss?"

"Who could forget? After moving heaven and earth to get him over here from Idaho for the funeral, you and Maxine won't allow the poor man to speak. It was great fun to see the look on his face when he realized he was off the program."

"Did you make the contact with him or did Andy Stack?"

"Stack invited him. I handled all the details. Believe me, that holy roller flies first class all the way."

"Well, he's no angel. The reason I'm asking is I need a cover reference." I explained that I wanted to approach Gordon Bliss on the pretense of considering his group as the possible recipient of a large donation. "It would put him off his guard for long enough to start talking to him."

"I think we can do better than that."

"You're just itching for a challenge, huh? Maybe you can help me find out something about a doctor named Morton who was killed in Bellingham in 1969. His death may have had some connection with a young woman named Isabelle Zangrilli who died in 1967, supposedly from bleeding following an illegal abortion, also in Bellingham."

Ambrose whistled. "Zangrilli? Any relation to the mob family back in New Jersey?"

"Well, she was from New Jersey."

"Hmmm. A little unusual, but you're right, it's a challenge. I'll see what I can find. Get a good night's rest and I'll call you first thing in the morning."

Amazingly enough I slept better than I had since I arrived in Seattle, although I woke up a few times wondering where Raoul was. Evidently, sleeping with a cat was addictive.

As I was eating my room service breakfast, a messenger brought a packet. It was from Ambrose, but before I could open it, the phone rang.

"Hello, Ambrose."

There was a momentary pause, "How did you know it was me?"

"You're the only one who knows I'm here, right?"

"True. Ahem." He regained his momentum, "You'd better get to the airport. I've booked you on the 9:00 o'clock flight to Boise. The flight information is in the packet. You got the packet, right?"

"Just now."

"Good. I've arranged an interview for you with the Reverend Bliss at his home at noon. You didn't want to lunch with this person for any reason did you?"

"Good lord, no! Ambrose, I marvel at your efficiency."

"Well, the Madrone Foundation carries a certain clout, and Mrs. Madrone authorized me to wield it on behalf of your interview. I hope the Reverend is not pinning his hopes too much on a donation. I glanced at his dossier before I sent it over. Have you seen it?"

"Haven't had time to open it." I pushed aside the remains of the breakfast and did so.

"You'll see when you look at it. Mrs. Madrone doesn't mind using her name to set up an interview with these people, but she'd never in a million years give them a penny."

"That doesn't surprise me. Please thank her for me, though. I'll check back with you when I get back in. Oh, I suppose it's too early to have anything on Isabelle Zangrilli or Dr. Morton . . . "

"Ahh . . . "

I hadn't realized Ambrose was capable of purring, but having heard Raoul at it, I recognized the human equivalent.

"Look at the packet, hon."

I glanced at it as I dialed homicide, not really expecting to find Gonick or Lasker in before 8:00 a.m. Come to think of it, I wasn't sure Lasker could or would take a call. I had never heard him speak. But Gonick answered on the second ring, and I was still startled enough by what was in the file in front of me that it took me a moment to remember why I had called.

"Sorry to bother you so early," I said after introducing myself. "But when I was in her apartment the other day clearing out some of Nina's stuff, I looked at her computer. There were no data files on it. Nothing. Someone wiped the memory and took all her data diskettes. Your department might have taken the diskettes but they sure wouldn't have been erased her hard drive. Maybe whoever killed her did."

He talked to someone else off the line and a moment later I heard pages rustle. "No computer diskettes on my evidence list. You do anything to the machine?"

"No. But the data on the hard drive might be retrievable."

"We'll get someone over there to bring it to our computer geek. He eats those things for breakfast. Maybe he can reconstruct it."

I put the packet from Ambrose in my briefcase and left for the airport.

Gordon Bliss had an office at his home in a rural neighborhood outside of Boise. Mrs. Bliss, Gordon's pink-cheeked wife, said he was expecting me and led me through a house that smelled of pine needles and furniture polish. The place mixed ski lodge architecture with farmhouse fussiness. A cozy clutter of magazines and knick knacks gave a homey look to the room. Mrs. Bliss, plump and blond with streaks of gray, looked like the perfect conservative wife. Hobbies and volunteer work.

The hallway leading to the study displayed pictures of Bliss shaking hands with various gurus and statesmen. The gurus and statesmen wore robes, loincloths, and Hong Kong sharkskin suits. In every picture Gordon Bliss wore the same plain gray suit—the one he had worn at the funeral or its clone.

As Mrs. Bliss led me into the study, I looked from her to her husband, still staring at a computer screen at the far end of the room. The last thing I would ever have guessed was that they belonged to one of the more notorious cults of the 60s. They might have an unconventional religion, but they worked hard at being acceptable middle-class citizens.

The study was the old-fashioned kind with thick velvet drapes, a Turkish carpet, and several bookcases full of beautifully bound but often read volumes. A few Japanese calligraphy samples framed in lacquered bamboo graced the walls between bookcases.

Bliss put on a welcoming smile and came from behind his desk stretching out one arm with the expectant look of a man who is only a handshake away from a handout.

Then he recognized me, and froze. He reached out unseeing and supported himself on a bookshelf as if suffering a mild coronary at the very sight of me. The blood rushed to his face.

"You!" he managed to gasp. "They said . . . The Madrone . . . But . . . " His eyes darted frantically to the door. Was he afraid of eavesdropping or a sudden entry by his wife? "You don't even have the decency to use an intermediary the way she did."

I once read in a cop's memoir that you take control of an interrogation in the first thirty seconds or not at all.

This guy was offering it to me on a plate.

I crossed the room, pulled up a chair, and sat down uninvited across from Bliss's chair. I unzipped my briefcase, took out a binder, and folded it open to the pad clipped inside. I crossed my legs at the ankles, took out my pen and uncapped it.

"That's the trouble with intermediaries," I said. "Things get lost in transit. You'd better explain."

I still had at least fifteen seconds to spare. Of course there was the slight problem that I didn't know what the hell we were talking about.

Bliss tottered back behind the desk and fell into his chair heavily. He bent over the blotter and put his head in his hands. For a moment I worried he might be having a genuine coronary or possibly a stroke. I felt so little sympathy for him that I wasn't much worried about whether the shock of seeing me killed him. I just didn't want it to kill him until he gave me some answers.

Then I heard his voice, a little muffled, but audible. "I

don't know why I thought I would get some peace when she died. After all, she managed to draw blood from me for years without ever leaving Seattle by using that ruthless little blood-sucking weasel. Why should it stop just because she's dead?"

Okay. Obviously the "she" must be Nina.

The blood-sucking weasel sounded like a gardening tool to beware of. But I was pretty sure he was referring to a person, a person with a big house, a straight-razor collection, and a muscular girlfriend.

"It's the amounts I'm interested in," I said sternly. "I think our little weasel friend might have been skimming. I can deal with that, but I need to know how much exactly did you give him and in what form?"

Gordon Bliss met my eyes. For a moment I thought he might be realizing that I wasn't exactly sure what was going on. But no. Besides, the folder from Ambrose had given me a few threads to follow.

Bliss swallowed convulsively. "He beat me up, you know. The first time. He just got out of the service I guess, and he was trained for that sort of thing. Hell, that was twenty-five years ago, before I had any health problems. I thought I could take him because he was so much smaller than me and he looked so wispy. But shit, he pulled a knife on me and damn near cut my nuts off. I couldn't even call the police. A few words from him and they might have arrested me as well. Even if they didn't, I'd be a dead man . . . " He slammed his fist down on the desk in fury.

"He cut you did he?" That was interesting. More proof that Stack knew how to use a knife, even though he was too short to have been the one who assaulted me in the barn.

Gordon's face grew even redder as he caught my drift.

"I think he killed her. If she found out he was holding out on her and demanded her share—zip!" He made a cutting gesture in front of his throat.

I could see why beating up someone like him might be enjoyable. "Don't waste my time, Bliss. It started with the paternity suit. She threatened to expose you."

Bliss laughed bitterly. Then he leaned back in his chair. I didn't want him getting too comfortable but I was groping in the dark here.

"That stupid paternity suit. You women think the world begins and ends between your legs."

"Now there's a pathetic accusation coming from the author of *X-Rated Ashram*! Come on, you're the one who thinks that. And look where it got you."

"Okay. Okay. I thought I could juggle a couple of stupid affairs on the side. I thought I was bored with my wife, but now I realize how truly terrifying she can be when she forgives someone. She doesn't know about the kid," he said softly. He almost but couldn't quite meet my eyes. "You're probably threatening to tell her as well."

Watching him cringe was almost as irritating as hearing him bluster. "We'll see."

"You know what she said when the doctor told us about my prostate problem?"

I shrugged.

"She said, 'There is a God.'"

I sidestepped religious debate with a shrug. "If she's so tough why didn't you sic *her* on our little weasel friend?"

Bliss shuddered, "Some things she shouldn't know. It's bad enough paying for silence. I can't leave my marriage. It would bankrupt me and cut off my income. Eastways still pays the bills. All I'd need would be to alienate my wife while the IRS is sniffing around our nonprofit status. Although, going to prison for tax fraud would be a picnic compared to what my life would be like if she knew I'd been taking money off the top for this." He shook his head. "At least now she leaves me in peace to write my porn."

I tapped my pen on his well-polished desk. "Spare me the soap opera. How much did he take? How often?"

He rubbed his eyes. "It was easier back then. The money came in like water through a firehose in those days. I hardly missed the fifty thousand I gave Nina that first year for the kid. She told me she just wanted the value of the property she had donated. You know the Center is built on what was once her family farm. With her holding the kid over my head and Stack standing there with a knife, it didn't seem like the time to point out that she'd already gotten the tax deduction for the donation. I thought that would be the end of it. It even seemed cheap at the price to get rid of the problem. She signed a paper saying I'd contributed to support the kid and she accepted it in lieu of legal action. I knew it probably wasn't legally binding, but it was something, and there was no way to talk her into an abortion."

"After what happened to Isabelle Zangrilli."

"Yeah," he said very softly, looking down at the desk. Then he looked up and saw I had noticed the computer screen, which held a balance sheet. Most of the numbers were five or six figures. He saw me looking and punched a button darkening the screen, then flinched a little as if expecting to be hit.

He let out a ragged sigh. "Then that little jerk came back and told me they'd found documentation linking me with Morton."

With the suddenness of a cloud covering the sun, the shadow of what must have happened came over me. "He threatened to tell the Zangrilli family that you got Isabelle pregnant and then took her to the abortionist who killed her."

"Right." Even though he had lived with it for over twenty years the threat still had power over him. "Morton presented himself as an M. D. He'd done a few other girls for me—always made a little joke about did I want the bitch spayed too? How was I to know he was a veterinarian? It turned out he wasn't even a licensed veterinarian, he'd flunked out of school. The way Isabelle's family killed him . . . " he shuddered.

"I know." It was in Ambrose's report. He had even managed to get hold of the coroner's report, which indicated torture.

"Her family had no idea she was in Eastways. Isabelle had been very careful not to tell them about our group. She wanted to protect us."

I gripped my pen hard. The very thought of the way Bliss had betrayed so many people filled me with rage, but I wanted to do this correctly, so I said coldly, "Stack never even needed documentary evidence. Just the threat to tell your name and address to Isabelle's relatives."

He nodded, staring at the desk top again.

I wrote a few four-letter words on my tablet just for show and turned a page. "You always paid Stack cash?"

"Yes. He picked it up in person every month at my office downtown."

"How much?" He wrote a figure on a piece of paper and pushed it across the desk at me, "Only two thousand?"

"It's all I could spare—twenty-four thousand a friggin' year for chrissake—it wasn't easy to hide it either. My wife probably thinks I have a mistress." He looked up with a sickly smile on his face.

I wasn't amused. I wanted the interview over as much as he did. "When was the last time?"

"At the funeral. He said he would accept a contribution then in lieu of this month's payment."

"The same amount as usual?"

"Double. I had to go to a bank. I don't carry that kind of cash on me."

"Interesting." I stood up.

He stood up as well, "Wha-what are you going to do?

Do you have the documents? Do you think you could cut back some on the amounts? I mean, if he's been skimming . . . She wasn't getting the full amount anyway. I'm not a well man. The last ten years or so the donations haven't been coming in the way they used to. This is just not such a spiritual age."

I snorted at him. "Oh, I think it's more spiritual than you are. Don't bother to see me out. I'll be in touch."

I passed his wife standing outside the door. I wondered if she had been listening. The house didn't seem quite so cozy anymore.

Chapter Thirty-Five

No one answered when I called Stack's home from the airport. At his business number the receptionist said he was there but not available and he usually worked all day Saturday. I told her to give Stack the message that I needed to talk to him about Nina's estate and I would be there around five if not before.

The initial $50,000 Nina had collected from Bliss with Andy's help must have gone into buying the apartment building. Her bank records had revealed as much. I wasn't sure whether she believed it was child support money or a fair exchange for the family property she had donated, or both, but she certainly had gone about it without leaving loose ends. The higher prices she had put on each piece of clothing she sold so cheaply must have been her own slow method of laundering the money.

But what about the cash Andy had extorted from Gordon Bliss in Nina's name? She couldn't have approved of that, and it must have gone straight into Andy's pocket to bankroll his fledgling diet business. I tried not to think about that because it was hard to drive safely and pound on the steering wheel and scream at the same time.

Okay, I said to myself, if Stack hadn't existed, his patients would simply have taken their diet frenzy down the road to enrich some other self-anointed weight loss expert. But only Andrew Stack could have blackmailed Gordon Bliss in Nina's name. Would he be blackmailing on his own, now that Nina wasn't alive to contradict him? Or did he now intend to collect in my name, as Gordon Bliss feared?

If I had been angry on the way to the building, seeing the lobby of the Stack Attack Headquarters put the match to my fuse.

The lobby had been designed with a feminine clientele in mind. Very few men would feel comfortable in that mauve and pink womb of a lobby. The closest thing to a male presence were three larger-than-life-sized cutouts of Andy Stack. Formal, in an Italian designer suit, grinning wildly and holding up the Daily Meal Stack—a fold-out menu plan of many pages which each participant purchased in a personalized version. Another cut-out wearing a headband and Stack-logo sweatsuit held the Stack Machine—a rubber-handled torture instrument that came with its own set of exercises. Last, but not least, the cardboard Andy nearest the receptionist wore a chef's hat and apron and held up StackSnaks, the sacramental wafer of the starving.

In my current mood I even had a bone to pick with the furniture, which appeared to have been selected with the idea of making fat people squirm. The low-slung, squashy sofas like puffy, pink Venus Flytraps, ready to grip like quicksand even a moderate-sized person. The chrome-framed mirrors enlarged the space and cowed the customers as well. Andy Stack didn't know how lucky he was I didn't have a rock at hand.

The receptionist half stood, half perched on a bar-stool

behind a glass podium desk designed to show off her re-
markable slenderness. Just the lady to inspire the quivering
masses of cellulite-haunted womanhood with the proper
self-abasing, cash-spending mood.

She sized me up with the smile of an unleased cheetah
crouching to run down a sacrificial heifer. Assessment
glowed in her eyes. Commissions must be a big part of her
salary. She was underestimating me. Never a wise idea.
The heifer she saw was only Dr. Jekyll. She hadn't seen Ms.
Hyde yet. If she made the leap she was tensing for, it would
be charging cheetah meets Godzilla.

"Good afternoon," she trilled. "Are you a client or a new-
comer?"

I refrained from roaring for the moment. Gave her a
chance to be businesslike. I introduced myself and explained that I needed to see Andy Stack "about an urgent
matter." She said something about needing an appointment. If she behaved herself I would let her live. "I called
earlier." I looked at the slots with little pink phone message
slips. Andy Stack's was empty. "I see he got the message.
I'm a friend of Nina West."

The name meant nothing to her. Obviously she didn't
pay attention to the large-size clothing store on the prem-
ises. Well, why should she notice it? She was slender young
woman in her twenties who probably had an anxiety attack
if her home scale registered three pounds over usual. For
her the existence of clothing for any female over size fourteen was an unfortunate and ugly secret, which would become unnecessary after the diet revolution when no
woman of my current size or larger would exist. Except in
freak shows perhaps. For a moment I thought of the writing on Nina's wall, "Kill the Whales." Someone had simply
taken Andy's basic business plan to eliminate fat people
into the realm of blood and knives.

But the receptionist was chirping at me again. "He's so

good about giving complimentary memberships. Of course, once you've tried the facilities you'll want to come back often and maybe bring friends. How much do you want to lose?"

Okay, she was going to die. "I won't dignify that question by asking whether you mean dollars, pounds, pesos, or deutschmarks. I have no intention of losing anything, except my temper—if I don't see Andy Stack. And pronto."

Her eyes were beginning to show some alarm but she dug down and came up with a note of cheerful woman-to-woman concern into her voice. "You shouldn't give up on yourself so easily. You have such a pretty face."

"Gee, that might almost be a compliment, if it wasn't an insult. What's your name?" For the second time in the afternoon I unzipped my briefcase, and whipped out my notepad.

"Merrilee, and yours?" The chirp was fading fast and the glowing smile had already shut down.

"I already told you mine, Merrilee. It will be in the report." I wrote it down. "Last name?"

"Hoffman. Um, why do you want to know?"

"I'll need all of this for my report."

"Oh, my god." Merrilee's veneer cracked in a large way. "Where are you from, really?"

"I can't say. But if you want me to put in a good word for you, you'd better start by letting people state their own business when they walk in here, rather than grabbing their leg like a rabid badger."

Merrilee had turned pale, "But that was the pitch. I mean, I was taught to start that way. Did they change it last week? I was sick last week, no one told me."

"What! A healthy girl like you sick? Do you use the Stack products yourself?"

"Of course I do! Look, anyone can get a cold."

"Easier still if you've been undermining your health by unwise dieting."

"Gosh! You're not from the FDA are you? Or the FTC?"

"Were you told to expect someone from the Federal Trade Commission? We like to use the whole name. The Food and Drug Administration, you say. So they finally picked up the ball on the Stack problem, huh?"

"No! I mean—look what do you want?"

I snapped my notebook shut. "Now that should have been your first question, shouldn't it?" She was too easy. I was on a roll. Might as well move on to someone more challenging. "I would advise you to treat people with decency, but it may be beyond your ability. Where's Stack's office?"

"First door to the right, but he's not . . . "

"I'll wait for him there. You let him know I'm waiting. If he isn't out in fifteen minutes, Ms. Hoffman, I'll come back and we can chat some more." I was down the hall and closing the first door to the right before she could utter another word. I assumed I wouldn't be alone long in his office.

In fact, I barely had time to check out the parade of framed ads and magazine covers featuring Stack and his diet enterprises.

I had dropped out of the diet-as-holy-grail quest fifteen years earlier when I met Nina. It had been almost that long since I paid much attention to the latest fads and fat wranglers. Stack must be hot right now. The magazine covers were all within the past five years.

He had no shame. The American flag was featured prominently in his layouts and he had diet suggestions for schoolkids and grandparents, the whole family right down to the dog, although his main audience was paranoid single women. Stack was touted as a caring diet monger. A patriot whose commitment to fitness and America drove him to attack the monster of fat and rescue its imprisoned victims.

I'd just finished scanning the wall when the door flew open and Andy scurried in, looking as usual as if sparks should be flying from his electrified hair. "So you came to visit, at last." Today he wore a yellow and red Hawaiian shirt with a brown raw silk suit. It made his brown eyes snap in contrast. For all his warm words he was on guard.

I stood stiffly for a moment while he hugged me. He backed up to look at me from arm's length as if he had been missing me for weeks. Perhaps he was assessing the cold glare I gave him. He took my hand and pulled me toward the door, "You've seen the reception area and my office, let me show you the consultation rooms where the real work gets done."

He led the way down corridors of small offices, each with a gleaming medical scale and a couple of cozy chairs pulled up to a table. "See, it's like sitting down with a friend to plan how you're going to solve a problem."

"You mean like sheep sitting down to plan their own fleecing?"

He stopped, his mask of warm concern vanished. His sharp brown eyes turned mean. I saw the vampire weasel Gordon Bliss feared. "The receptionist said you were on the rag. Would you like to tell me what's bugging you?"

I slowed my pace and forced myself to relax enough to breathe carefully and notice the layout of the place. I might want to dodge out the nearest exit one jump ahead of a security guard. "You know, Andy, much as I appreciate your helping Nina get what she needed from Gordon Bliss, I have to say you're a lot like him. I just came from a little heart-to-heart with Gordon over in Idaho."

He gave me an assessing glance and kept walking toward a room we could see ahead of us through floor-to-ceiling windows onto the hallway.

He went in. I followed him. "Look, here's Susan." It was a room of mirrors. A row of exercise bicycles stood next to a couple of Stairmasters and several treadmills. One wall held racks of barbells and free weights. A Polaris Tower bristled next to it. The gym was sparsely populated at nearly 5:00 p. m. on a Saturday. Susan was one of the few people in the room. She was intimately engaged with a leg-press machine.

"Hello, sweetie." He unwisely planted a kiss on her wet brow then stood up and wiped her sweat from his mouth. I was surprised she didn't snarl at him. A man shouldn't wipe his mouth after he kisses his woman. It makes both of them look bad.

Susan let out a big puff of air and looked at him a little hazily. "I'm not finished, babe. Go away for half an hour, would you?"

"Of course, sweetheart. You know where to find me."

He led the way back to his office in silence and went behind his desk. "You're not in a touring mood," he said. "So let me show you this."

He opened a drawer, put his hand deep inside to release another control, and as I looked over his shoulder I saw a compartment hidden at the bottom of the middle desk drawer. He pulled out a small picture album. He handed it to me. I sat on the chair across from his desk and looked through it.

It was a about four by six inches, palm-sized. There was no title. All the pictures were Nina. At different ages. Different sizes.

Most fat people have such a sequence of pictures. The first picture in the book showed Nina as a teenager, with the glowing energy of youth. At that age she must have been around a size fourteen—the largest size on the rack in most women's clothing stores. Of course she felt fat and everyone told her she was unacceptable.

In the next picture she was a little heavier. She had started to make her own clothes and I recognized the flow-ing lines and fanciful designs of the mid-sixties.

In the next photo I scarcely recognized my old friend. She had lost a substantial amount of weight. She was wearing a tight sweater, very short micro-mini skirt, and an expression of frenzied animation. I had seen enough desperately dieting women to understand the forced gaiety in her face.

Well, here it is, the Holy Grail. I'm finally at a normal weight. Why do I feel so crazy? I'm always thinking about food. I'm terrified to eat. Men's heads turn when I walk by, women see me as competition. I'm getting the attention I always wanted. Why do I feel so driven and hopeless? What will happen to me if I gain weight again?

Over the next series of photos she did.

Gradually, the flesh crept back on. Her body testified that normal for it was not the size of the Nina in the micro mini. In the last few photos I thought she looked glorious. Glowing with health and confidence, wearing clothing she had designed to show off a body she had come to accept and even celebrate. This was the Nina I'd known and loved.

As I looked at the last picture I realized that every one of Stack's clients would call it a "before" picture and would suffer any pain or indignity to get to the slender "after" mode, never facing the fact that for many of them it was unnatural, even damaging to their health, and impossible to maintain.

I looked up at Andy and realized I was crying without knowing when I had started. He came around to perch on the corner of his desk a few feet from me. He had a box of tissues within reach, and he held it out for me to pick one. He watched me intently. He knew his way around crying women. "So?" I said, sniffling a little, "She was beautiful. You wouldn't have kept her pictures if you hadn't thought so."

"She was the one great love of my life. But she was out of control."

He reached out and touched the tears under my eyes, then put his finger to his lips and licked it.

I thought of him kissing Susan and wiping his mouth

afterward. A knot of dread formed in my stomach. Andy took the book out of my hands and turned the pages.

"Here, look," he said, pointing to the picture of Nina at her thinnest in her mini skirt.

"We were in high school together. It was a small town. All any of us wanted was to get out of high school and out of that town. Nina thought a fat girl had no chance at all. Hell, I understood. I was a short, skinny kid. But I was always doing exercises, lifting weights, any guy who thought he could beat me up just because I was littler was in for a nasty surprise. Nobody tried more than once. I protected Nina when kids made fun of her. They threw rocks. The two of us threw 'em right back. I taught her how to throw to hurt too.

"Finally I convinced her to work out with me, follow my diet plans. We found a diet she could afford. Her mom was dead by then but we made sure it was something her father wouldn't kick at. And she got skinny and pretty. You see the picture."

"I see it. She doesn't look too happy to me."

"You're right. She couldn't take it. She wasn't used to the attention. She wouldn't stay on the program with me. I told her, 'This is it.' She'd have to be on this diet or one like it for the rest of her life. She'd always have to work out. But it was worth it because she was so beautiful like that. She didn't understand. All these guys were suddenly falling all over themselves to ask her out and she thought I was jealous."

"Well, weren't you mad at her if she was suddenly dating other men?" I asked.

He put the book down on the desk, and leaned back on his hands, "Of course I was. But it went beyond jealousy. I was like that Greek sculptor, Pygmalion, the guy who fell in love with the statue he created. Only Nina stepped down off her pedestal and went partying."

He looked aside. His jaw clenched. It was nearly thirty

years ago and he was still deeply hurt. "We quarrelled and she went off to California. I went into the Army. It was 1968. I could easily have been sent to Vietnam, but I was stationed in Germany. When I got back, Nina was back in town too. Her dad had died and she inherited the family farm. She gave it to those ESP people. Everyone thought she was crazy. She was starting to get fat again. I didn't want to see her.

"Then one night in 1970 she came by my house. She cried. Told me she was pregnant. That old goat Gordon Bliss knocked her up. He wanted to give her some money from petty cash and the name of an abortionist—a total quack."

"Dr. Morton from Bellingham."

He looked at me strangely, the chain of reminiscence nearly severed. "How did you know that?"

Instead of answering I asked. "What did you do then?"

"I said, 'Hey, what do you want from me, applause?' She just turned and walked away. I let her go.

"By the next morning I knew I had to see her again. I went to the Eastways Center. But she was gone. One woman took me aside and told me Nina had gone to Seattle. I finally found someone who knew how to reach her and I went to see her there. She told me a lawyer had got her some information about paternity suits and she was going to talk to that scumbag preacher. I asked to go with her. Hell, I was the closest thing Nina had to family. She needed help with that low life. It was like the old days, protecting her from bullies. He paid her. I made sure of that, then she went to Seattle and had the baby. I think she arranged for it to be adopted, but by the time I moved to Seattle the kid was out of the picture. She gained back all the weight she'd lost and more, and told me she would never go back to following my program. You seem to agree with her on that point."

"Yes, it's called self-acceptance."

His lips curled, "If you say so." He tugged at his hair in anguish, "I loved Nina. But I refused to be seen in public with her the way she was. I hated having people stare and snicker at us, with me being so short and her being so big. I'm too old to throw rocks any more when people make fun. I told her, but she didn't seem to care. Then one day when I was at the gym after working at some shitty sales job, I realized I could do for other women what I did for Nina. It's become a holy crusade for me.

"Ironic isn't it? I never had a weight problem. I only studied about diets and women's exercise for Nina. And she was the one woman who wouldn't follow my program. You may wonder why I offered Nina practically free rent for her boutique here in the building."

He gestured to the building, the pictures of himself with celebrities on the wall. "None of this would have happened if I hadn't tried to help Nina with her problem. I owed her something."

"Not to mention the money you extorted from Gordon Bliss all these years in Nina's name, for not revealing his identity to Isabelle Zangrilli's family. If they tortured and killed the incompetent abortionist think what they would have done to the man who knocked her up and then sent her to him."

"What!"

"Don't try to lie. Gordon didn't want to become another small clipping in the newspaper violent crimes section, so he paid you for your silence."

"That's a pretty wild accusation, do you have any proof?" He leaned back against the desk and folded his arms.

"I have documentation on how Isabelle died. And the bizarre slaying of Dr. Morton, a Bellingham veterinarian. Gordon Bliss confirmed it."

He half turned away from me. For a moment he was so

still that I realized I had never seen him when he wasn't seething with energy. He turned back and seemed utterly and serenely calm. "So what?" he said. "Do you actually think Gordon would accuse me? If your story gets out he wouldn't be alive to confirm it."

"I think Nina found out about your blackmailing Gordon Bliss in her name. She wrote me a letter saying she was writing her memoirs. I think she was going to expose you for what you are—a criminal rather than a patriot. Now I don't know if after all these years Isabelle Zangrilli's relatives would kill Gordon Bliss. But that kind of publicity certainly could kill your business."

Andy regarded me with his new icy calm, "Just try it."

I felt as if I had somehow come close to the truth without quite reaching it. "If you killed Nina you also took her computer diskettes and wiped her computer memory. But the police have the computer now and they may be able to restore the files."

Neither of us said anything for a moment. There was a small, timid knock at the door and Susan opened it and stood in the doorway staring. Her cheeks were flushed from her workout and her hair was wet and pulled back into a ponytail. Her eyes widened as she took in the scene.

What she saw might have looked compromising, with me sitting on a chair as Andy braced against the desk, bent over me, so close that his knees nearly touched mine. He straightened slowly and walked purposefully to meet her at the door. Susan watched his approach with an unreadable expression. I couldn't tell if she was hypnotised by him or terrified of him.

"Jo and I are finished for now, Susan. Are you ready to go home?"

"Yes," she said to him, then she looked back at me with unspoken questions in her eyes. "May I have a moment alone with Jo?"

He didn't like it. "We're really running late, Susan. Can't it wait for another time?"

"No. It can't." She set her jaw and asked with unexpected firmness, "Would you like to go on now and I'll meet you?"

"I'll wait." He brushed past her rudely as if she were a stranger in a crowd he was jostling past without apology.

I stood up as Susan came into the room. She saw the album Andy had left on the desk top and opened it up. She thumbed through the pictures briefly pausing at each. At the end she went back, as Andy had, and looked at the picture of Nina at her very thinnest. Then she flipped to the very last picture in the book. She closed the book without comment and put it down on the desk top.

"I tried to call you at Maxine's, Jo. She said you'd moved out. I need to talk to you privately. There's no time now, but would later be okay?"

"Sure." I gave her the 800-number. For some reason I hesitated to give her the hotel name. "If you need to get hold of me in a hurry they can always reach me from here."

"Thanks." She turned and walked to the door, gestured to me to follow, but before I reached the door she asked, "What if I were in trouble. Who can I call? I mean, my brothers might come, but they're so far away."

"Are you in physical danger, Susan?"

"I—I'm not sure."

"Are you covering up for Andy?"

"Maybe we should get married right away, not wait. What do you think?"

"I don't think you should marry someone you're afraid of."

"You know they can't force you to testify against your spouse."

"Susan, I can't make someone behave sensibly, but if you're giving Andy an alibi for the time when Nina was killed, you might consider that you're also the only person who can testify for sure that he wasn't with you. If you try to hold that over his head, he might end up killing you as well."

"I'll keep that in mind." She stared at me with an intensity that was almost frightening. Was she terrified or determined? "Bye."

She opened the door for me to go out first. Andy was fuming in the hallway. He took her by the arm a little too roughly for my taste and glanced at me over his shoulder as they walked off. I went in the opposite direction toward the Exit sign.

Chapter Thirty-Six

The next morning was Sunday. I found a florist who was open and she put together a bright handful of red tulips, white freesia for scent, with daffodils and irises for yellow and purple. The store also sold stuffed animals and wine but I settled for a tin of chocolate chip cookies. I brought the whole thing over to Maxine's as token of apology.

There was no answer to the bell. Although I had the keys to the building's front door on the ring of keys to Nina's place I had left Maxine's keys on her kitchen table, and even if I'd had them I wouldn't have used them after the anger she had shown when I left. I was surprised to find that what worried me most was how Raoul was doing. That cat was really getting under my skin.

I let myself into the building and went downstairs to the basement. I knocked on Hope's door. No answer. I took a deep breath and went to knock on Mulligan's door. Awkward, but it was the next logical course.

Mulligan answered, wearing a sweater and jeans. I felt a rush of pleasure just to see him. It turned to dismay as he blocked the view into the room with his body. Someone was with him. Someone he didn't want me to see. He looked at me and then at the flowers. He raised his eyebrows. "What's up?" he asked.

"For Maxine," I explained. "But there was no answer at her apartment, I thought she might be at Hope's but there's no answer there either."

"You probably didn't knock loud enough." He came into the hallway, pulling the door closed carefully behind him. He crossed the hall and hammered on Hope's door. "Hey, wake up! Jo's here."

"It's a little early for them on Sunday morning," he explained, backing into his apartment, so that I still couldn't see past him.

"It's nearly noon," I protested, but he had closed the door.

Hmm. Definitely someone he didn't want me to see was in there. Joan perhaps? Or was there yet another woman in his life? No wonder I was attracted to Mulligan. He was starting to look more and more like a beefy, overgrown version of my ex-husband—the adventurer, photographer, and Romeo of the seven seas. If that turned out to be the case I would have to concede I was not a genius at picking men.

William answered Hope's door, naked to the waist and wearing blue jeans, looking as if he had just gotten to sleep a few minutes earlier. "Oh, hi," he said. "Hope'll be out in a minute. Want to come in."

I felt silly holding my flowers and tin of cookies. But I perched on the sofa till Hope shuffled out of the bathroom, bundled up in a terry cloth robe, her hair wrapped in a towel. She looked unusually normal with her hair covered and her motorcycle bad girl clothes set aside. "What's going on?" she asked.

"Well, I wanted to bring these flowers to your mother. To sort of apologize. I also wanted to check on the cat."

"I can let you in. She's probably gone out for brunch. She likes to do that on Sundays. You want to come on up?"

"If you think she wouldn't mind. She was in a pretty bad mood the last time I saw her."

"Oh, she's sobered up. There's no predicting her moods. But she likes flowers. Come on." She led me upstairs without another look at William, who was wandering back toward the bedroom.

Hope let me into Maxine's and called out, "Mom!" The only answer was Groucho's greeting screech. "Hello, Groucho." She made some bird noises at him, which caused him to rock back and forth on his branch and caw. "Grouch's cage is uncovered. That means she's already fed him and gone out. You can leave the flowers on the coffee table. It'll make her day. What else did you get her? Cookies, huh? I'll have to come up and talk her out of some later when she gets back."

I looked at Hope, a little surprised. I had never seen her so cordial. After running from me, begging a heart-to-heart talk and most recently nearly accusing me of murder, her latest mood surprised me. "Are you feeling all right, Hope?"

She had the good grace to be embarrassed. "Yeah," she said, looking at her feet. "Thanks for the help with the lawyer. William talked to him yesterday and agreed to turn himself in tomorrow." She paused, a little shy, "You didn't have to do that."

"I think Nina would have wanted him to have the money."

Hope nodded. "Are you staying here tonight?"

"No. I've got a hotel room." I cast around looking for Raoul. Sure enough, he came ambling in. I sat down on the sofa and stretched out my hand for him to sniff at thoroughly. I must have passed muster. He hopped up to the sofa and took possession of my lap. He curled up there and began to purr.

Hope laughed. "Well, I'll leave you two together."

"Hope, did Maxine ever talk to you about your father?"

She stopped and looked at me suspiciously. I expected her to say something about Maxine's dead husband.

"Yeah, yesterday she told me that guy Gordon Bliss, the religious nut, was my father." She rolled her eyes at the ceiling, "Just when I thought I was starting to cope, right?"

"Did she say anything about, uh, William?"

"About William probably having the same father? Yeah. Maybe we can get a family discount at the shrink." She glanced back to see if I was shocked as she turned to leave, "Like they say at Disneyland, you know?"

"What?"

"It's a small world after all." She left.

For a little while I thought of nothing but petting Raoul. The cat was all for it. He settled into a steady outboard motor purr, except when I scratched under his chin, which caused him to accelerate to a double barreled purr on alternating frequencies. He rotated his blue gray whiskers forward and extended his head serpent fashion so I could reach the entire length of his neck. He must know Nina was dead. But he accepted it and he accepted me.

Why was I so hard on Nina? She had done the best she could for her son, for the people like me who came to her with emotional wounds, for refugees from her religious group, even for this cat. In her situation could I have done better? Had I ever done anything even half as difficult? Just The prospect of taking on the care of an extremely agreeable twenty pound furball like Raoul seemed more than I could handle.

Raoul stood up on my knees, planted his front feet on my collar bone, and pressed his snub nose close to mine with a goofy expression of pure affection.

Okay, so I'd take the cat. In fact I could take him right now if I changed hotels. I could get the cat carrier from Nina's apartment and call Ambrose about that suite at the Waverly.

I left a message for Ambrose. Raoul was not keen on my leaving to get the carrier, but when I gave him some milk from Maxine's refrigerator he put aside his protests and managed to drink it. I told him I would be right back.

I didn't start to get scared until I reached the door of Nina's apartment. I took a deep breath and unlocked the door. The place looked the same.

For a minute and a few deep breaths I studied the driftwood sculpture, hanging on its fishing-net frame. For the first time since Nina died, I considered how I would transport it in order to return it to its maker. Driftwood pieces of various sizes were suspended along the net from a driftwood log at the top, as thick as my wrist. A few small nails held the whole thing up. It probably wasn't very heavy, even though it did take up most of the wall. Unless one of Nina's other friends wanted it, I'd let the artist use one of his own walls to display it.

I was in the utility room looking for the cat carrier when I heard someone open the door and come in. I thought it must be Maxine, but I admit I hoped it was Mulligan.

"Who is it?" I called out and went into the living room.

It was Eric. He had a strange look on his face even for Eric. It was similar to a smile but not quite. His eyes glowed with a strange, angry light. I didn't like it. Then there was that white coverall he wore like a painter's smock or a lab coat. I realized too late—a butcher's apron. I stopped dead cold and stared.

"How did you get in?"

He held up a ring of thin metal rods, "Skeleton keys," he said. "They usually do the trick."

He dropped the keys in his coverall pocket and pulled

something out of his belt. It was a long knife. I had never seen one quite like it.

"Eric. You should know that I just talked to Mulligan and he's on his way up. Put the knife away."

He looked down at his hands and smiled even more broadly. He didn't seem to have heard me. "Great knife, huh? It's a butcher knife. Got it the summer I worked at the meat plant. Lazy people use a mallet. An oldtimer showed Eric the real way to do it. Done it to cattle, sheep, you name it. Nothing to it once you know how. A narrower knife works better for killing pigs, you go in through the eye. But for human pigs, this is best. Eric should have got you in Twila that way. More time here. Without that busybody old woman. Hated to kill her. Had no choice. Thought about letting you go. Too risky killing people in the same building . . . Except—" He took a step toward me.

"Except for Nina. You killed her here in the building, didn't you?"

"No!" he cried out as if I were the one threatening him. "No. I didn't kill Nina. I loved her."

We were both shocked. But the shock vanished when he looked at me again and that awful light flickered in his eyes. "But you." He took a step toward me. "You went to see my parents."

"Yes."

"My father thought you were my girlfriend."

I opened my mouth and screamed as loud as I could. He didn't like it, but it didn't stop his slow advance. I circled around the other side of the living room.

"Stupid enough to kill someone in the building, except—" The twitch of a smile was back. "Eric doesn't live here any more. Once you're dead meat, Eric's out of here. Should have gone awhile back when the phone got tapped." He slashed at the air experimentally with the knife. I flinched. "How long did they think ol' Eric wouldn't notice that?"

He was still between me and the door. I got as far as the edge of the driftwood sculpture and grabbed the net.

I could feel the small nails give.

He rushed at me.

I hauled down and forward as hard as I could. The net tore off the nails that held it to the wall. The long thin log at the top hit me on the shoulder coming down. I grabbed it and swung the net with its driftwood weights out over Eric.

He stumbled when a large chunk of driftwood smacked him in the ear.

I dropped the edge of the net and ran for the door.

He made a grab for me as I went past, but tripped on the coffee table, which was snared in the net as well. He turned and followed me, the table trailing after him. I heard his labored progress behind me as I raced to the door and fumbled with the doorknob.

As I opened the door he was nearly upon me, but the net dragging the coffee table caught on the door frame. Panting in frustration, kicking at the snared coffee table, Eric tried to disentangle himself. At last he gave a roar of rage and pulled free of the table as I broke out into the hallway and screamed again.

Eric followed me into the hallway pulling the net and driftwood after him. I headed for the stairs. An apartment door downstairs slammed open and the stairwell was suddenly full of tall, burly men, and a couple of strapping women, charging up the stairs from the flight below.

I stood aside and let them thunder past. Looking at their backs as they raced up the stairs to where Eric stood, netted on the landing, I saw police uniforms and dark nylon jackets with POLICE and SECRET SERVICE stenciled in large letters on the back. I thought I saw one that said FBI, but no one stood still long enough for me to be sure.

The group paused as one for a second at the landing, taking in the sight of Eric and his knife. Then, as I saw them fall on Eric, strong arms pulled me close and shielded me as another couple of men ran past up the stairway to join the three or four who had leaped on Eric while he slashed at them frantically.

I stood blinking in surprise, realizing it was Mulligan who was holding me. "Come on," he said. We went down to the next landing. The door to Eric's apartment stood open. His computer screens flickered in the dimness.

"Who are all these people?" I asked. I noticed Mulligan was one of several men who wore a sports jacket rather than a uniform.

"The uniforms are Seattle PD and most of the plain clothes people are our unit, telephone company security. The guys in raid jackets are Secret Service and FBI," he said, gesturing with his chin. "The rest are local fraud squad. We were in Eric's apartment with a warrant," Mulligan explained. "We've been building a case on his computer crimes—hacking into local banks, airlines, the phone company, buying things on phony credit cards—not to mention all the stolen phone company equipment we've found in his place. He's been selling cloned cell phones. That was his most recent scam. We've been watching his place for a couple months.

"But we haven't been following him. We had no idea until we came in to confiscate his computers. He's got a couple of those butcher aprons that have been washed, but still show signs of blood, cardboard boxes of women's clothes that might be souvenirs from Captain Ahab's victims, and a scrapbook of clippings—newspaper articles on the killings. I'm glad we picked today to raid the place."

Our eyes met and I realized what great restraint I was showing in not kissing him.

He looked away and continued to explain. "It sure looks like we got him dead to rights as Captain Ahab. We were waiting for him to come home when we heard you scream." I noticed he kept his arms around me, which was good because I was holding on for dear life.

"He wasn't going home," I gasped, suddenly realizing how close I had come to Nina's fate. "He said he knew his phone was tapped. He was leaving."

"Well, I'm glad you had the sense to scream," he said, running his hand along the side of my face, then looking around to see if anyone was watching. "You know these floors are like amplifiers, you can hear everything from the apartment below," he concluded.

"I'll keep that in mind for the future," I said.

I looked into his eyes and saw that he wanted to kiss me as well, but it was clearly not the moment to start something we wouldn't be able to stop.

"It's not a problem in the basement apartments," he said.

"Perhaps you can show me when you get off work," I said.

"At least we won't have to worry about a killer on the loose," Mulligan said.

"Yeah," I said. But even as I spoke I couldn't help but think how adamant Eric had been that he had not killed Nina. He had even used the "I" word. *I didn't kill her,* he had said. *I loved Nina.*

Chapter Thirty-Seven

Mulligan had details to take care of that would fill the next twenty-four hours. I decided to take the cat, head for the Waverly Hotel, and let him call me there when he was done. After I had given statements and talked to representatives of half a dozen law enforcement agencies, I stood waiting for a word with Mulligan.

While I was waiting I noticed my old friends from homicide, Gonick and Lasker, conferring in a corner of the narrow landing. "His alibi checked with the airline, but with his skill, he might have hacked into their computer and put his name on a passenger list. We're checking further," Gonick said. "They may have got him for the Ahab killings but he was a southpaw. You know what that means." Then Lasker nudged him. They noticed I was listening and moved their conversation well out of earshot.

Finally I found Mulligan and told him I was going. He said, "Wait. I'll take an hour and follow you over there. It might be a couple days before I get another chance to talk to you."

If that's what you want to call it, I retorted mentally, surprised to find that I was suddenly nervous.

Raoul wailed piteously from the moment he was put in the cat carrier and caterwauled during registration at the Waverly, but Ambrose had told them to expect me and they were amazingly cat friendly. I was glad Mulligan had come along to carry Raoul's feline survival equipment, though. There is something indelicate about handing a litter box to a bellhop, even when it's swaddled in several large plastic trash bags.

When we got up to the room and I opened the door to the cat carrier, Raoul suddenly fell silent. His owlish gray head popped out of the carrier door. He ventured out cautiously, looked around, and began to explore the room, his velvety gray nose quivering with intensity.

I looked at Mulligan. Suddenly there seemed to be a vast gulf between us. He bridged it by pulling me close, but it was the hug of two exhausted wrestlers.

He pulled back and examined my face. "Look I've got to get back and we need to talk."

"Seriously, what is your first name?"

"Huh?"

"Come on, you're not the coy type. I just make it a point not to sleep with men whose names I don't know. Just call me an old-fashioned girl."

He ran his hand over my head. "When we've got more time, I'll explain, okay?"

"Okay. And thank you."

"For what?"

"For showing up with the U.S. Cavalry to rescue me."

He chuckled. "You know I think the Cavalry was about the only unit that didn't get involved today."

"But Mulligan?"

"Yeah?"

"Next time come alone."

"I promise."

I spent the night with Raoul, who was not in the least shy about joining me in a strange bed.

The next morning I left him sitting by a window that looked out over a busy street and went to find breakfast.

When I got back to the hotel there was a message waiting for me. "Susan called. Emergency. Please call back."

Chapter Thirty-Eight

I didn't realize until I got that message how much I had put my suspicions of Andy Stack on hold in the horror of discovering that Eric was indeed the Captain Ahab killer. Eric had denied killing Nina and, if what I heard Gonick say was true, he had probably been out of town defrauding the telephone company when Nina was killed.

If Stack had killed Nina, Susan might be in danger as well. If nothing else, Stack was an abuser of women, and I wanted to find a way to help Susan to get free of his clutches. But I worried that it might be a trap. Could Andy be forcing her to call? Even cops are cautious about domestic disturbance calls. Maybe I could get Susan to meet me somewhere to talk.

That was my plan when I called the number Susan had left on the message. She answered on the first ring. Her voice was quaking and she sounded as breathless as if she had just sprinted to the phone.

"Jo! Could you please come? I'm afraid."

"Susan. Is Andy there?"

For a moment the phone went silent and I thought she had hung up.

"Susan, hello. Are you in danger? I'll come, but I'd better call the police immediately."

"No! No, he's not . . . I have to get away now while he's out." She took a gasping breath. "Please. You've got to help me. I'm afraid." The terror in her voice was so palpable that I started to shiver in sympathy. My mind raced. Who could help me help Susan?

Then she said softly, "Please. I don't think I can do it on my own. Will you come?" And she hung up.

I tried to call Ambrose before I went to get the car. No answer. I left a message on his voice mail, telling him where I was going and asking him to call on the cellular phone.

There were no cars visibly parked outside Andy's house. I didn't know where the garage was.

The front door was slightly open. I didn't like that. I heard an odd hoarse sound like gust of wind whistling through a crack.

I pressed the door open cautiously. It swung back against the wall. No one behind it. I advanced through the front hall, left the door wide open. There was no sign of anyone in the front hallway. I advanced into the huge living room. Someone was sitting on the sofa facing out that sweeping picture window, head tilted forward. Sitting with an unnatural stillness. Asleep? Unconscious? Was it Susan? Was I too late?

"Susan?" No response. As I came up behind the sofa I saw that it was Andy. I waited for him to react. Nothing.

I moved around to stand in front of him. I got as far as the edge of the sofa. The floor in front of him was puddled with blood that had gushed down the front of his shirt and trousers to soak the sofa and drip onto the hardwood. The blood had been congealing but not for long.

That whistling sound again. It wasn't from Andy. He was

long past making any sound. I looked up. It was Susan. The sound was her breathing. She was hyperventilating, her eyes were round and staring. She held a blood-stained knife in her hand. Her right hand. The wildly hysterical thought occurred to me that Andy must have canceled the wedding.

"Susan. I called 911 on my way over," I said, struggling to find a soothing tone of voice, desperately wishing what I said were actually true, which of course it wasn't. "The paramedics will be here soon to help you." As I spoke I edged my hand down into my purse and slid out the cellular phone. I didn't dare take my eyes off Susan. I hoped I was pressing either "0" or the redial button. I dropped the phone into my jacket pocket, watching Susan as I did so. "I don't understand Susan, did he threaten you?"

Her mouth turned down as if she were about to cry, but instead she yelled, "Don't talk down to me!" She took a step toward me. "You think I'm weak and stupid, don't you?" Her voice had returned to the quavering, helpless tone she had used over the phone, but now I could hear the undertone of white hot resentment and fury.

I started to edge away toward the nearest door, which was the hallway down to the kitchen. "I wouldn't talk down to you, Susan. Hell, you fooled me. You fooled everyone. I thought Andy killed Nina and you were covering up, giving him an alibi. We did know it was a man who called to report that there was a body in the apartment. That must have been Andy, right?"

"Yeah." She relaxed a little.

"I figured Andy must have called so the body would be discovered while you two were still away for the weekend. Except that you hadn't been gone the whole weekend. That must have been the part you were lying about. But why, why did you do it?"

Susan shuddered. "I knew he went to visit her a lot because I followed and saw he had a key. So I stole the keys and copied them. Then I let myself in while they were talking. She was real mad at him. She said she'd ruin him for using her that way. She must have meant her body. You saw those pictures, how could he let her gain that weight back again like that? He said he loved her."

I heard the beep of the phone and a tinny little voice talking—I must have punched redial, it sounded like Ambrose's machine. I talked to cover the sound, "But Susan, they were old friends."

"Yeah, but he still wanted her. When she said she wouldn't let him use her anymore, he said he loved her, he'd always love her. He never talked to me like that!"

Her voice was thick with tears and rage. "She told him he had me now. And he laughed and said I was just a puppet. He was getting bored with me. Maybe he wouldn't even marry me. She said maybe she should teach me to stand up for myself. That fat old bitch! I showed her I could stand up for myself alright. I came out of the hall where I was listening, marched in, and slit her throat, right there on the bed.

"Andy tried to stop me but he was on the other side of the bed and it was too late. We both stood there, like paralyzed. Then he said to wait and not move. He went and got a shower curtain. Made me walk out on it so there were no tracks. He wrote on the mirror to make it look like those other killings. He did something to her computer. I don't know what. He even stole one of her coats to cover up my clothes."

She shuddered. "I hated wearing her clothes, even to get out of there."

She looked at the floor and shuddered again. "But at least, I thought, because we shared that secret we'd always be together, protect each other. Then he talked to you yesterday. This morning he told me he was going to turn me in for Nina's murder. He said he couldn't live with himself and with me like this. I sweated blood for him. I did everything he wanted and still he wouldn't . . . " Her face twisted into a grimace close to tears. She said through clenched teeth, "Well, he didn't have to live, did he? It's all *your* fault!"

I made a sudden dash for the hall and raced down it and through the dining room, throwing chairs down behind me as I went. I ducked through the butler's pantry into the kitchen, slamming the door behind me. I ran the length of the refectory table, pulling out chairs behind me. The kitchen island was no real cover, but I went behind it and threw open the cupboards over the stove, looking for some sort of weapon. A black trash bag fell out of the first cupboard I opened and spilled out its contents, blood-soaked clothes, a shower curtain, and computer diskettes.

Susan threw the door open, stormed in and ran into a chair.

I heard her come in and whirled around to face her under the hanging ropes of garlic and peppers. I backed into the stove and bent to look in the bulk supplies on the lower shelves of the island, grabbing the first bottle I could reach.

It was olive oil. I unscrewed the lid and sluiced the contents all over the floor between the long table and the island just as Susan wrestled past the last chair, bloody knife in hand.

She hit the olive oil and skidded feet first into the tile base of the island as I searched frantically through the shelves for the jar I wanted.

It was there.

Susan hauled herself to her feet and came around the island holding onto the edge of the butcher-block.

Her breathing was loud in the tiled room. As she found

her footing, she raised the knife in front of her in one hand, the other arm raised for balance and to grab me if I should try to elude her.

I forced myself to wait until she was within striking range and then tossed the spice jar lid off to her left. As she flinched to the right, I drew back my arm and drenched her face in a cloud of finely ground pepper.

Susan drew back gasping to breathe through the powder that now coated her sweat-damp face. I dropped the jar and unhooked the huge iron skillet that hung from the pan rack above. It was so heavy, it took both hands to heft it. I grasped it in both hands like a tennis racket and set myself for a backhand swing, but Susan had dropped to her hands and knees, coughing and choking.

The knife clattered to the floor as Susan crumpled onto her side, reaching out as if for air and shuddering as she choked in more pepper. I stood over her with the skillet for a few seconds, but her heaving turned into a desperate sucking noise and she began to twitch all over. Her fingers grasped the floor near the knife. I kicked it prudently far out of reach, rested the skillet on the countertop, and pulled the cellular phone out of my jacket pocket.

"Hello, Jo!" It was Ambrose on the line. "Are you okay? I called the cops and the paramedics."

"Bless you, Ambrose." I listened, thinking I did hear sirens. "I'm glad I caught you."

"I heard all that, I might have it on tape, but the reception was terrible, what did you have the phone stuck in a handbag or something?"

"I should get off the phone and call homicide," I said, keeping one hand on the frying pan and a watchful eye on Susan. "There's evidence here they'll want," I added, looking at the trash bag that had fallen on the floor behind the kitchen island.

"That's gratitude for you," Ambrose said. "Better let me call homicide. You'd only screw it up."

Chapter Thirty-Nine

One of the cops that afternoon told me as a casual aside that pepper gas had been known to cause fatalities. After listening to the paramedics mutter about massive tracheal spasms I could imagine how breathing pepper could kill someone. Later in the day I learned that Susan would survive. I was still too much in shock to realize they were saying I hadn't killed Susan with the pepper. It would take awhile to get my mind around that.

The afternoon wore on, Gonick and Lasker appeared. They were not in charge of investigating Andy's murder, but the detectives who were on the case showed them the black plastic trash bag that had fallen out of the cupboard. A friendly argument ensued about who got what evidence.

They were chipper, even chatty. When asked if their computer expert had been able to retrieve the files from Nina's computer hard drive, Lasker even managed to say that they had. He left it to Gonick to elaborate that the files had contained a brief description of Andy's blackmailing efforts and Nina's plan to talk to him as well as a threat to publish the information if he didn't stop. If the diskettes matched the files Andy had tried to erase from Nina's computer, it would help the case against Susan.

When I said Ambrose might have gotten Susan's confession on tape, Gonick grew even redder with pleasure under his sunburn and Lasker stopped scribbling long enough to actually speak the words, "Where can I reach this Ambrose?" Then he turned back to his pen and paper to write down the number.

The next day when I dropped by Maxine's apartment, Ambrose was there sitting on the sofa comparing notes with Maxine and Hope. The tin of cookies I had brought the day before sat open on the low table in front of the sofa next to a tray that held a teapot, sugar, lemon, and cream.

Groucho spread wide green wings at my entrance and hurled himself at the bars of his cage, biting the metal in welcome. Maxine thanked me for the flowers and cookies. Evidently all friction was forgotten and she made it clear without saying so that she had forgiven me for inheriting Nina's building. I asked if anyone had seen Mulligan.

"He was here earlier but he's had all these men coming in and out of his apartment. Well, some of it must be about arresting Eric," Hope said seriously. "But do you think maybe Mulligan could be gay?"

Ambrose cast an eloquent look my way. He refrained from rolling his eyes, but the corner of his mouth twitched. "Well, we were going to invite you to join our tea party, Miss Josephine, but it sounds like you have other plans," he said.

"Well, I'm just going to go check. I have some unfinished business."

Mulligan was in his apartment. He let me in. Although the place was neat as a pin, he seemed rushed. I couldn't help casting a quick look into the bedroom, where the crisply made bed mocked me.

"Jo, I took this apartment under false pretenses because I wanted to keep an eye on Eric. The phone company has been onto him for a couple of years now, and when I came to work there everyone talked about how he was a legendary nuisance but no one could get any hard evidence against him because he covered his tracks so well. We had no reason to think he was anything more than a clever hacker and a thief. We did know where Eric lived though. Hell, I was ambitious, and just divorced, so it wasn't like I had a social life. I took this apartment just to keep an eye on Eric. But what happened with Nina was real. I wasn't expecting it, but it was real."

"Now that you've got Eric, what will you do?"

"We'll make a case against him, of course. But as far as my life . . . " He sighed. "I don't know."

"Yeah. Me either."

"Still." He put his hands on my shoulders and pulled me close for a kiss that defied description. When we came up for air and hugged for a moment, he said, "I don't want to lose you."

"I feel the same way," I said, breathless, feeling my resolve to explain start to seep away. "I need to warn you though, I'm not a good substitute for Nina. I've lost my only friend and I'm just starting to try to get to know some new ones. I don't know what will happen in a couple of weeks when I go back to work. I love my job and it means I'll be traveling a lot."

He looked at me sadly. "Yeah."

"One other thing—about your name . . . "

He looked at his watch, "This is going to take a couple days to clear up."

"It's just—" I stopped, not sure what I wanted to say.

"Thor."

"Huh."

"My name is Thor." He had turned redder than I thought possible.

He was so embarrassed, I started to blush as well. "Look, this is the most important case I've ever worked on. I've got to get back to work."

"I understand." I did. We walked up to the foyer in silence. After a brief kiss, he muttered, "I'll call you." And disappeared into the Spring drizzle.

"Yeah, you do that—Thor," I said, after the door had closed behind him. But I had to smile. Okay. The name explained a lot.

I turned to Maxine's door and knocked. I was free for the day and that tea party was looking pretty good after all.

About the Author

Lynne Murray was born in Decatur, Illinois and grew up in Texas, Alaska, Washington, and Southern California. She now lives in San Francisco. She has published numerous articles in local and national newspapers and magazines and has written and directed a play. She is the author of two other novels, *Termination Interview* and *Death Flower*.